WOMAN IN THE MIRROR

Winston Graham is the author of more than thirty novels, which include *Cordelia*, *Night Without Stars*, *Marnie* and *The Walking Stick* as well as the highly successful *Poldark* series. His novels have been translated into seventeen languages and six have been filmed. Two television series have been made of the *Poldark* novels and shown in twenty-two countries. *The Stranger From the Sea* has now also been televised. *Tremor*, Winston Graham's latest best-seller, is also available from Pan Books.

Winston Graham lives in Sussex. He is a fellow of the Royal Society of Literature and in 1983 was awarded an OBE.

By the same author

ROSS POLDARK
DEMELZA
JEREMY POLDARK
WARLEGGAN
THE BLACK MOON
THE FOUR SWANS
THE ANGRY TIDE
THE STRANGER FROM THE SEA
THE MILLER'S DANCE
THE LOVING CUP
THE TWISTED SWORD

NIGHT JOURNEY
CORDELIA
THE FORGOTTEN STORY
THE MERCILESS LADIES
NIGHT WITHOUT STARS
TAKE MY LIFE
FORTUNE IS A WOMAN
THE LITTLE WALLS
THE SLEEPING PARTNER
GREEK FIRE
THE TUMBLED HOUSE
MARNIE
THE GROVE OF EAGLES
AFTER THE ACT
THE WALKING STICK
ANGELL, PEARL AND LITTLE GOD
THE JAPANESE GIRL (short stories)
THE GREEN FLASH
CAMEO
STEPHANIE
TREMOR

THE SPANISH ARMADAS
POLDARK'S CORNWALL

WINSTON GRAHAM

WOMAN
IN THE
MIRROR

PAN BOOKS

First published 1975 by The Bodley Head Ltd

This edition published 1997 by Pan Books
an imprint of Macmillan Publishers Ltd
25 Eccleston Place, London SW1W 9NF
and Basingstoke

Associated companies throughout the world

ISBN 0 330 33904 4

ACKNOWLEDGEMENT
The author is grateful to J. M. Dent & Sons Ltd and the Trustees for the Copyrights
of the late Dylan Thomas for permission to quote one verse of 'And Death Shall
Have No Dominion' from *The Collected Poems of Dylan Thomas*

Some of this book is based on an earlier novel by the author,
The Giant's Chair, published in 1938.

1 3 5 7 9 8 6 4 2

A CIP catalogue record for this book is available from
the British Library.

Typeset by CentraCet Limited, Cambridge
Printed by Mackays of Chatham plc, Chatham, Kent

For Rosamund

CHAPTER ONE

I

'THESE DAMNED local trains are always late,' said the railway official as he got in.

He was speaking to his companion but the jerk of the carriage as they moved off enabled Norah to nod in agreement. Not that she welcomed the intrusion. All the way from Brecon in this leisurely train she had been lucky enough to have the compartment to herself: the local people divided at her door like water about a rock – she was a stranger and it was enough – but these men had no such prejudices.

They were both in dark suits, one a good deal the elder and senior in position, so it was only through their conversation that she knew their business. The older one made no attempt to hide it and scarcely ever stopped talking, in a soft Welsh voice, except briefly to pull up the window when the train gathered speed. The younger, a very dark man, thin with sharp bright eyes, glanced at her legs, then up to her face, assessing her, ready to smile if she did.

She did not, being sleepy and hot and restless after a tedious journey. London to Bristol and Bristol to Brecon was reasonable enough; then across country in this little local train with three carriages and an engine shaped like a bathroom cistern. They had already stopped a dozen times and taken on and discharged a large number of black-clad passengers. She had thought at first there was a funeral; but unrelieved black was apparently the universal best wear of the country people around here, as Welsh was the universal language. She had hardly heard a word of English until the two men came.

The afternoon sun was streaming in on her, and it was too late to move now. At times the train would take a sharp curve and in the shade she would begin to wake up; but always it twisted back again to bring the sun full in on her face, and back would come drowsiness weighing on her eyelids to the rhythmic clanking of the wheels.

She almost dozed; and woke to hear the older man saying softly he wanted to kill something. It sounded disturbing at first but what he was saying was that they intended to kill this line as soon as ever they could.

'It's no good, Tom. You talk about the viability of the railways. They can never be viable while money is trickling away supporting these useless and totally uneconomic branch lines. This is one we would kill tomorrow if we could get government sanction.'

'It's not at all badly patronized,' Tom said.

'A few people going to market or visiting relatives. A few school kids in the morning. What's the use of that, with a whole string of stations to maintain, track to keep up, wages to pay? To make anything at all we've got to cut and kill. It's a surgical necessity.' There was a quiet rancour in his voice: it amounted to enmity, as if this line – and perhaps other lines like it – had done him a personal and unforgivable injury. They were passing through a wooded valley with steep, rocky sides. Below the line was a placid river with bone-white pebbles and cows standing hoof-deep in the water.

Tom said: 'People round here would miss it. For many it's the only means of communication.'

'They'll find others. Cars are cheap. Buses can run. You've got to chop off the small arteries to make the larger ones healthy. It's part of modernization. We've got to make the government see that.'

To Norah, who had come to learn quite a lot about arteries when her father died earlier in the year, the metaphor seemed inapt, but it was not her business. The train chugged on, and mercifully it changed course so that the sun now fell only on her feet. They stopped at another station, and the station-master, a man with a long red nose, was telling the guard the winner of the two-thirty. A hen was picking at the grass between the lines.

The country now softened into rich pasture land. Perhaps she was nearly there. She had always pictured Althea Syme living among wide lawns and shady trees.

As it happened she had first met Mrs Syme on a train; but not one at all like this; a great green French boat train two years ago when John Faulkner had been first taken ill, in his Paris flat, and Norah had been sent for. Althea Syme had been in the same compartment,

3

also travelling alone. She was instantly sympathetic and her offer of help, though not accepted, was kindly and warmly meant.

They had met a number of times since then; in Paris, in London, and then in Bournemouth, where Norah had gone with her father and where the two women had seen a lot of each other. 'I took to you the moment we first met,' Mrs Syme said, 'because you're awfully like the daughter of an old friend of mine. But since then a rapport has grown up, don't you think? I hope it's not misunderstood. It's – a little unusual between an older and a younger woman – the generations usually have so little in common – but I hope we shall continue to keep in touch. Any help I can offer you, you've only to ask.'

Another station. The engine was breathing like an old man who had to sit up in bed with asthma. The name was Pant-y-Dwr. Appropriate. In many of these stations the station-master's house was built into the platform and flush with the booking office. From where she sat she could see directly into one room; a table laid for a meal, spotless cloth, big china teapot, blue pattern plates, a white cat asleep on a chair. Was all this to be changed, disrupted, destroyed – by the railway people *themselves*, if the government would but give permission?

A creaking of couplings and they were off again. What was the appeal of Althea Syme? She was a woman who somehow contrived to be good-looking in spite of her features. Spectacled, with a long, clever upper lip, over-plentiful carelessly combed brown hair

looped low on her forehead. Not much sense of dress –
she always chose things that made her look bigger.
There was something luxuriant about her, a bit tropical:
the leaves of the tree had grown over-large. But such a
quick mind and so youthful an approach to life that
Norah never felt she was with a woman in her mid-
fifties.

For Althea was nothing if not enterprising. She
lectured all over the place on political economy and
hygiene; she wrote gardening features for the Press. She
was always travelling abroad. She found time to write
to the papers on matters of moment, particularly if they
concerned women's rights, and she had the good fortune
to be known to editors, so that most of her letters got
in. Where women met, the name Althea Syme meant
something.

She had been a widow nine years, owned an estate
and property in Montgomery and Cardigan, and had a
son of fifteen to whom she claimed she gave the
maximum freedom in all things. Norah admired
enterprise and originality and a refusal to conform,
and in all these things it seemed to her her friend
excelled.

A month ago she had received a letter:

30th August, 1951

'My dear,
    I had not heard of your father's death. Why
didn't you write? Will you take as said the
stereotyped expressions of sympathy, which you
know I sincerely feel? Your plans no doubt will be

vague as yet, but if when things are settled you should like to spend a few weeks with me here, don't wait for a further invitation, *please*.'

A week later another letter which, characteristically, had carried on where the first left off.

'Or better still. Are you working yet? I imagine not, because you told me you'd not be returning to the job you gave up when your father was taken ill. Well, I want a secretary. Indeed, I *need* a secretary, as I have just sacked the one I had! It would be of course entirely a business matter, and I would pay the going rates, but how agreeable it would be to mix business with pleasure! A month's trial (on both sides)? It's deep in the Welsh mountains. But perhaps you won't mind that. Do come.'

Another river winking and glinting over the stones. The train at last was going faster, gaining on the down grade.

The older man said: 'Like it or not, Tom, conurbations are the thing of the future. Centralization of city, town, village, hospital, school. In the mid-twentieth century we can't afford to straggle all over the countryside in hamlets and cottages with tiny pubs and churches and women's institutes and the like. As the population explosion goes on the towns will grow and grow, but the isolated districts of Scotland and Wales and

Cumberland will shrivel and die. *And* on the whole, not altogether a bad thing.'

'Not a bad thing?'

'Well, these are odd districts. I was born here, you know. You Cardiff people who travel up here twice a year haven't really a notion. You think Wales is civilized. All right then, so it is. But don't include these mountain districts. And I'm not talking about before the war, boy. Last year I met a farmer who'd lost some sheep, and he was as sure as took no contradiction that someone'd put the evil eye on him. *And* he knew who it was, too. He'd been to see an old woman who gave him some things in little linen bags that he was to hang over his door ... And at the little pub where I shall spend tonight, the wife there had erysipelas for a year and the doctors could not touch it, but she went to see a white witch and in three days it was gone.'

So they were superstitious, Norah thought. Did it matter? Except for this railway there probably hadn't been much change to mark a thousand years. In the days when Edward the Elder was driving the invading Danes out of the Severn Valley those mountains would still have been there in the distance, mist-capped and rain-swept, or gleaming like bronze helmets in the sun. There would be this same moss-green valley winding among the sombre hills, and single-storeyed cottages not dissimilar from those now sheltering among the trees. What got into a man that, having been born here, he had such a desire to uproot what the landscape had long since absorbed – this out-of-date little train chuffering past unpainted signal boxes and rusty stations? The sacred needs of British Rail? The peremptory demands of grey-faced accountants?

'And mind you, there are many other things go on in these parts besides the charming of braxy. On more than one occasion when I was a lad . . .' The train went under a bridge. '. . . Some say malicious gossip, of course, but I can tell you, boy, it was nothing of the sort . . .'

A long tunnel; but when they came out of it the sunshine had gone. It was as if they were in a twilight world. The train slowed to a stop, and just for a moment it seemed to her that the two men had climbed out and that her father got in and sat in the seat opposite her. He was wearing strange grey clothes which gave off a peculiar smell, and he looked thin and pale and drawn. Her father hadn't liked Mrs Syme. He had thought the friendship unhealthy. Perhaps he had even been jealous. Now, sitting opposite his daughter in the carriage, he took her hand in his icy hand and seemed to be speaking a warning, which was drowned by the shrill whistle of the train.

She just managed to choke back the beginnings of an exclamation as the younger railman turned to look at her. The train was slowing. This was a station of more importance; new houses about, a timber yard. The two men were really going now, rising, picking up their briefcases, hands on the carriage door. She rose quickly also.

'Excuse me. Is this Morb Lane?'

'Llanidloes,' said the older man pleasantly. 'Your station is two stops farther on.'

II

'MISS FAULKNER?'

A big dark man in a chauffeur's uniform. Althea had said she would be met.

Morb Lane seemed pretty much the end of the line. The empty train was shunting off towards a cluster of points and a few old small locomotives which had apparently been put out to grass. In the distance a clump of fir trees were grouped like the spires of a cathedral.

'I'm Timson, miss. This is all your baggage?'

A surly face, over-square, obstinate, and cropped hair that bristled about the back of his neck. They made no conversation on the way, which first was on a fair tarmac road, then through two villages leaving clouds of dust behind them, with farm hands leaning on pitchforks. They turned up a road with an AA sign *Impracticable for Motorists* and soon began to climb. The big car filled the narrow way. Potholes developed, with here and there ridges and outcroppings of rock.

The country here was wild: moorland and hills with this track winding through. An old mine of some sort, and then Timson had to open a gate and had some difficulty in keeping a flock of sheep on the other side while he drove through. She offered to help, but he said politely, thank you, no, he was used to this.

They drove into an even more barren area, with mounds of shale and ruined empty cottages; then a deserted church with stones piled against the gate, and beside it a house that might have been the vicarage, with frameless windows and a gaping roof. Perhaps the railman's prediction of dehabitation was already in process. The minor arteries did not need to be cut, they were shrivelling away.

The sun was low now, the hills in shadow. They turned into a shaly valley with two ruined engine houses beside the road. A tall battlemented cloud peered down it, pink-tipped. Mountains all round. Then she saw the house.

Not the expected. This house might have been stolen from the Cotswolds, being of good mellow stone but straggling, with different cambered roofs of grey tiles sloping up towards the ornamental brickwork of various grouped chimneys. It was a big house, of only two storeys but with a few attic windows in the roof, and the windows at one end uncurtained. If she had not known it to be only a hundred and twenty years old she could have mistaken it for Elizabethan.

And its north-eastern end was built almost flush against a precipice which rose fifty feet and then sloped away for perhaps three times that height to a great granite rock. The cliff would offer protection from all the cold winds but some danger, one would have thought, from falling stones. Very surprisingly no garden was visible, only this bumpy road which led through gateposts across a field which itself ran up to the foundations of the house like a green tide.

Getting out of the car while the chauffeur took out

her two bags, Norah looked back to see the long valley in the premature twilight of its guardian hills. They stood out over it, here swelling gently, there craggy and dark. You could see one old mine building and some ruined cottages. In the background on the right the bulk of a much larger mountain was outlined against the bright sky.

Then she heard the door open, and turned to be greeted by Althea Syme.

III

INSIDE, THE house was hard to evaluate. It seemed not so much a house built to a plan as a collection of oak-panelled living-rooms put together arbitrarily to suit different tastes. The rooms were dark and mostly large, low-beamed but pleasant, with a lived-in look about them; some good Swansea porcelain, plenty of books, but too many family portraits which didn't seem to have much merit as paintings. Leading the way upstairs Althea explained that the house had originally been built to accommodate two quite separate families, so there was a tendency to duplication.

As you mounted the first flight you came to a wide landing with three doors and two passages leading off, with, at one side, eight stairs leading down to another short passage ('our bathrooms,' Mrs Syme explained, 'grouped together, I'm afraid, and shockingly inconvenient'), and at the other a staircase leading up. These stairs were narrower, thinly carpeted and steeper. At the top was a heavy oak door hinged back on a chain, and beyond a square passage with two doors.

'I always thought to put you up here if you came,' Althea said, breathing deeply with the effort. 'If you don't like it tell me at once and come down to the next floor. Miss Harris, my previous secretary, was down there. But if you do decide to stay here you can have your own little flat and do what you like with it. And there *is* a bathroom of one's own, which is an advantage. A trifle primitive by London standards but . . .' floorboards creaked under her weight, 'this,' opening the door, 'is your bedroom.' She padded across it and opened a door beyond. 'And this, if you decide to stay up here, can be your sitting-room. It's a mess and only half furnished at present, but some of the rooms downstairs are so overcrowded you can take your pick of anything except the grand piano. You could even have that if Gregory were not taking lessons – and incidentally making very smart progress.'

'I'm looking forward to meeting him,' Norah said.

'There's one slight problem up here. As you can see, we don't have electricity, but there's coke-fired central heating on the ground floor and in a few of the first-floor bedrooms. If the weather turns cold you might be driven down.'

'Not now, certainly.'

'No, not now. And of course the heat does tend to rise.' They stopped and looked at each other. Althea smiled and said: 'Well, my dear, how *are* you?'

She put her arms round the girl, and they kissed.

'Fine,' Norah said. 'Absolutely fine.'

'I can see that. And as pretty as ever. You've lost weight.'

'A bit.'

'It suits you ... But tell me seriously, within yourself. You're better? I mean after your father's death?'

'Yes, fine. But as you know, we were pretty close, so it's just taking a bit of getting used to.'

'I know that. I know ... I think it'll do you a lot of good here. I know it'll do me a lot of good to have you.'

Norah laughed. 'Well, thanks. You're – very kind. Honestly, I ...'

'What?'

'Well, I'm very glad to *be* here, Althea. I've been looking forward to it. Thanks for your thoughtfulness.'

They looked at each other again, then the older woman sighed and blinked. 'I'll leave you before we get emotional. Dinner's at seven-thirty. I have an elderly cousin staying here at present, so there'll be just the four of us.'

'What kind of dress?'

'Oh, cocktail sort of thing – a little smarter than daytime. It's a pandering to suburbanism I encourage because it prevents general slackness. In the country one can so easily get into squalid habits.'

She went to the door, and Norah turned to open her case, but Althea stopped.

'And Robert?'

'Oh that,' said Norah, and hesitated. 'It's over.'

'Really?'

'Absolutely ... A major break. We – ran into a complete dead end.'

'Are you sorry?'

'Well ... I think maybe sorry's the wrong word. Licking my wounds.'

'As bad as that?'

'Well ... Naturally one doesn't emerge without a few flying splinters.'

Althea stood with her hand on the door. 'Tell me about it sometime.'

Norah smiled. 'I don't know ...'

'As you please, my dear. I can tell you my own feelings are a bit mixed on the subject. I only met him a couple of times. But there was something that suggested to me that you were neither of you particularly right for the other. I'd never have said so; but if it is over I can say so now.'

'We were right and we were wrong,' said Norah. 'It's probably the most dangerous mixture.'

'Don't I know,' said Althea Syme.

When she had gone Norah reflected that the last sentence had been spoken with some feeling, and that she had in fact heard little of her friend's own marriage. That was a confidence that had not come yet; Althea usually talked only of her life since she became a widow.

The girl looked out of the window. The front of the house might be without a garden but the land at the back sloped away from the house and the cliff in a high degree of cultivation, with steps and rocky eminences and sunlit grassy levels, towards a small ornamental lake bordered by flowering plants and fringed with reeds. As the last sun faded behind the hill the lake mirrored every detail of tree and sky and rock.

She looked about her bedroom. Her coming had obviously been the occasion for some re-furnishing. The chocolate and cream chintz curtains looked as if they had been hung that day and matched the counterpane on the bed. Two white rugs on the floor smelt new. Yellow roses in a vase. The furniture was Victorian but shone with polish.

The sitting-room was about the same size, but renovation had not extended this far. As Althea said, it was rather a mess: horse-hair chairs, a sagging sofa in worn velvet, a rocking-chair, much scratched; even a rocking-horse. The whole room smelt musty and neglected. There was a bookcase full of formidable old books: Darwin's *Descent of Man*, *Crockford's Chemical Dictionary* for 1916, *The Metallurgy of Lead* by J. Percy; and on a dark side-table was a frame with big beads on rails such as children once used for learning to count. These must be long pre-Gregory, surely Edwardian at the latest.

She thumped the window open – the smell was rather unpleasant – and went to take a bath. In a room which clearly had been a boxroom the bath stood on tall crabbed feet in one corner as if left there temporarily while the plumbers went to lunch, but she tested the tap marked 'hot', and found it as good as its word.

IV

FORTY MINUTES later something rattled in the depths of the house, and Norah put down her book, tightened the belt of her frock, flipped at the upstanding collar tips, and went down the two flights to where a maid, called Alice, was waiting to show her into the dining-room. Only Althea was there, in regal purple, newly powdered and smiling.

'*That's* nice. I've not seen it before, have I? Warm yourself before the fire. The evening's turning chilly.'

Norah murmured a compliment about the room and Mrs Syme said: 'The picture over the mantel is Watts's painting of my grandfather. It was his father who built this house, at the time when the valuable lead mines were extending all around the district. Jonathan Syme and Daniel Nichols owned three mines in this vicinity and between them they built this house to accommodate their increasing families. Jonathan had eleven children and Daniel eight – it was a vigorous age. Jonathan's eldest son, whose portrait that is, bought the Nichols out and made the two houses into one. Of course the mines are long since derelict. If I wanted to sell the house I could scarcely give it away, but it suits me well. Ah, Gregory darling, come and be introduced to Miss Faulkner.'

She had learned a lot about the boy from the talk of a doting mother; so reality was a shock. He was like an unflattering replica of her friend: the same largeness, the look of clumsiness about the feet, the dull opacity of skin, the shag of coffee-coloured hair, the spectacles; but all exaggerated so that, while his mother in spite of all had distinction and looks, he was almost ugly.

'How d'you do, Miss Faulkner.' His voice had broken late, still cracked as he spoke. When she took his hand it lay in hers like a dead animal, and she had a moment's revulsion, which she was careful not to show as Althea was watching her.

He was like his mother physically but seemed the reverse in temperament. While she was assertive and outgoing, ever talkative and extrovert, he was ingrown, quiet, closed off from the world, stood with shoulders bent and hands clasped listening, listening. The spectacles pointed the contrast. Mrs Syme's small, alert, friendly eyes were always visible, her glasses were a pane through which she observed everything more clearly. Gregory's were a wall. Lenses twice as thick cut off his eyes from the outer world, caught the light and reflected it, never let it through.

They sat down to dinner at a long table. This did not encourage easy conversation particularly because of the two oil lamps down the middle. Althea was at one end and Norah at the other, and in order to see her hostess she had to bend her head to one side and peer past the lights.

Nor did Althea's cousin, the Reverend Rupert Croome-Nichols, add to the occasion. He was tall and thin, with one of those jack-knife bodies that always seem to be either folding or unfolding, grey silky hair growing in a peak low on his forehead, and a face deeply indented with ravines so dark that one speculated whether soap and water had recently penetrated them. Throughout the earlier part of the meal he was silent, but when his hunger had been appeased he turned to look at Norah and asked her if her father had been to Oxford. Surprised, she swallowed hastily and answered, yes.

'Ah, I thought you looked as if your father had been up. Can usually tell in the children. I hope when you have children you'll send them there.'

Other conditions favourable, Norah thought it possible.

'Ah, I was up in 1911–12. Vintage years, those. Lassiter was up with me. Not that I approve of this movement he's founding. All these movements: Buchmanism, Toc H, Salvation Army; they all take people away from the Church proper. What good does it do? Prior was up at the same time, too. Bishop Prior. What year was your father up?'

Norah couldn't remember.

'Ah. '11, '12 and '13 were good years. A lot of good people up at that time. Most of 'em wiped out, of course. All fine young chaps. Remaking the world. Never had a generation like it since. And – er – hm . . .'

'Gregory,' said Mrs Syme, 'is going to Oxford. Aren't you, duck?'

'Yes, mother.'

'If he can get in,' said Mr Croome-Nichols. 'All these examinations these days. Often keeps out the right sort. I was a Westminster boy. Westminster and St John's. It always tells.' He put a large forkful of food into a deep corner of his mouth and reluctantly withdrew the fork, turning his eyes up as he did so. 'But there's a lot of favouritism in the Church – always has been. Your father a clergyman, did I hear?'

'No. He was in NATO.'

'Ah. The Church isn't what it was. Panders too much to public taste, tries to keep up with the latest fads. Panders. The lower classes are well catered for. What I say is, after all, the upper classes have souls. It's the Church's duty to cater for them. I told the diocesan conference so last time. Didn't please the bishops. What did your father die of?'

'His heart.'

'You should have written,' came Althea's voice from behind the lamps. 'I mightn't even have heard.'

'I have pains at my heart sometimes,' said Mr Croome-Nichols. He put another large forkful of food deep into a corner of his mouth. 'Have often thought I ought to see a doctor about them. After all, sixty-three is sixty-three. But chief trouble is my chest. Get phlegm in the mornings. Cold weather doesn't suit me. I dread the cold.'

'It's mild here generally,' said Althea, 'but sometimes we have frightfully hard weather for a short time. This is now mainly a sheep-farming district, and last year one farmer lost fifty sheep in the snow. It's interesting to see how well some of my half-hardy shrubs survive these cold spells. I'm convinced with such shrubs it's very much more the quality of the *ground* they are in than the air temperature. Round the lake at the back of the house there's an acre or more of fine loamy soil, and almost anything will grow there.'

'I saw it from my bedroom window. It looks lovely.'

'And all done in six years,' said Althea Syme. 'Seven years ago it was a wilderness of bracken and birch saplings.'

'Simon will be surprised,' said Mr Croome-Nichols. 'I shouldn't be surprised if he were astonished. And – er – hm . . .'

His habit of ending sentences this way was disconcerting. It was as if a sudden impulse of discretion had just stepped in to prevent him saying something he should not: Conversation was left in the air, suspended over a precipice.

Alice relieved them of their plates and set the dessert in front of them. Norah looked up to find Gregory's shining round spectacles turned speculatively towards her, but after a quick stare he looked away.

'Simon,' said Althea, 'is my nephew. We're expecting him on Wednesday. He's been abroad for some years and won't have seen the improvements. I'm sure he'll like them.'

'No one knows what Simon will like,' said Mr Croome-Nichols. 'Not even Simon.'

'What time is he coming?' asked Gregory.

'We haven't heard. Probably in the evening.'

They went on talking for a few minutes, but now between the exchanges there were silences which did not stem from Mr Croome-Nichols.

After dinner she was shown some of the rest of the house, but still didn't get a very clear impression of its layout. There were too many portraits in all the principal rooms, and on the whole they were not an engaging flock. A part of the house, Althea explained, was no longer used, for it was simply too big to keep it all up, and this accounted for the uncurtained windows.

Bed early; and up in her own rooms stare down through the casement window over the sloping roof towards where the lake had borrowed tinsel from the stars. The bulk of the mountains gloomed behind.

The depression that had been quietly waiting to pounce all day suddenly fell on her like a kidnapper's cloak. She struggled with it, knowing from the experience of the last few weeks that it must be fought off before it could gain a proper hold. This invitation of Althea's was only for a month's trial. If, in spite of Althea, one found her environment too depressing it would be easy enough to make an excuse and leave.

But come. Why make decisions and then regret them? Her hostess was as likeable and as kind as ever, and, thank goodness, being a woman, understanding – the rest of the company could well improve with a little effort. It was early days yet. A month would pass in a flicker. Must try to get to know Gregory. Tomorrow the sun would be shining. Gorgeous country! One hardly imagined anything left so wild and untouched in this crowded world.

She turned into the sitting-room. It was a peculiar smell, the one attaching to this particular room, half stale, half antiseptic. Probably the furniture. More than ever it contrasted with the freshness of her bedroom. The lamp she had set down on the table when she came in was not far from the rocking-horse, and so the rocking-horse cast a giant shadow on the wall behind.

As she turned from the window some trick of her eyes or of the light deceived her, so that it looked as if the horse and its shadow were moving slightly. Very slightly the shadow seemed to move on the wall.

She picked up the lamp and all the shadows lurched about like drunken men. She went back into her bedroom, stared a moment closely at herself in the mirror, fancying a blemish on her cheek, then seeing it was not. She searched her face for signs of the self-doubt that she thought she detected in her character. Heavy-lidded thoughtful eyes stared back at her. Weakness, indecision? How did they show? She began to undress, hanging her frock, folding her underclothes more carefully than usual, as if to delay the moment of nakedness.

Where was Robert now? It all stemmed, of course, this depression that hovered, it stemmed from her loss not of one man but of two. Her father's wise, urbane companionship, his elegant good humour was something she would be short of for the rest of her life. 'I am not resigned to the shutting away of loving hearts in the hard ground.' Who had written that? An American: Milleis was it? Well, *she* was not resigned. 'Lovers and thinkers, into the earth with you . . .' To Hell with life.

But the choice had not been *hers*. Robert was someone she was going to miss, differently but distinctly, if not for the rest of her life, at least for a while yet. All very well to be flippant with Althea, talk of flying splinters. But it was more than that. And the choice in this case had been hers . . .

Had it? Was there a true element of choice in rejecting his complete unreasonableness? That was, if she wanted to remain a person in her own right. Unreasonableness on her side too? *He* thought so. But this was no lover's tiff. The gap was unbridgeable. She was sick of men and their ways. To Hell with them too ... Young men anyhow. Why were older men so much more understanding? Had they too been impossible when young?

With a shiver, avoiding sight of herself in the glass, she dropped her nightdress over her head. And her other friends? Margery and Daphne living it up in their bedsitter. Olga doing her usual tour of the theatre agencies. Pete playing New Orleans jazz. Mark tuning his car.

A last look out of the window, then she went to the door to see if there was a key. There wasn't. Nor to the door leading to the sitting-room. Although it was not important to have a key to either she would, illogically, more have preferred to cut herself off from her sitting-room than from the house downstairs.

She slipped into bed. Good sheets. She had expensive tastes in sheets and used them extravagantly at home. A cool fresh sheet was halfway to a good night's rest.

She thought she heard something move in the sitting-room. Silly. She had just been in there herself, and floorboards often reacted after being stepped on. She blew out the lamp and lay a few minutes looking up at the dark. As her eyes adjusted themselves the square of the window lightened and let in an oblong foot width of night sky between the parted curtains.

This had all obviously once been someone's nursery. Many young Symes. Generations of them, growing and fading. Girls and boys hurtling up and down the narrow

23

stairs. Clear young voices. Childish cries, childish ailments, childish fears. Childish deaths. Climbing on and off the rocking-horse. Laughing and quarrelling, sulking and dreaming. The patter of little feet. She must remember to ask Althea all about it tomorrow. Why did the thought of little feet pattering in the room next door seem vaguely disturbing?

It was not until she was on the verge of dozing off that she thought she recognized the peculiar smell in her sitting-room as the same smell her father had brought into the railway carriage in her dream on the train.

CHAPTER TWO

I

GREGORY SAID in a querulous voice: 'How long is he coming for? Everyone is so close about these things.'

'I can't enlighten you, boy. No concern of mine. And – er – hm . . .'

'I think it's a concern of us all! If he intends to come and settle here and upset everything . . .'

'Simon's not the sort to settle. You'll see. He'll be off back again in a few weeks. He's never been able to stick it here. Not since the war.'

'Mother's so pathetic at times; she still treats me like a child. As if I didn't know all about her anxieties.'

'Then you know more than I do, boy . . . Look, these declensions will never do . . .'

A firm hand closed on Norah's shoulder. She started as Althea Syme said: 'I see you're looking in on my dear infant's studies.'

Norah went red. 'I *stumbled* on them. I can't find my way round this house yet. Where is the library?'

Althea laughed and led her across the passage. 'You're not the only one. When I first came here as a girl I was for ever walking by mistake into the down-stairs lavatory. Come and see my garden.'

It was the second day. Unfortunately there had been no sun yesterday, a fine drizzle had set in early and they had all stayed indoors and it had been very depressing. But this morning, Wednesday, was brilliant, the rain had washed the atmosphere, and the mountains had a Mediterranean clarity.

So for the first time they walked around Althea's well-publicized garden, the one that served her as copy for so many of her articles. Norah suitably admired, and not disingenuously. She liked gardens, and she esteemed someone who knew so much about, and was so passionately concerned in, their creation and upkeep. Her friend talked learnedly but amiably about telopeas and aralias and mahonias, and they wandered down to the lake.

'The *nyssa sylvatica* is nothing much yet, but in a month if the weather holds, it will be the most brilliant thing in the garden . . . It may have occurred to you to wonder, my pet, why it is that I, whose married name is Syme, should appear to claim the family as my own.'

'No, it hadn't . . .'

'In fact it is my own. I happen to be the only child of Henry Syme's fourth daughter. My husband, Captain Syme, was also my cousin. So I can't escape, you see.'

'What I *have* wondered,' said Norah, 'is why in the first place the house was ever built so close to the cliff.'

Althea smiled. 'So close to Cader Morb? For luck of course. Cader Morb is supposed to be lucky, and financially at least he's done his stuff.'

'Wouldn't the luck have held good if the house had been built twenty yards farther away?'

'Jonathan and his partner were superstitious men. In winter sometimes they say Jonathan used to go out by himself and talk to Cader Morb.'

Norah stared up at the sharp cliff surmounted by the jutting cone of bare rock. 'Yes, I can understand that. You haven't, by the way, even mentioned yet what I have to do.'

'What you have to do?'

'As your secretary. Typing and things. When d'you want me to start?'

'Oh, that. No hurry at all. Settle in first. Explore the countryside while the weather lasts.'

'I'm not even sure how good you expect me to be. Before my father was taken ill I suppose I was an average decent secretary. But I'm a bit rusty. And, you know, I didn't have much settled education. I was evacuated, and then after the war we were always moving about. I don't even know that I'll come up to your standards.'

'You'll do all I need, I promise you. Anyway, I'm not altogether convinced about formal education. That's why I thought it better for Gregory to develop without the constricting influences of a public school.'

'I thought he was at one.'

'I took him away. He isn't really the type.'

They walked on in silence. This was the tricky subject.

'I don't suppose Mr Croome-Nichols would approve.'

27

'Of what?'

'Of taking Gregory away from school. He seems to think very much of formal education.'

'Look at this rhododendron. *Auriculatum*. One of my few failures. I don't know if there's lime here, but they do well enough on the other side of the lake. Tell me, Norah, as a friend, what do you think of Gregory?'

They walked on a few paces. The sun, having dodged a mountain tip, was just flooding back over the garden.

'What do I *think* of him? How can I say? He seems very nice. I've hardly met him. We talked a couple of times yesterday, but it was only a few sentences.'

'I'd like you to get to know each other.'

'Of course. Gladly.'

'Don't be put off by his shyness. You know what causes it?'

'No.'

'His sight. That's really why I took him away from Radley. He was at such a disadvantage.'

'I'd no idea. I'm so sorry.'

Althea took a deep breath. Her bulk swelled with it. 'Sometimes I worry quite a bit.'

'How much can he see?'

'Oh . . . adequately at close quarters. But not much beyond short range. It makes him introverted.'

Norah was tempted to remark that taking him away from school would be likely to make him even more introverted, but she did not.

A blackbird was twittering at some real or fancied alarm. Althea said abruptly: 'Don't suppose I can't take an objective view of someone as close to me as my own son. I was never exactly a – a desirable woman – at least not like you – I have always been too heavy; but I think I have been able to make *up* in some way. He, poor duck, seems to have inherited the worst of my looks. You have to admit that for a boy of his age he's – unprepossessing. Of course that wouldn't matter so much if it were not for his sight ... However, he's got an absolutely first-rate brain. Very acute, very mature. But he badly needs taking out of himself – bringing out. Sometimes he's capable of astonishing misjudgments, and I'm convinced it's only because of his lack of contacts.'

Norah said: 'Perhaps your nephew will be able to help.'

'Who?'

'Mr – Simon Syme, is it?'

Althea bent down to look at a shrub. 'These magnolias – they take such a time to overcome the shock of moving. You can build a house in twenty months; a garden takes twenty years.'

'I think you've done wonders.'

'Oh, yes, but you know of course most of these trees and shrubs were brought here half grown. It's the new technique. They come with a great ball of soil or in massive pots. It's very expensive but it *furnishes* a garden, gives one a head start. It's only a few shrubs, like magnolias, arbutus, embothrium, that obstinately refuse ...'

'The design, the layout was entirely yours?'

'Yes. You see, I never lived here permanently until the end of the war. My husband, as the eldest son, never wanted to live here – he didn't like it – so Simon's

29

mother and father occupied it instead. When my husband died I decided to take up journalism – as a hobby, you understand. Gregory was a little boy, and this enabled me to stay with him most of the time. At the same time it gave me an outlet for my energies. Thomas died in 1942.'

'I never knew – was it the war? Being a captain . . .'

'It was the result of the war. We were in London through all the worst of the bombing. Gregory and I moved back here in 1945.'

'No one began a garden ever before?'

'The lake existed. A few common trees. The Symes, I'm afraid, were only concerned with the profits to be got underground. When those failed they invested their money in property in Aberystwyth and Barmouth. I am the first gardener.'

II

AFTER LUNCH Althea took Norah at her word and dictated half an article and a few letters. Moving weightily about her study, she delivered herself, and Norah took it down easily enough and afterwards typed the pieces out and left them to be read later. Her shorthand was certainly rusty but it would soon pick up. Then she went downstairs and dutifully sought out Gregory.

Coming on him apparently by accident, she tried to get him into conversation but like yesterday this was not a success. He answered in monosyllables or with the minimum of words necessary. He was not as fat as he looked. It was really big bones and the way he dressed. His face was almost expressionless, bland, and his glasses blinked indecipherable morse.

Presently she said: 'I'm going for a walk, but I've no idea which way would be best. Can you suggest where I could go – maybe some favourite walk of your own?'

'I'm afraid I haven't got a favourite walk. I don't go out much.'

'Which is Plynlimon? Do you know if it's a difficult climb?'

A long, rather slim forefinger pointed. The nail was dirty. 'That's Plynlimon.' He indicated the great bulk of mountain which last night had stood like a fortress against the setting sun.

'How do you reach it? Are you doing anything special this afternoon? Would you show me the way?'

Just for a moment she saw his eyes, dark brown and small but with large pupils. His spectacles showed ring upon ring of light. 'Did Mother suggest I went with you?'

'I think she'd be quite pleased if you were to come.'

'Perhaps she would, but that's not the same, is it? Cousin Simon'll be here this evening, won't he?'

'I believe so.'

'Well, why don't you ask him to go out with you when he comes?'

She flushed. 'I don't know anything about what your cousin will want to do. I was asking you.'

He half turned away, muttered something which ended in: 'It's no good pretending.'

She said sharply: 'Pretending what?'

'Innocence . . . That you're a total stranger. That you don't know anything. Anything about Simon. You know your way about all right . . .'

'Look, Gregory,' she said, 'I haven't an idea what you're talking about, so I don't know whether you mean to be as insulting as you sound. Your mother . . .' She stopped.

'Go on.'

'Perhaps if you come out for a walk you'd be able to explain what you mean by suggesting I'm not a total stranger. Do you mean to this district or what?'

He said: 'I think I'd rather not come, thank you.'

She went out of the house, very annoyed. The trouble with Gregory was not his bad sight but his bad manners. A couple of slaps across the face would cure a lot.

In her irritation she began to walk at random, climbing the turfy hillside with an energy that was fuelled by anger. As her anger cooled so her steps slowed; but by then she was high above the house, looking down on it as on a toy in the sun. A worm of lazy smoke marked its habitation. In front of the house the slaty valley threaded its way downwards between the hills towards the ruined cottages and the old mine building. Behind was the limpid mirror of the pool. And at the side the great Cader Morb, or whatever it was called, dominated everything as a Swiss alp does the village at its foot. She pictured all the early brood of Symes and Nichols being born in that house and being influenced by the shadow falling over them. With a father who on wet and windy nights went out and talked aloud to it, one could well come to believe that it had a life of its own, perhaps associate it with a god to whom propitiation must be made. She could imagine a sort of spiritual emancipation for the child who for the first time climbed the rock and sat on its hoary head and saw all the greater mountains beyond.

Gregory needed to be put up there daily. The boy was stupidly suspicious of everyone who came to the house, jealous of his mother's friends, abrasively ill-mannered. Fifteen of course was an awkward age. She remembered how her polite and gentle cousin Jonathan had become an oaf for about twelve months around that age. What could there be in Gregory's mind to connect her with his cousin Simon? Perhaps to a suspicious boy the fact that they were arriving in the same week was enough. But suspicious of what? Why did he resent strangers coming here? No wonder the other secretary left!

Still walking without obvious direction, she had nevertheless been following a sort of sheep track, which now led round a corner of the hillside and left the house and the valley out of sight. It was a gossamer afternoon of early autumn, the sky clear but not lustrous, the sun warmly peering. Her original idea had been to make for Plynlimon, the highest mountain in the district; but it was farther away than she had thought and would take all of a day. This day was already far spent.

A stream trickled across her path and she picked her way over it, stumbled on the last loose stone and wet her feet. She sat down for a few minutes, took off her shoes to let them dry. She spotted the beginning of a ladder on one ankle, so bubbled some spittle on to her finger-tip and dabbed it on the end of the flaw. Then seeing how damp the stockings were she unhitched them and pulled them off, rolled them in a ball and stuffed them into a pocket of her jacket, wriggled her bare toes in the dusty heather. It was hard to take too sour a view of things in such country and on such a day. It was all experience, all part of life. You couldn't exactly do this in London when you came out of the office for lunch.

She was not at all sure that she really wanted to go back to office work anyhow. The brief dictation and typing session today had revived an unfamiliar and unwelcome sensation. *Nothing* to do with the Symes, this – just memories of the drudgery of her last secretarial job. Well, she had to do something; her father had left two thousand pounds. Anyway, she *wanted* to do something. If it had not been that he was so obviously failing, she would have enjoyed looking after her father. It was so much more constructive in human terms. Should she then have been a nurse? Could she still be? Plenty of drudgery in that, and not much money. A doctor's receptionist? An air stewardess? All the airlines were expanding. Something to feel one was of use. When she left the Symes ... If she left the Symes ...

She put her damp shoes on again and went on up the hill. A few grave sheep looked their concern and moved away at her coming. Two or three were lame, hobbling among the stones. They kept their feet better than she did, for the slope was steep and twice she slipped. At the top an old dry-stone wall, part fallen down. She climbed over it and saw that she was at the top.

Another green and brown valley; but the farther side was sheer, being cut here and there by shallow ravines where the water drained. A stream at the bottom. It was the same one she had crossed: it curled round the foot of the hill she had climbed. The hill swelled like a great animal in the centre of the one broad valley, and the curious old stone wall ran along the top like a vertebral cord.

She began to walk and slither down the other side. Wanderings such as this on her own would make a lot of things tolerable. To be away from people and rush and the smell of petrol. Poor Althea – she was to be pitied for having such a son.

She came to a gate in another wall. It was broken and hung on one hinge and led into a stretch of vivid green turf. She stood leaning on a post, wondering whether to go farther aware that the sun was not so high, aware that the smiling hills would not smile when dusk began to fall –

She heard a cough – a clearing of the throat, and this was so close that her hand on its way to pull open the gate stayed frozen. She had been so isolated that for a moment –

There was a click. She turned sharply to see a man come from behind a boulder. He was putting his camera back into its case as he came forward.

'Sorry,' he said. 'Hope I didn't startle you. I expect you thought you were alone.'

Late thirties probably – long-faced, broad-shouldered, a hint of accent, open-neck shirt and Daks trousers. She couldn't find her voice.

'Hope I didn't startle you,' he said again. 'I was watching you come down the hillside. Then when you got by the gate you seemed to provide just the sort of foreground that was needed. Painters can juggle with their subjects. Constable could paint in a cow or a sheep wherever he wanted one. Unfortunately photography can't lie – or not to that extent. And it was – you were just the foreground I needed.'

'Failing the cow,' said Norah indistinctly.

He took a pipe out of his pocket and drew smoke from it. Then he dabbed his pocket to make sure it was not smouldering. 'That was Constable's style, not mine . . . One can hardly expect this weather to last much longer so I've been out most of today. Are you staying round here?'

'Round here, yes.'

He knitted his brows at her and then smiled. 'The attitude really was perfect: body just sufficiently taut, one foot on the bar of the gate, head raised, hair blowing. Like a poppy in the wind. But I had to get your head round a bit: hence the cough. Have you ever done model work?'

'No.'

'You should.'

The shock had left her now. She was half amused. But the amusement was not entirely friendly. 'I thought there was no one else for miles.'

'Being up here gives you that impression, doesn't it –

sometimes even that there's no one else in the world. It's why I come here. It's one of the few places left.'

'Left for springing booby traps?'

He eyed her. 'I suppose it *was* rather startling. But I'll give you a print. It'll be worth it. You'll see.'

An odd face, almost an actor's face, the features more prominent than life. Handsome if you liked gaunt artistic-looking men.

'Do you do it professionally?'

'Scare people? No.' He laughed. 'I photograph professionally, if that's what you mean. Name of Christopher Carew.'

If he thought this might have meant something to her he was disappointed.

'Mainly I freelance but I do some commissioned work for the glossies. And yours?'

'My name? Norah Faulkner.'

'Hullo.' He put his pipe in his mouth and offered her a hand. 'Nice to know you. I've done one or two professional assignments round here, but this is holiday. I have a cottage over the hill. I'm one of these absentee house-owners the Welsh don't like – here for about six weeks in a year. You on holiday? I suppose you are?'

'Well, sort of. Not entirely.'

As she made a movement he said: 'No, please don't go. We've only just met. Have a cup of tea. I was just going to have one. It's so rare to meet anyone round here except a farmer or a few sheep . . .'

'Or a cow.'

'I see you're going to pin that one on me. Look, sit

37

here. I've got a Thermos behind that rock. There's a cup and I can drink out of the lid.'

'Well . . .' Why not? At least he was cheerful and fairly young. More than would be offered her if she turned for home. She sat down and presently he squatted beside her; long legs doubling under him, and poured her a cup.

'I'm here on my own this year, and though I'm fond of myself the company eventually palls. Sugar?'

'One lump, please.'

'I take three. It's a good principle, I find, to have half of what you would like of any sweet thing.'

'Quite the ascetic,' Norah said.

He laughed, more wholeheartedly. A flock of birds rose at the other side of the valley. Then he knelt up and handed the cup to her.

'Don't think me presumptuous,' he said. 'Probably you already do; but I believe, I have a feeling that some good use could be made of this accidental meeting, if you were willing. Strictly business, of course. These photographs I'm doing at present are chiefly for my own pleasure but they're being taken also with an eye to a book on mid-Wales sometime or other. And that crack about Constable wasn't just stupid. A degree of foreground interest helps to make a composition. Where are you staying – Aberystwyth? Could you spare a couple of days? I'd pay.'

She smiled for the first time as she shook her head. 'Sorry. My time's not entirely my own. But thank you for suggesting it.'

'Pity. Got an invalid mother or something?'

'No. I'm staying about two miles from here – and working, more or less, as a secretary.'

'Good Lord. Secretary to a sheep farmer? But seriously, d'you know this country well?'

'I only arrived on Monday.'

'I came on an assignment two years ago – never thought of coming back; but the countryside captivated me – hence the cottage. Everything's so remote and forsaken. When you climb to the top of that ridge over there you can see across twenty miles of mountains. It's like a northern Greece. And in the next valley – you see those trees?'

She turned to look at where a belt of firs filled a perfect rectangle on the slope.

'Well, like that, only all over the place. I can't find out if they've been planted or if they're the remains of a forest. They're there in single file, in platoons, in regiments, all in perfect order. If you painted it you'd want to call it "Wellington on Army Manœuvres". Then there's Plynlimon. And back the way you came Cader Morb is interesting because . . .'

'That's where I came from. That's where I'm staying.'

He stared. 'From Cader Morb? You don't mean Morb House?'

'Yes.'

He had put down his cup and was frowning at her, brows uneven with surprise. 'You mean to say you're Mrs Syme's secretary?'

'Do you know her?'

'Yes, it was to photograph her garden that I first came down here.'

39

'How extraordinary!'

'It is extraordinary.' He turned and knocked his pipe out on a stone. 'It's more than extraordinary, it's fantastic. Did they kidnap you?'

'What d'you mean?'

'Well, you're hardly their type, are you?'

After a moment Norah said: 'They happen to be my friends.'

'Friends but not relations?'

'Since you ask, no.'

'I thought not. And you only came on Monday? That's why you still look so fresh.'

She put down her half empty cup. Whatever her private views were likely to be, she didn't appreciate his.

'Oh, I've never quarrelled with them,' he said, sensing what she was thinking. 'I've no old score to pay off. Indeed, I had dinner with them when I was down last year. But honestly ... Old Croome-Nichols, for instance. He believes in one God, one Church and one Oxford college, world without end amen. For a clergyman it simplifies the outlook. Has he asked you what your income is yet?'

She stood up and stared past him at the mountains.

'Oh, I know. They're your friends. And I admire your loyalty. But wait until you know them better. Only don't wait too long. I'd hate to meet you next year and find you'd grown a hump back and a beard.'

'I think I'd be more likely to do that by sitting here.'

'That's a nasty one.' He rose to his feet, tall and rather stooping, a vigorous and emphatic man. 'Well, let's not quarrel. I've no wish to quarrel, even with them. But it's an opinion I hold. Sit down and talk again.'

'Thanks, but the sun is getting low. It'll take me half an hour to get back.'

'Oh, all of that. You're farther away than you think. Like me to come with you?'

'No, I've a good sense of direction.'

'That house, you know. It photographs well but I'd hate to live there. Anyway, it's got a funny sort of reputation.'

'What d'you mean?'

'I mean with the Welsh. They won't work there, and they won't pass by it after dark.'

'I suppose somebody once saw a sheet flapping.'

'Maybe. I grant you that. Country districts are all alike. But ... Althea Syme ... She's surely as phoney as they come even by civilized standards. Isn't she? Don't you think so?'

That settled it. 'Well,' Norah said, 'thank you for the tea.'

'But like my opinions it was a bit on the strong side, eh? All right, I'm sorry I spoke. One tends to exaggerate to make a point – the Symes may be quite harmless. But I'm not awfully interested in *them*. Can't *we* meet again sometime? I have nearly another two weeks here. Nant-y-Bar Cottage is where I live.'

'I'll remember.'

As she moved away he walked a few paces with her, eyes appreciatively looking her over: 'Is it afternoons you usually go exploring?'

'I've no idea. There's no routine yet.'

'Have you a car?'

'No.'

'Then perhaps it's too far to suggest we might meet for a drink in Llandathery?'

'Where's that?'

'About a mile from my cottage. A tiny village with a pub called the Dyfri Arms. I could come for you.'

'Well, thanks, but I've hardly settled in yet. I don't know what Mrs Syme's plans are going to be.'

'Let me know when you can. I shall be about this part, usually in the afternoon . . . Goodbye.'

'Goodbye.' It was a bit difficult to climb up to the wall and then go slithering and sliding down the other side with any degree of dignity or elegance but she didn't much care. To Hell with him and his dogmatic opinions. It was going to take her all her time to be back before the sun set into the mountains.

Cooler already. A hint of autumn mist in the air. Soon the sun would be dying, not only for today but for all the year. Beautiful as it all was today, one could see how grey and cold and barren it would look in the winter. This was not a friendly land. It was still unconquered, little different from when the Bala limestone had first cooled among the slate and the volcanic rocks. From the days of Caractacus men had ridden over it and fought over it and, sparsely, had lived here. But it had never been taken over and tamed, as England had. It was man who lived on sufferance here, not the land. Perhaps if two or three generations of a family lived in the mountains they became affected by it, slightly 'different' as a result, recluses or eccentrics. Could one ever see Gregory marrying and begetting children here to carry on the line? Or would he inherit and eventually die alone, the ultimate eccentric and recluse?

It took her forty minutes to get down, and she chided herself for feeling slight relief when she came round the corner of the last hill and saw the house miniatured below in the long deep shade of the evening. Then as she came nearer she saw the Syme car at the door and the chauffeur handling luggage. A man got out a few moments later to be greeted, as she had been greeted on Monday, by Mrs Syme at the front door. Mr Simon Syme had arrived.

CHAPTER THREE

I

THEY HAD all gone in long before she reached the house and she saw nothing of the new arrival until dinner. But she saw Doole, the butler, who had been on holiday and had returned while she had been out. One seldom pictured a butler under fifty years of age, but Doole was scarcely thirty-five. A personable young man, powerfully built, quick-moving, on small, dancer's feet, with black hair close-cropped but worn low, and a shadowed chin. His eyes were a trifle too active for a well-trained servant.

No one else was about, but soon after she got upstairs to her room there was a tap on the door and Althea came in.

'Well, my pet, did you have a nice walk?'

'Marvellous. I could have gone on for miles.'

'I used to do a lot here when I was a girl, but unfortunately walking isn't my speciality these days. Otherwise you'd have a companion.'

'I tried hard to persuade Gregory, but no go.'

Althea frowned. She was in maroon silk tonight; the colour was good but as usual there was too much to the frock; she needed austere, simple lines. 'Maybe in a day or two.'

'He'd come with me if you told him to.'

'Oh, I know. He's nothing if not dutiful. But the essential thing is he should want to go with you of his own free will.'

Norah slipped out of her day frock and went to the wardrobe with it. 'I must say he behaved rather oddly. He seemed to think I knew something about his cousin Simon or that I was connected with him in some way.'

'Oh?' Althea was sitting in the easy chair. The oil lamp, just lighted, was flickering as if the wick were damp. 'That's strange. I expect your coming the same week . . .'

'He seemed – grudging – jealous. Is he jealous of me because I'm a friend of yours?'

'Maybe. Or he may be a little jealous of Simon. Are you sure you didn't misunderstand him?'

'What I am sure of is that I didn't understand him at all!'

'Simon, as I expect I've told you, is the son of my husband's brother. He's always been difficult, a non-conformer. He wanted to be a painter and failed. I think . . .' She paused.

Norah was uncertain which frock to wear. If one went by one's hostess one ought to be fairly formal. 'Yes?' She chose the green chiffon. (Shades of Paris . . . there'd been a shop round the corner from their apartment where they copied *haute couture*.)

'Well, I suppose Gregory has always been terribly proud of this house and the land we own. He's not really happy anywhere but here. I think the thought of Simon coming may upset him a bit; he may fear that a much older cousin will usurp his position. But of course as long as Simon lives I can't refuse him a home . . .'

'I see. But why does that . . .'

'What?'

'Oh, never mind. Perhaps I got the wrong impression.' Norah stepped into her frock and pushed the zip halfway up. She began to fiddle with her hair. 'I met a man today who says he knows you.'

'You met a *man*?' Althea's smile in the mirror was both incredulous and crooked. '*Here*? A farmer?'

'No, up in the hills. A photographer. Called Christopher Carew. He's on holiday. Has a cottage somewhere near.'

'Oh, at Nant-y-Bar! Yes. He photographed this house and garden. Interesting person. Rather a ladies' man. I'd no idea he was here again. He should have let us know.'

'He's here for another two weeks,' Norah said with a hint of malice.

'Alone?'

'I believe so.'

'Well, we must have him over some time.'

'Who is he? What is he?'

'Ah, I see he's made a hit.'

'Well, hardly!'

'I know very little about him. He came originally from the Midlands but he has a successful studio in Chelsea. Married twice but I believe the marriages haven't turned out well. I met one of his wives – a pretty little thing and well bred but not his equal intellectually. At times, of course, he tries to be *too* clever.'

'Oh? In what way?'

Althea stood up. 'Tell me, why don't you part your hair a bit more and allow that piece of hair to come forward as a fringe? It's freer. More natural.'

'All right, if you'd like me to I will. Like this?'

'Yes. Like that. I think it suits you, makes you look younger.'

As Althea moved to the door Norah said: 'Could you do up this zip?'

'Of course.' Althea came up behind her and put a hand on her bare shoulder. The signet ring was cold. Then she zipped up the frock. The hand for a few seconds remained as their eyes met in the mirror – the girl in the vivid green dress standing cool and unblemished beside the lush handsome woman in maroon whose skin was faintly pitted with too much powder.

'Thanks,' said Norah, moving away. 'See you in about fifteen minutes.'

'You really have the most satiny shoulders,' said Althea. 'Really *the* most. Don't wait to come down. I think we shall all be prompt tonight.'

II

WHEN SHE did eventually reach the room where they had drinks a thin fair-haired man of about forty was talking to Mr Croome-Nichols, and Mrs Syme was showing a book of photographs to Gregory. The new-comer did not look round when she came in, and Mrs Syme said:

'Ah, you met Christopher Carew. These are the original photographs he took of the house. I was telling Gregory you'd seen him.'

Norah bent to look at them. They were professional work of the highest class – the detail and the composition could not be faulted. They also had the quality of making the subjects more attractive than in fact they were. Whatever Christopher Carew's acidulous gaze might privately make of his subjects, his public eye had a rose-tinted lens. Althea had had twenty pictures of the house and garden bound into a book.

After a few minutes she said: 'You haven't met my nephew Mr Simon Syme. Simon, this is my new secretary, Miss Norah Faulkner.'

The newcomer turned, his face lit with what might have been a very attractive smile, but it was wiped from his face in a flash.

'God . . .'

He had a thin, sharp nose, blue-grey sensitive eyes, stony fair hair which had probably been brighter as a young man. He was staring at Norah as if he had been struck across the face.

'So you *do* notice the resemblance,' said Althea with a brief laugh. 'I was very struck with it when I first met her, but to tell the truth it seems so little now that I had quite forgotten it.'

'Merciful Christ . . .' said Simon Syme. 'You're like – she's like . . . I . . .'

'Unpleasant,' said Mr Croome-Nichols. 'Use of such words. Blasphemy. And – er – hm . . .'

'Like Marion, yes,' said Althea, still smiling at her nephew's consternation. 'It's very superficial, but at first sight I admit one does get that distinct impression.'

'Never met Marion,' said Mr Croome-Nichols. 'Seen her portraits, of course. Maybe there is a likeness, I suppose. Not that I would have remarked it. But I never met Marion. Haven't met many of the Symes. Not many left now. All families die out in time. I'm the last of the Croome-Nichols. My father saw it coming. Can't get away from change and decay.'

Simon Syme abruptly lowered his eyes, and Norah felt as if the live current she had been grasping had been switched off.

'That's the trouble with the world today,' said Mr Croome-Nichols, thrusting out his neck. 'Too much change and decay. That's the trouble with the Church. The old order dying off like flies and nothing to replace it. Like the railways: needs reorganization.' He opened his mouth in a smile, then quickly shut it again. 'No laughing matter. Disestablishment offers no solution. Look at the decline of the Wesleyans. And – er – hm . . .'

'You travelled in the same train as Doole, didn't you, Simon?' said his aunt.

'Yes.' A conventional smile moved the corner of Simon's lips. 'I also offered him a lift from Machynlleth in the car you sent . . . which he naturally accepted.'

'Kind of you. Doole,' said Althea to Norah, 'is my butler back from holiday.'

'Yes, I've already seen him.'

'Very efficient, Doole,' said Mr Croome-Nichols. 'Only trouble, doesn't always know his place.'

'Rubbish. He's very good. I shall be happier now we're full strength again. Have you all finished your drinks? Bring yours with you, Norah. I know dinner's ready.'

III

ALTHEA WAS at her best that night, sharp and entertaining – Norah recognized her as the woman who had first fascinated her by the breadth and vigour of her talk – but here the surroundings were against her. In a restaurant in Paris it was different. Against the counterpoint of Croome-Nichols's dull remarks, Gregory's silences and Simon's absent-minded rejoinders, the performance was out of tune. Norah found herself unusually reluctant to join in, and she had to force herself to take part.

After that first shock Simon Syme never looked at her. Even when she had her head turned away he never looked at her, she was sure of that. He had a pleasant face, deeply furrowed with lines about the mouth yet surprisingly young-looking, unsophisticated. She thought he was younger than she had first guessed. Most of the time he seemed scarcely to be there, to be deeply preoccupied with other things, and there were times when he answered his aunt in a flat and uninterested voice. Yet Norah was certain that he had been talking to Mr Croome-Nichols in a lively and engaging manner when she first came into the room, and twice during the meal he showed animation – once when his aunt said something about the Symes and he said brusquely: 'There are too many in this house. Walls are full of them. You've changed more than I like,' and once when Picasso was mentioned and he said: 'I saw him twice, before the war, at the Deux Magots in Paris. The young men round him really were like disciples. For them he was the centre of the universe.'

But he never looked at Norah, and after dinner he excused himself with a headache and went to bed. He had been given what Mrs Syme called 'the master bedroom' at the end of the devious passage leading away to the right from the main stairs and therefore a long way from the two main bathrooms; but the room, although Norah hadn't seen it from the inside, had, she knew, the three tall Gothic windows at the southern end of the house and therefore must have a fine view right down the valley; apparently it was the room his parents had always occupied.

When he had gone Althea prevailed on Gregory to play the piano, and this, to Norah's surprise, he did very well. He played Mozart, Scarlatti, MacDowell, Mattei, Grieg; chiefly the simpler pieces and some of them arranged; but they were all done with competence. His fingers were long and slender, his touch precise and delicate and easy. It was like listening to a talented girl. This at least was one area in which his mother didn't over-estimate him.

It was not a house where there was much to do after

dinner, and they were all soon ready to call it a day. But there was one thing on Norah's mind, and she followed her hostess into the library where she had gone to fetch her book.

'Althea.'

'Yes, my pet?' She was carrying a little night lamp, and this for the moment gave her spectacles the opaqueness of Gregory's.

'I've been wondering all evening about this extraordinary resemblance I seem to bear to your niece. It is your niece, isn't it?'

'Yes,' said Althea smiling. 'But it's not an extraordinary resemblance, it's a superficial one. I remarked on it, you remember, when we first met.'

'Mr Simon Syme seems to feel it very much.'

'Oh, he did for a moment. I think it soon passed.'

'I thought it upset him. All evening he seemed . . .'

'I don't think it was that. He tends to be moody. And probably the journey tired him.'

'Is Marion . . . ? Where is she now?'

'Marion is dead.'

Norah watched the slow rise and fall of Althea's cameo brooch. It moved like a piece of flotsam on a slow swell. 'I wondered.'

'Yes . . . she was drowned some years ago. It was a frightful thing at the time.'

'What relation was she to Simon?'

'His sister.'

'*Well*, then! It would be specially startling for him – and unpleasant! Shouldn't you at least have warned him?'

'Well, it was a long time ago, you know. I told you –
when I first saw you the likeness struck me, but afterwards I forgot it. Perhaps I should have mentioned
something to him, but I wasn't even sure he would
notice it. And this evening it never occurred to me.'

'But isn't that why Gregory connected me with him?
Because I'm like Marion, who was Simon's sister?'

'Oh, no,' Althea laughed and shook her head.
'Marion died seven years ago. I doubt if Gregory ever
saw her. I think it was just one of his fancies because
you were arriving at about the same time.'

The gilt bindings of the rows of books grinned as
Althea moved her lamp. Norah said: 'How old was she?
Marion, I mean. Quite young, I suppose?'

'Twenty-three.'

'But that's my age now . . . !'

'I know.'

'How did she come to be drowned?'

'It's a long story. Not a happy one, as you can guess.
She was just going away.'

'Away?'

'She had just been married. Less than a week.'

Norah waited. Presently she commented: 'How
awful. I'm very sorry.'

Althea said: 'Yes, it was frightfully bad luck.' As
Norah was clearly expecting more she added: 'It's not a
thing we really talk about even now, even though it's so
long ago.'

'Well . . . no, I see that. But all the same, if I'm at all
like Marion I think you should have warned Simon.'

'I'll apologize to him in the morning, if you wish. But

don't think any more about it. For Heaven's sake don't let it *worry* you. Every family has its tragedies, and I don't want this one to depress you.' Althea patted her shoulder. 'I'm sorry if you think I should have told you more. Go and sleep on it. It'll all look different in the morning.'

Upstairs in the bedroom Norah was a while getting undressed. It had been an eventful day, quite different from the first. She felt as if she had already been in the house a week. She thought of Gregory Syme and his blunt ugly face with its myopic glass shields, his sharp broken voice, his slender fingers delicately and precisely playing Mozart. She thought of Christopher Carew with his boisterous natural way, his sardonic humour, his casual smiling eyes looking over her figure and knowing pretty well. She thought of Simon Syme, old-young, worried, withdrawn, sensitive. 'Merciful Christ!' he had said. Why *hadn't* Althea warned him?

She thought of Althea Syme, perhaps another enigma, and a new one. 'You really have the most satiny shoulders. Really *the* most,' with a little gentle squeeze to emphasize. There had never before been any signs of *that*. So ignore it this time. Of course Althea had always admired her, passed the occasional complimentary remark about her figure and her looks – but always with discretion, without any emotional loading to the words. In fact in their own ways they *were* fond of each other, admired each other; but not in an overt, physical way. Her chief reason for accepting Althea's invitation to come here had not been her father's death but her break-up with Robert Jenkin – Althea with her sharp perception probably guessed that now. It had offered her an opportunity to get right away; still more it was an opportunity to enjoy the companionship of someone who, because of her sex, would make no physical demands on her. So this was disconcerting, this development, disconcerting if it were anything more than a stupid misunderstanding. Admiration, of course, was quite another thing. There was no reason at all why one woman shouldn't admire another.

Anyway it was unimportant – forget it. Althea had been at her best tonight. She seemed to have almost total recall. Once she had read, seen, done a thing it was *there*; could be quoted, remembered, described at will . . .

Before getting into bed she parted the curtains and looked out at the garden and the dark glower of the mountains. An hour ago there had been a first pared disc of moon but it was already set. Wind stirred against the window pane, trying it for strength. She blew out her lamp and got into bed.

Usually she went to sleep quickly and tonight would have been no exception, but just as she was drifting quietly off she heard the tapping. She opened her eyes again and lay still, listening. Tap-tap-tap. Tap-tap-tap-tap . . . Tap-tap-tap. Not loud. Just a faint noise. It wouldn't so much have mattered but it seemed to come from her sitting-room. That was the disconcerting thing.

She took a few breaths, allowing the slight alarm to escape. The tapping stopped. There, it was nothing.

Probably the pipes in her bathroom. Water produced the oddest effects. Except, of course, that her bathroom was the other way. But still . . .

The patter of little feet?

She drowsed, and then the tapping began again. Stopped . . . Irritating. Then something moved in her sitting-room.

She sat up in bed, in the dark, groped for the matches, half found them and then they slipped through her fingers to the floor, making a loud rattling noise. She got quickly out, felt about on the carpet for them. It was suddenly essential that she should not be in the dark. Matches found, one head broke, the second flared, she knelt up, took the still warm glass off the lamp and lit the wick. Yellow light sought out the corners of the room. The door into her sitting-room was closed.

But something had *moved*. She couldn't be certain what but she was certain something. A footstep, or a cushion had fallen, or a book had moved on the table.

She took two or three more breaths. Ridiculous to get in such a panic. A mouse. Or even a bat. Not the most desirable thought but much to be preferred to her first ideas. Anyway, she'd never sleep if she didn't find out.

Her dressing-gown was behind her own door. She fetched that, tied it tight as if for protection, picked up the lamp. God, for electricity . . . !

She got to the door and grasped the handle. Very quiet now. She was panicking in an old house. Every old house was full of creaks.

She took a breath and turned the handle and pushed open the door.

Her lamp flung its light uncertainly about the musty room. She held the lamp high above her shoulder and peered. The room was quite empty, the curtains undrawn, her own books unmoved on the table, no cushion disturbed. Then she saw something which at first she put down to the unsteadiness of her lamp, but presently knew had no such explanation. The rocking-horse was gently rocking backwards and forwards, its shadow moving against the wall behind.

CHAPTER FOUR

I

ANOTHER FINE day dawned, though Mr Croome-Nichols said the barometer was dropping. Norah was up early, having eventually leaned a chair against the door leading to the sitting-room, so that if anyone opened the door the chair would fall. Thereafter she dozed fitfully. Twice when dropping off to sleep she had heard the tapping again. Now in the morning light, while she did not disbelieve the evidence of her own ears and eyes, it all looked less menacing. The sitting-room was just a sitting-room, musty smelling and poorly furnished, the rocking-horse rocked easily and quietly at her touch; it certainly didn't make a tapping sound. The wind had been rising last night. Perhaps funnelling down the small chimney it had created a sufficient current of air . . .

At breakfast there were only three of them. Norah said: 'Is Simon not well?'

'Oh, yes. He's gone out painting. He often spends his holidays that way.'

'Did you say he had been abroad?'

'Well, only to Ireland. That's recently. But he has been quite a traveller.'

'One of those young men,' said Croome-Nichols, 'who find it more pleasant to travel than to arrive.' He opened his mouth and embedded a forkful of bacon.

Norah said: 'What does he do? For a living, I mean.'

'I'm afraid Simon hasn't settled to very much,' Althea said. 'He's constantly changing his field of interest, and as a result . . .'

'Gathering no moss,' said Mr Croome-Nichols. 'But then, does he need to? When I was a young chap of his age – and – er – hm . . .'

'When you were a young chap of his age,' said Althea, 'you were already vicar of St Medwyn. Simon isn't so young: he's rising thirty-five. But he'll never settle down. I predict he'll be away again after a few weeks here.'

'Has *he* never married?' Norah asked.

There was a moment's silence. 'No,' said Althea.

'Nor ever likely to,' said Croome-Nichols. 'Or so I'd guess. Not that I know him,' he added after a moment, disavowing responsibility. 'Only came here myself three years ago, when I retired. Althea wanted a tutor for Gregory, and as my grandmother was a Nichols it all seemed very appropriate. Kept it in the family. Of course I know *about* Simon. Difficult not to. And – er – hm . . .'

After breakfast there was another article to take down and the first one to re-type – Mrs Syme had written in a number of alterations and corrected a couple of spelling mistakes – Norah could never spell 'cholesterol' – but by twelve she was free. It was much cooler today so she put on a light coat and went out.

The higher mountains were cloud-capped, and now and then a screen of white wool would detach itself and drift across the sun. There was little wind in the valley, and sheep could be heard lamenting across a field. It was a lonely sound. Norah walked in the garden towards the lake, and then drew back as she saw a man sitting at an easel near the water. Her first thought was to keep out of his way altogether.

Then she checked the impulse. She had liked Simon's looks last night. His thin sensitive face was as quick to change its expression as a young boy's, so unguarded and then so closely guarded. If they were to live in this house together for a couple of weeks it would be pretty silly to try to avoid him. Much better plunge in now. Deep end first and swim for the shallow.

Not liking herself much, she walked towards him. 'Good morning, Mr Syme. Another lovely day!'

He started and put down his brush. She tried not to look at the picture but smiled directly at him, seeing his eyes go raw, go eager, go dull.

'Morning . . . Yes . . . very fine.'

'Mr Croome-Nichols is saying rain before nightfall. Perhaps he knows the signs.'

Simon Syme shook his head. 'It won't rain yet. Those clouds mean nothing.'

There was a pause. Out of the corner of her eye she saw that he was not painting the scene before him. He was painting a different-shaped lake bordered with silver birches, with reeds in the water and a windy sky.

She said: 'I hope I'm not disturbing you.' It wasn't

exactly scintillating stuff, but she could think of no other way of keeping the conversation going.

He looked down, and again she felt that relaxation of tension. 'I'm afraid I don't remember your name.'

'Norah Faulkner.'

'Miss – er – Faulkner. No, it's time I stopped. Three hours at a stretch is long enough.'

'Do you paint a lot?'

'Yes – quite a lot.'

'You mentioned Picasso last night. Did you study painting in France before the war?'

'Very briefly. Afraid my father didn't intend it should be my career.'

'Well, it was through *my* father that I got to know Paris, because he worked there for a time.'

'It's a cold city, very unfriendly to the outsider. Like a cold beautiful woman.'

'But unspoiled, thank Heaven,' she said.

'Unspoiled by the Germans, certainly.'

'That's what I meant.'

'Yes.' He smiled. 'But the traffic's very bad now, isn't it? Very blatant and noisy. So I gather.'

'It's bad. When were you there last?'

'Just before the war. What *I* meant, if I may explain, is that more cities are destroyed by their own inhabitants than by invaders.'

She said: 'Mr Syme, I hope the fact that I look a bit like your sister – I hope it doesn't upset you. Honestly, I'd no idea when I came that I was like *anyone*. Althea did mention something when we first met but she never

61

spoke of it afterwards. It never occurred to me –
obviously – that it might . . . upset anyone here.'

'Oh?' His stony hair looked less faded in the morning
light; the lines of his face contributed to the charm of
his smile.

She looked away from him, up towards Cader Morb.
A thin wreath of cloud was moving off its tip like a
scarf blowing in the wind.

'And does it?'

'Does it what?'

'Does my resemblance to your sister Marion upset
you?'

After a minute he said: 'Listen to those sheep. "And
full grown lambs loud bleat from hilly bourn." That
was Keats, wasn't it? "And gathering swallows twitter
in the skies." I love the peace of this part of Wales, if
one could only dissociate it from memories.'

'You haven't answered my question.'

'I'm trying to. Two people grow up together and
become very close – closer than an ordinary brother and
sister. As children we played together for hours upstairs
in the nursery. In the winter those are long hours, dark
hours – no other children anywhere for miles. Can you
wonder that our concern for each other becomes a little
ingrown, preoccupied, that we know so much of each
other's thoughts?'

He stopped. He seemed plunged into solitary recol-
lections on which it would be unseemly to intrude.

She ventured: 'Like the Brontës perhaps?'

'The . . . ? Well, yes. But there there were four. Here

there were only two. Could you blame me or I blame you for feeling the loss of the other?'

She waited, but he didn't go on. She watched him pick up a brush, dab it in green and touch his painting experimentally. She said: 'So my being here brings it all back?'

'No . . . I think your being here brings it all forward.'

'Whichever way you like . . . Do you want me to leave?'

He said: 'How can I want that?'

The whole conversation had been full of awkward pauses. She felt he was constantly evading the point.

'Well, you've only to say, Mr Syme. I mean that. Your aunt may have told you that I'm here on a month's trial. I may in any case leave then. But I'll leave tomorrow if my being here still upsets you.'

He straightened up from the painting and smiled at her again. 'No . . . I think we should all live more or less dangerously. It's a good principle of life. The greater the trial the greater the triumph.'

Norah frowned. 'I don't quite see what you mean . . .'

'Never mind. Never mind.'

'But I do mind.'

'Well, let me put it this way.' He turned and looked back at the house. 'There are too many Symes in that place, as I said at dinner last night. It's not just the three of us, of course, Althea, Gregory and me. It's all those who've lived there for the last century and longer. Althea's made it so much worse, so much more pervasive – I've

63

counted over thirty canvas faces hanging on the walls. That's all been changed since I went away – most of them were shut away in cupboards where they more properly belong. It would be a mistake for you in any way, in *any* way, to become one of them – perhaps I should say one of us.'

'I don't intend to.'

'No ... no, well, that's fine. Well, then, there's no problem, is there?'

'I don't know.'

He put down his brush in a jar and stared for a minute over the lake, his lean, clever face contemplative.

'I was always fond of Aunt Althea, you know.'

'Were you? Aren't you?'

He said: 'But my fondness, if I analyse it, was slightly patronizing. Sorry for the egoism. Perhaps that was something of a fault. You see I always thought of her as having one of these acquisitive brains that gathered up nuts of information like a squirrel and hid them somewhere and then dug them up and pretended they were a discovery of her own – competent, second-rate, uninventive. But now I'm not so sure ... There is a creative ingenuity about ... Will you tell her all this?'

'Not if you don't want me to.'

'What I'm not certain about at this stage is whether she wishes me good or ill. What do you think, Miss – er – Faulkner?'

'Good, surely. But how could I know? I know nothing of your family.'

'So you say. This is what we have to discover, isn't it?'

'I don't think I like being considered a liar,' she said.

'No ... no, that wasn't what I meant.' He laughed pleasantly. 'We're not getting very far, are we? Sorry, it's my fault. Let's not fence any more. You asked me a question. Does your being here upset me? The answer is no.'

'Thank you.' Norah was still uncomfortable but she smiled back at him.

He quickly lowered his eyes. 'Fine. That's settled. Would you help me carry my things back to the house?'

She did so, and as she did so she saw the picture more clearly. In the rushes at the edge of the lake he had painted a woman's figure, naked, lying face upwards in the water.

II

BY THE afternoon post came a flat package for Norah. She tore it open and found the photograph taken of her yesterday by Christopher Carew.

Well, there it was, the professionalism again, the composition of foreground and background, the fine detail, the differing shades and shadows. Even the foreground, she had to admit, was not altogether a failure. She knew that her parted lips and wide eyes were parted and wide from shock; but anyone looking at the picture and not knowing would see it only as an expression of enjoyable excitement. She looked as if any moment she might leap the gate.

On the back was written: 'See what I mean? Please come again.'

She might have done that; but Mr Croome-Nichols was right and Simon wrong; by the time she had helped Mrs Syme with her bills it was raining.

She went up to her room and into her sitting-room and read a book for an hour. She used this room – indeed entered it – with a continuing reluctance. With its air of desuetude, its slightly acrid, disinfectant smell, its faded curtains and worn furniture and the memory of movements she fancied she had heard, it didn't make her feel comfortable or at home. After a while she put her book down and stared about. This presumably had been the day nursery where twenty years ago Simon and Marion had played together – besides probably many generations before. They must have slept in her bedroom. These were the beads on the frame by which they had first learned to count. This was the rocking-horse Marion had ridden hour after hour as a child through the long winter afternoons. Marion had been drowned. So Simon painted her as he had once seen her lying naked face upwards in the lake was that it? – the lake as it had been before Althea turned it into a garden. Perhaps Marion still came up from the lake – sometimes and sat on this horse and rocked gently backwards and forwards, her long hair dripping and weedy. Perhaps she had been here last night, tapping with her foot on the floor.

Oh, rubbish. Take a grip of yourself. She got up and went over to the rocking-horse, pushed it. As before it rocked easily but made no sound. It was about two feet from the wall and, deprived of the shadow cast by a lamp, it looked old and worn and harmless. The wall-paper on this wall of the room was slightly different from the rest, less faded and the pattern smaller – as if perhaps it had been added a few years after the rest, when the original pattern was no longer obtainable. In one or two places it had a bulge as if the paste had dried and allowed it to come away from the plaster behind.

The only ornament on this wall was a faded print of a Dürer engraving beside a cupboard, and a spotted mirror, in which she now stared at herself. What had Marion *really* looked like? – clearly not fair like her brother. There must be a photograph somewhere or even a painting. Surely Simon would have painted her. Were they really alike, she and Marion? Twenty-three Marion had been. Her age now. But that was seven years ago. It would make her thirty now, if she had lived. Four years younger than her brother. It was about the right age-gap for a romantic attachment between brother and sister, a sort of love affair without sex, an intimacy grown right through from childhood: thoughts, memories, ideals shared.

She picked up her book again but she had not made a good choice. Her father had often laughed over W. W. Jacobs, so today she had taken this out of the library to read a casual story or so. Two light ones to begin, pleasant, old-fashioned fisherman's stories, mildly amusing; then the third, a nasty hair-raising tale of murder and possession. It wasn't the proper reading for a dark afternoon.

She went back to the cupboard on the wall. Two

days ago she had opened it and found an untidy litter of things which had not seemed worth sifting through. Now she picked them over.

Many of them were childish. A mouth-organ, a top, a skipping rope. In the back she found a pair of blue slippers. They were a bit small for her, possibly were Marion's. A school photograph of about thirty girls – impossible to pick one out; a photograph of two young men in RAF uniforms. On the back was written: 'To Marion, my very own love'. One of the men was Simon. So the other . . . ? Or had Simon written it?

An exercise book full of scribblings and drawings. Childish writing: 'Marion Mary Syme, Morb House, Llandathery, Montgomeryshire, Wales, Great Britain, Europe, The World'. Marion had also had some talent for drawing. There were dozens of crayon sketches of a boy of about fifteen with a mop of fair hair. Sometimes he had a round smiling face, sometimes it looked narrow and preoccupied. There were also one or two more mature drawings; one of a boy and a girl climbing a tree and he was holding her by the ankle; another of what looked like an execution; the axe had come down and the head was just splitting from the body; it was Simon's face and the executioner was a girl. Another where a boy and a girl were locked in a fight, yet appeared to be kissing. There were several more in which both boy and girl had goat's heads, and then a whole series of naked pictures in which none of the people had faces. At the very end was a drawing of a devil with a tail where his sexual organs ought to have been.

Norah shut the book, shut the cupboard and dusted her hands. Then she went into the bathroom to wash them. It was good to be out of that room. The rain was still falling and the house was quiet and prematurely dark. She returned to the sitting-room and got her book, careful not to take any notice of the rocking-horse which she half persuaded herself had been moving gently when she returned.

She went downstairs. The first landing was dark and silent, almost darker now than at night when a small light burned. The design of the house was very eccentric. This big central landing was platform-like, with Althea's bedroom and Gregory's and another opening directly off it, while beside Althea's bedroom the eight steps led down to the bathrooms. At the other side was the long meandering creaking passage down which at night Mr Croome-Nichols was seen to jerk his way, and at the very end of which Simon's bedroom commanded a view of the valley. Near the stairs going up to her rooms were steps down to the other passage whose destination seemed to be a green door leading to the staff quarters. Norah wondered about the unused part of the house and how one entered it. Perhaps they were two quite separate entities.

She decided it was not the day for exploring – or she was not in the mood to do it. She went down to the ground floor. As she passed Mrs Syme's study there were voices which sounded as if they were raised in argument. She heard Althea saying something emphatically. It could have been Simon's voice answering.

She walked on towards the first drawing-room,

turned over some of the music on the piano, then pressed her nose against the window staring at the weeping valley. A break in the clouds low over the west. The Jacobs book was still in her hand, and she turned and went into the library to put it back.

There was a scuffle and two figures broke apart; one stood up rapidly, the other got more slowly from a chair. Alice the parlour maid and Doole the butler. First instinct to apologize and withdraw. She checked that and went across to a bookshelf to return her book, as if no one else was there.

'I beg your pardon, miss,' Doole said, 'I came to look for Mr Syme and . . .'

She caught the glint of his dark eyes as he spoke. Disadvantage of a young butler. But the normality of having interrupted a little petting was curiously reassuring.

'Is it time for tea?' she asked. 'I believe it's after four.'

'Any time, miss. Usual, I wait for madam to ring.'

'Then I'll wait.'

He went out. She looked along the rows of books. There was a fair selection of modern novels in the study, but in here nothing seemed to have been added since the middle thirties.

'I'm that sorry, miss,' came suddenly from Alice, who was still in the room. An attractive Welsh lilt.

'About what?'

'About finding me and Doole like that, you know.'

Norah picked out a book. 'Oh, it's not my concern, Alice.'

'So I hope you won't mention it to madam. It would be the push I should get.'

'And Doole?'

'Oh, no. Oh, no, Mrs Syme would give me the blame.'

'Wrongly?'

'Well, maybe it is half and half, like. Though it is hard to keep away from him in this house . . .'

'Mrs Syme won't hear anything from me.'

'Thank you, miss.'

Norah put the book back. She didn't feel in the mood for Tolstoy. The girl had still not left the room.

'Are you fond of him, Alice?'

'Who, Doole?' Reassured, Alice came a step or two out of the shadow. 'Goodness, no, miss. There's times he's a bit of a swine, like. Er – begging your pardon, that is.'

'So why . . .'

'Oh, I dunno.' Alice broke off. The mysteries of physical attraction and repulsion went too deep for her. 'It's a bit lonely, like, up here. And he's not so bad when he's in a good mood, you know . . .'

Norah could not help her. She felt sympathy and a gulf. She had never been able to accept love and sex as that sort of a second-rate game. But she didn't think it entitled her to feel superior about the mysteries of physical attraction and repulsion. Even with her break from Robert Jenkin so fresh in her mind – and her determination not to allow herself any new involvement until the old had had a long time to fade – even with this she was aware of new and potent influences at work in her in the last few days.

Alice said: 'Others 've come and gone. The other maids, yes. Mostly the English girls. They miss the bright lights and the city streets, like. But I've stayed. I'm used to the quiet. Madam likes me. But if it was whether I went or Ted Doole, it would be me.' She made a movement to the door.

'How long have you been here?'

'Three and a half years, miss.'

'You don't remember Mr Syme's sister, then? Miss Marion Syme.'

'Oh, goodness no. It would be a long time before, you know. There has been no one here so long as that. I am the longest, then Timson, then Doole. They've all been changed.'

'Are you a local girl?'

'No, miss. I'm from the north. Abergele. The local girls won't come here.'

'Why not?'

'I dunno, miss. They say it's unlucky, like.'

Norah took out another book, stared at it without seeing the name. 'Have you ever seen a photograph of Miss Marion Syme?'

'No, miss. Never, miss. Only . . .'

'Only what?'

'Only the paintings.'

'What paintings?'

'Those that was on the walls, miss. Three of them. One in the dining-room, one in the back hall, you know. One in . . .'

'They were taken down?'

'Oh yes, miss, quite recent. Early this month. Taken up to Mr Simon's bedroom, they was.'

'On whose orders?'

'Oh, I suppose he asked for 'em, you know. Madam had some other portraits brought in instead.'

A gleam of sun fell across the garden and then died again. The rain was over.

Norah said: 'Alice, do you notice any likeness between those portraits of Miss Marion and me?'

The girl smiled. 'Why yes, miss, I thought there was a likeness when I first saw you. Doole's remarked on it too, he has. You might be sisters, like. Of course, it is only going by the paintings, mind. You can't really tell from those, can you? Did you know Miss Marion, miss?'

'No. I believe she died six or seven years ago – was drowned or something.'

'Yes, indeed, they both were.'

'Both?'

'Miss Marion and her husband. My goodness, I don't know, but that's what people say . . .'

She broke off as the door opened and Gregory peered in. Heliographs blinked from his eyes.

'Mother wants you,' he said to Norah. 'She's in the study with Cousin Simon.'

CHAPTER FIVE

ALTHEA WANTED to dictate some letters; it seemed a routine matter, except that Simon was there and that when he moved to go Mrs Syme said: 'No, stay. Stay and make sure that this is what you want me to say.' He had got up when Norah came in and had smiled cheerfully at her – it was a smile that warmed her and made her feel more welcome in this house than anything had before – but once she began to take dictation he seemed to lose interest in his surroundings and to draw into himself. Althea was her usual serene self – like a great lake scarcely ruffled by the storm that had blown. But there had been a storm, of that there was no doubt.

The letters were business letters of a routine kind; one directed to a solicitor in Aberystwyth, another to an estate agent, a third to a bank, a fourth to an insurance company. One dealt with the collection of rents, another with outstanding mortgages, a third with the sale of shares. Syme property was evidently extensive – they were a wealthy family. Much of the money seemed to be in the form of trusts.

'Would you like me to type these now?' Norah asked when they had done.

'Any time. After tea or tomorrow morning. Oh, I have asked a friend of yours to dinner tonight.'

'Of mine?'

'Well, you met him yesterday. Christopher Carew. He telephoned an hour ago so I told him to come for drinks at seven and stay for a meal. You don't know him, Simon, do you?' Mrs Syme explained about him. 'You may have a good deal in common. Photography these days is an art.'

'Not so much an art as an artifact,' Simon said. 'It's surely a sort of – of halfway profession. Isn't it? I'd rather make chairs. That seems to be more genuinely creative.'

'I found him quite interesting,' Norah said.

'If you like him,' Simon said, 'that's a recommendation.'

Althea looped back her hair. 'Very gracious of you! I hope your mood is changing.'

'I don't say gracious things,' Simon said; 'I only try to speak my mind; and if Norah likes this man I'm prepared to sink my principles.'

It was the first time he had used her Christian name, and he put a sort of affinity, of affection into it.

After tea she typed the letters and made three copies at Mrs Syme's request. She and Althea talked for a while. It was in the old friendly way, chatting and laughing and exchanging points of view. Yet when the older woman brought up casually the subject of the quarrel and break-up with Robert Jenkin, Norah found herself reluctant to confide the whole story, as she had fully expected to do sooner or later. Some barely acknowledged change in her feeling for Althea had created a little hedge of reserve. She was herself surprised to find it there, barring the way to complete frankness on her part.

Presently it was time to change for dinner. She was interested to see how Christopher Carew would behave. Whatever his private opinion he was clearly not going to miss an evening out; she heard his voice before she entered the room, and when she did he was leaning against the mantelpiece talking emphatically to Althea Syme. He was in brown twill trousers and a maroon smoking jacket; the wide tie, the big cream shirt, the handkerchief loosely hanging, all matched his large bony good-humoured features and helped to build up the picture of the artist at ease.

They were discussing a book on landscape gardening which was to come out at Christmas and for which he had contributed some of the photographs.

'Oh, I believe you've met my young friend, Miss Faulkner. You know Mr Carew, Norah.'

He smiled. 'Yes, I wrote a poem about her, she looked so pretty standing at the gate. But I couldn't get it to scan. Maybe if she came again she could help me with the trochees . . .'

'Is that a new breed of cattle?' Norah asked, smiling back.

'*Touché.*' He turned to Althea. 'But look, your garden is still so *new*. Even with these pre-fab methods you employ, you can hardly . . .'

'What a ghastly description!'

'Well, whatever you call these transplants, you can

never compete with the great gardens that have had a hundred years to grow. When they . . .'

'You should have seen it *before*,' Simon said. 'It had had a hundred years to mellow before all these alterations were made. Now it's like a new shopping centre compared to an old village street. D'you know that thing? "By shallow rivers to whose falls, Melodious birds sing madrigals." It was *that* sort of garden. A shock to me to see the changes.'

'You've been away some time?' Carew said.

'. . . Five years – nearly six.'

'In America, d'you say?'

'Part of the time.'

'Where were you?'

'In America?' Simon hesitated. 'Oh, various places.'

'You used to write to us mainly from New York,' said Althea encouragingly.

'Yes, well . . .'

'I was in New York two years ago,' said Christopher. 'Stayed at the New Weston, near Rockefeller Center. D'you know it?'

'I don't think I do.'

'There was an exhibition of photography at – I forget the name of the hall – in West 49th Street . . .'

Presently they went in to dinner. Christopher sat next to Norah and kept her in the conversation. He was a stimulating man and rather, one supposed, a domineering one. Oh, dear, not again! When his eyes met hers they weighed on her with a significance she recognized, yet it was so momentary that no one else could intercept the communication, not even Simon, who sat opposite and for the most part had retired into his shell again. The meal certainly sparkled as no other had done. Christopher was good at keeping talk going without dominating it. She had to admire.

It was clear that Althea enjoyed his company. Sometimes there was a hint of archness in her voice as if she were ready to flirt with him. She responded mentally and physically to the stimulus.

After dinner they had coffee in the big drawing-room behind. Like the other rooms it had too many family portraits; Althea Syme took her guests on a conducted tour of them, and he politely went along, though he took the opportunity to give Norah a wink when the others were not looking. She turned and spoke to Simon, who had come up behind her.

He said: 'Portraiture's one of the most difficult things. I used to paint a lot of portraits, but it – in the end it's self-defeating.'

'How do you mean?'

He looked closely at her to see if she really cared. 'Well, it's a conflict, isn't it – between the painter's self and the sitter's. If the painter's self becomes uppermost it may turn out a good painting but a bad portrait. If the sitter triumphs then it becomes scarcely more than a good likeness.'

'Famous painters have done a lot, though.'

'Oh, yes. Picasso never cared about the sitter, of course. Rembrandt – well, his self portraits are supreme because here there is no conflict. I – perhaps I have always had too much difficulty in separating myself from other people. There's a great danger of being

78

swallowed up by other people, of being absorbed into them. It can become a complaint, a weakness if you like. To lose oneself may be desirable in a saint, it's death to the artist.'

She hesitated. 'Did you ever paint your sister?'

He sipped his coffee. 'Yes,' he said, 'so often that I almost became a part of her.'

She suppressed a tendency to shiver. 'I've never seen one of her. Do you have any here?'

'Yes ... in my bedroom. If you come up there I'll show you. Sometime tomorrow?'

'Thank you.'

'Or perhaps,' he said, turning away, 'it would be better not.'

A little later there was a discussion on Welsh poetry, and inevitably Dylan Thomas's name came up. Christopher thought him too much of the showman, Althea Syme was convinced he was a minor genius.

'Gregory,' she said. 'Where is that tape? The one that was made during the war of his reading his poems on the Third Programme. Simon's father,' she explained, 'was one of the first private individuals to buy a tape machine, and he would take down his favourite programmes off the radio and play them back when he wanted. You know it, Gregory.'

'Yes, mother. But it's out at the back somewhere. The machine hasn't been used for a year or more.'

'Oh, yes, I used it a couple of weeks ago to try out a speech. It must be in the library.'

'Well, it's too heavy for me to carry myself.'

'Go with him, Rupert,' she said to Croome-Nichols.

'I'd like you to hear it, Mr Carew, because it contains about half of his "Deaths and Entrances" on which I think his claim to greatness chiefly rests.'

In the movement which followed Norah found herself alone with their guest.

He said: 'Well, what did you think of the photograph?'

'I liked it. I think perhaps it's more honest than the photographer.'

'Honest?'

'Well, less hypocritical.'

'Because I've come to dinner? But I told you, I came last year. Of course one has one's private opinion.'

'Perhaps it would have been better to have kept it that way.'

'But honestly, my dear. *Aren't* they an odd lot? D'you think young Gregory was come by naturally or hatched over a peat fire?'

'And Simon?'

'*Can* he paint?'

'Yes.'

'How well?'

'I think quite well.'

'He's the best of them. But *honestly*,' he stopped; 'that's the second time I've used that word and this time I mean it – I rang up and fished for an invitation chiefly to meet you again.'

She looked at him. 'Why?'

'Because I very much wanted to.'

'How much hypocrisy in that?'

'No hypocrisy. Only a gross understatement.'

She was the one to look away then, aware enough of the message and softened by it, but not wanting it to mean anything to her.

'When are we going to meet again?'

'Are we?'

'I hope so. Look, we can't talk now. Can you meet me tomorrow afternoon?'

'It depends. If Mrs Syme needs me . . .'

'Come if you can. Same place, same gate; about four.'

'If I'm free I'll walk that way . . .'

Althea came back followed by Mr Croome-Nichols carrying the tape recorder. Doole served more coffee while she threaded the tape. As they settled back the rich rotund voice of Dylan Thomas came into the room.

> 'And death shall have no dominion.
> Dead men naked they shall be one
> With the man in the wind and the west
>   moon;
> When their bones are picked clean and
>   the clean bones gone,
> They shall have stars at elbow and foot;
> Though they go mad they shall be sane,
> Though they sink through the sea they
>   shall rise again;
> Though lovers be lost love shall not;
> And death shall have no dominion.'

The sonorous voice went on, reading one poem after another. It cast a spell over the room, and when Doole had withdrawn there was no movement or attempt to talk. It lasted for about fifteen minutes and then a discreet BBC voice said: 'That was Dylan Thomas reading a selection of his own poetry ... This is the BBC Third Programme. We now have ...' The voice faded out.

'Well,' said Christopher, 'I confess they're impressive. *Minor* genius one might just admit; but in these last few years he's been too much the extrovert to do anything as good. He ...'

The tape had not been switched off and had been clicking a time or two. Now a young woman's voice said:

'Hullo, everybody, this is the BBC Third Programme. Here is the News, and this is Marion Syme reading it.' The voice burst into laughter which was echoed by voices somewhere in the background. 'At one o'clock today the engagement was announced between Flying Officer Richard Healy of 201 Bomber Squadron of the Royal Air Force and ...' 'Do shut up, Marion,' a voice interrupted. 'You know you can't hold me to it. A tape can't be used in evidence ...' There was more laughter and the tape chilled into silence.

Simon was standing up, his coffee cup askew on its saucer and a trickle of coffee dregs dripping.

'Oh,' said Althea, 'so sorry. I'd forgotten this was on the same tape. Just high spirits at a time when – but of course, Simon ... Switch it off, Gregory.'

The boy got up and went towards the instrument. Before he got there Marion's voice came again. It was imitating Dylan Thomas, sombre and round-vowelled.

'They shall have stars at elbow and foot; though they go mad they shall be sane, though they sink through the sea they shall rise again; though lovers be lost . . .'

Click. Gregory had switched it off.

'Excuse me,' Simon said. He dropped his coffee cup with a smash in the hearth and left the room.

There was silence.

'I do beg everyone's pardon,' Althea said. 'It was *quite* inexcusable of me, but I'd *entirely* forgotten there was anything more on that tape. Gregory, you should have been quicker to switch it off.'

'How was *I* to know . . . !'

''Fraid I'm rather lost in this,' Christopher said. 'Is it something . . . ?'

'Marion was Simon's sister. She met her death in unfortunate circumstances seven years ago. Simon has never quite got over it. Hearing her voice, I suppose, would bring it all back. I *am* so sorry. I expect he'll return in a moment.'

The nasty feeling at the back of Norah's neck and spine was receding only slowly; for the voice had not been altogether unlike hers.

She said: 'D'you think I might go and see if he's all right?'

'Of course, my pet, please do. Don't bother, Mr Carew, Doole will clear up the mess. Will you have another brandy? Gregory, what is on the other side of the tape? I think it's some of Priestley's wartime broadcasts . . .'

In the main hall there was no one about. Six Symes, dimly seen among the shadows, looked down their noses at the intruder. A window was open, and in the rising breeze one of the hanging lamps gently swayed. As she shut the casement Simon's voice came from the front drawing-room.

'. . . hanging about the house like this . . . your own quarters!'

Timson came out. He was in a grey suit, not his chauffeur's uniform. Truculent, big-faced, he glanced at Norah, then hunched his shoulders and stepped past.

As she went in Simon was moving towards a drawing-room window which also was open. His profile was sharp and nervous, like a fox's. He shut the window and stood peering out at the intangible night. She coughed.

As he saw her his eyes caught light from the lamp before they dulled over.

'Why have you followed me?'

Confronted with the blunt question, she was not sure. A lot of her impulses these last two days had been confused, and this was one of them. A wish to help him, to free him from some incubus. A feeling that by helping him she might be able to throw off some of the fetters of her own disquiet.

'I thought you were not feeling well.' It sounded lame even to herself.

'Did Althea send you?'

'No.'

'I'm glad . . . But in the first place she brought you here. *She* brought you here, and I wonder how much she has told you.'

'Nothing.'

He moved nearer to her, peering at her in the soft white light. 'But *don't* you know? In your heart don't you know everything?'

'Nothing.' She didn't lower her gaze.

Eventually he put his hand up to his eyes, turned away. 'I suppose not ... I suppose you're only being kind.'

'Not even just that,' she said, the words coming out unexpectedly.

'But you *are* kind. I feel such an unexpected sense of sympathy ... Norah, I want to talk to you, quite seriously. There may not be another opportunity, because this is a trial of strength and I am not sure when something may – when something may not be strong enough. Can you sit down?'

She sat on the edge of a chair. He took a seat opposite her, leaning forward, hands clasped between knees.

'This morning you asked me whether you should leave this house, and I said no, not to please me. Well, now I think you would be wise to go.'

'You think I should go.'

'There's no real alternative. If you are not in this then you are as much a dupe as I. But where I am guilty you are not. And I think there would be danger for you. I want you to take that to heart. Possibly there could be danger.'

The conversation's slipping away again, she thought. 'What sort of danger?'

He shook his head. 'I prefer not to go into that. Isn't it sufficient reason to tell you that so long as you stay in this house you're – putting yourself at some risk?'

'Is this to do with your sister?'

He smiled, but it was not the warm pleasant smile of which he was capable. 'Yes. Oh, yes. What else could it be?'

'But your sister has been dead for seven years.'

'For a while I wondered – tried to persuade myself. Sometimes I even hoped. But of course it's all in vain. I – but you see – if Marion died ... I – I was responsible ...'

'How responsible ... ? Are you not sure she's dead?'

He turned swiftly as the door opened. Doole stood there.

'Beg pardon, sir. Mr Carew is leaving and madam thought ...'

'Of course.' Simon got up. 'I'll come and say good night.'

As he moved to pass Norah she touched his arm. He stopped instantly. She said: 'Are you not sure she's ...'

After a moment he said: 'Yes. Recently I've been looking for her. But I'm sure now. But you see, even then, however hard you try, you can't lay the ghost.'

CHAPTER SIX

I

THAT NIGHT there were no noises to disturb her, and the following day everything went so normally that her unease was held in abeyance. She had had every intention of telling Althea of her conversation with Simon and asking if she might leave as soon as was decently convenient. But she changed her mind. Against her better judgment she had become caught up in the situation in the house and thought to wait one or two days more to see how it would develop. She was not at all sure of her own impulses and knew that this decision owed more to emotion than to reason. It was illogical to offer to leave if Simon told her to and then not to leave when he did. But she found herself suddenly too far involved to pack her bags and take the next train. She wanted to know *why*. An explanation of some sort was owing to her. It must come from somewhere – either from Althea Syme or Simon himself – before she left. But who would speak the truth? Plain asking might not receive a plain answer. In dealing with a devious situation one might have to be devious oneself.

She also thought it might be interesting to meet Christopher Carew again.

But she did not see him that day as arranged.

In the morning she had to take down an article Mrs Syme was writing on peat-loving shrubs for a gardening paper, and then to type out a speech she was delivering in Shrewsbury later in the week. After this she was told they were 'all' going to Aberystwyth in the afternoon, and would she come with them? It was a luminous autumn day, and she could hardly do other than accept. 'All' was indeed all: Simon and Gregory in the front of the big car with Timson, Norah in the back with Althea and the Reverend Rupert Croome-Nichols.

They went via Devil's Bridge and the road which ran along the edge of the cliff overlooking the River Rheidol. The valley spread out eight hundred feet below them, a vivid cucumber green dotted with the tiniest of toy houses and cattle too small to play with. Timson as usual drove at speed, and with the road turning and swooping high above the earth it was a stimulating experience.

In Aberystwyth Simon and his aunt went off to keep some appointment and the others were left to fend for themselves. Mr Croome-Nichols disappeared into an antiquarian bookshop, so Norah suggested to Gregory that they might look round the town together. She no longer had quite so much regard for Althea's requests, but to do this might suit her own ends as well.

The refusal she had half expected didn't come, so they went off, first along the promenade, then looking in a number of shops in the town. She made no attempt to open a conversation, and little was said. Gregory went into a bookshop and asked for a book called

Heredity and the Mendelian Principle by C. Stokes. He seemed annoyed that they had not got it and grudgingly left an order.

As they came out she said: 'It's hardly the sort of book a provincial bookseller would have in stock, is it? I would have thought . . .'

'There's the University of Wales here. It's not *just* a provincial town. Students want books like that.'

'I didn't know. Or I'd forgotten. Are you studying genetics?'

'Not *studying* it. Reading about it. What I want to take up is psychiatry – psycho-analysis. Uncle Rupert, of course, won't hear of it. He says it's anti-Christian. As if I cared.'

Seagulls were crying in the autumn sunlight.

Gregory said: 'I spoke to that man Carew about it last night, and he says they're opposites.'

'What are?'

'Christianity and psycho-analysis. He says, Carew says, that Christianity visits the sins of the fathers upon the children, while psycho-analysis visits the sins of the children upon the fathers. I thought it rather neat.'

'Yes, it is.'

'Anyway, as if I cared about Uncle Rupert's opinion.'

'What does your mother say?'

The goggles were trained on her. 'You think she lets me have my own way?'

'She says she does.'

'Oh, she *says* so. But it's easy to say things. To get your own way with Mother you have to fight. And then it's like fighting an eiderdown.'

Norah said: 'It's often the way with vigorous, intelligent people, Gregory. They dominate without realizing they're doing it.'

'Oh, she realizes she's doing it, with me,' Gregory said. 'But she thinks she's succeeding.'

They walked on.

'Whose idea was it you should leave Radley?'

'Oh, she's told you that . . . Mine, actually.'

'You didn't like it?'

'I was wasting my time. How could I be good at games?'

'But is that all you could learn there?'

'No, but I wasn't willing to play second fiddle to a lot of fellows who happen to be able to see to kick a ball better than I can. And it's all so *childish* – the jargon you have to learn, the things you can do and can't do, the little petty tyrannies. I got absolutely fed up.'

'Yes, well . . .'

'Anyway, I was needed here.'

He was tall and ungainly beside her. The way he walked his shoes might have been heavy boots.

'Needed?'

'*I* thought so . . . How long have you known Mother?'

'About two years.'

'And Simon?'

'Two days.'

'You think Mother's a clever woman?'

'Very.'

'So she is, in some things. In others she's stupid –

plain stupid. I could have helped her in a dozen things if she'd let me ... much better than you're helping her. I would have arranged everything better. But she still thinks I'm a child.'

They were heading back towards the car. She was more aware than she had been before of the difficulties of a boy of fifteen, in-grown, with an existence unbruised by contact with ordinary humanity. Book knowledge taught him demonstrable facts, not the incalculable uncertainties of real life. His young mind, alert within its cage, made its own clearcut judgments and decisions, but was lamentably short of outside criteria to measure by.

She said: 'Do you remember your cousin Marion?'

'I met her once or twice. And I've seen her portraits. She was like you.'

'Yes, so people tell me. You must have been very young when she died.'

'Nearly nine. But I remember.'

'And her husband as well?'

'Richard? No, I never met him. Why?'

She said: 'You were not in Morb House when that record was made?'

'We didn't live here then. We were in London during the war. Surely Mother's told you.'

'I wondered why the tape so upset Simon last night.'

'Wouldn't you be upset?'

She said: 'I'm not sure. It's hard to judge, I know. I've just lost my father. He meant a great deal to me. But if after six or seven years I heard his voice on tape ...'

'Unexpectedly.'

'I suppose it might give me a turn. But I don't think I'd be upset in that way.'

'Simon thought he owned his sister.'

'What makes you say that?'

'It's one of Mother's remarks.'

Norah stopped, looking in a shop window, not seeing any thing in it but the reflection of the heavy spectacled boy beside her, reluctantly stopping also, reluctantly waiting for her. 'Gregory, do you know anything about Marion's marriage – and her death? Because I'm supposed to resemble her I feel I'd like to know something more, and your mother is reluctant to talk about it.'

'Why don't you ask Simon?'

'You know I can't do that. But probably you're too young to remember. Perhaps I shouldn't have asked.'

To her surprise he rose to the bait. 'I don't really see what business it is of yours. Of course I know; it's my family, isn't it?'

'Is it private – secret – that you can't tell?'

'It was all in the war. Simon was in a bomber squadron, his plane went in the sea, he was saved; they invalided him out – in '44, I suppose . . . His sister came home to look after him – she'd been on war work. Then one of Simon's friends fell in love with Marion. Simon didn't like it. He disapproved. But it didn't stop them. After the wedding they were going to spend their honeymoon in Ireland. On the way across their boat was sunk and they were both drowned.'

She stared at Gregory's reflection. 'Sunk? By a U-boat or something?'

'No, it was a storm.'

'But – this was in the Irish Sea?'

'Where else?' he said impatiently.

'But – I thought...' She stopped and saw him watching her. 'I knew Marion had been drowned, but I thought it was...' She stopped again, no longer willing to go on. 'Why did Simon disapprove?'

'He wanted Marion to stay with him. He thought he owned her. He said that here was where she belonged.' Gregory hunched his shoulders and moved off towards the car.

II

THEY HAD tea at a little café and drove home in the scarlet evening with the sun shafting unconvincingly through clouds that crouched over the mountains and threatened storm. When the sun finally gave up, large sparse drops of rain began to fall on the car and distant thunder rumbled. Climbing the long winding valley out of Cardiganshire in the premature, brooding, thundery twilight, Norah thought she had seldom seen land wilder or more desolate.

When they got home Simon went straight to his room and Norah slit open a letter which had not arrived by post. It said:

'The cloud effect was great, you should have
come. But our meeting now has another purpose,
connected with the Symes, and I think it important I

93

should see you. Will walk over late this evening –
say ten-thirty – and hang around the conservatory
door at the back. Try and make it. C.'

Dinner was a quiet meal. During it Simon was at his
most charming to Norah, as if no thought that he had
asked her to leave had ever entered his head. When he
was in this mood it was impossible not to respond. But
after dinner he went early to bed, while Gregory played
the piano and Althea took on Croome-Nichols at chess.

Norah half listened to Gregory, half read a magazine,
thinking of her own life and the complexities of making
the right decision. If she were to leave tomorrow, just
ask for the car and leave and catch the next train back
to London, what did London offer? She could put up
probably for a while with Olga; it was a bit squalid but
warm and comfortable and undemanding. An employ-
ment agency would soon find her a 'temp' job while she
looked round. But the prospect wasn't ravishing. Perhaps there is a loneliness to all independence. She still
very much missed her father. His even temperament had
acted as a leaven upon her own. It was not only his age
that enabled him to see events in clearer perspective: it
was an innate sense of balance. She was much more like
her mother – tended to be contrary and to make
mistakes out of an excess of temperament but to
recognize them as mistakes soon after she had made
them.

She got up and wandered down the passage and into
the library. As she had thought, the tape machine had
been carried back there and set on a table between the

shelves. She lifted the lid and looked in. A tape was on the deck, and it looked very much like the one that had been played last night. She wondered how it worked. It looked fairly simple. There was a switch marked *On* which when she pulled it produced a green light. There was a knob with four slots: *Record*, *Wind on*, *Wind back* and *Play back*. There was a switch marked *Start* and a button marked *Press to stop*. The knob was set at *Play back*. She glanced round the shadowy library to see that no one was sitting hidden in one of the big chairs, then pressed the switch for *Start*.

Marion's voice loud and clear instantly filled the room.

' – love shall not.

And death shall have – '

In a panic she jabbed the button to stop. Silence settled again on the library like a heavy curtain that has been parted by a gust of wind.

After a minute she saw a knob marked *Gain* and turned it right back. Then she switched on again, slowly turning up the sound until the recording came through as an undertone.

There was silence and some clicking. Then Marion began to sing in a thin but sweet voice. At first she was just humming a tune, then she sang a little nursery rhyme,

> 'Once there was a little boy
> Wouldn't say his prayers
> When he went to bed one night
> Away upstairs.

> Mamma heard him shouting
> Dadda heard him call
> When they went to look for him
> He wasn't there at all!'

There was laughter at this, a man chuckling and the girl joined in. After that silence fell. It was queer waiting, not knowing what was to come.

Then the girl said sharply: 'Simon, come and look at my engagement ring! Don't you think the sapphire matches my eyes?'

The man laughed again and said: 'Don't be stupid, darling, your eyes are green. Anyway, Simon's sulking.'

'No, he's not. Are you, Simon. Simon never sulks for his Marion. *Simon . . . !*'

There was silence. Then a little whistle. It was a girl's whistle. Then the man's voice:

> 'Oh, whistle, and I'll come to ye, my lad,
> Oh, whistle, and I'll come to ye, my lad,
> Though father and mither and all should
>   gae mad,
> Oh, whistle, and I'll come to ye, my lad.'

Silence and clicking.

Marion's voice: 'Simon, come and look at my engagement ring. Simon . . . ! *Simon . . . . ! Simon . . . ! Simon . . . ! Simon . . . !*'

She went on repeating the name in a tense whisper. Unable to take any more, Norah switched off. The tape was not helping. It was not helping at all.

She rubbed her hands on her handkerchief as if to remove some dust or doubt. Then she walked out of the library and back to the drawing-room. Here the game of chess was just breaking up with the orthodoxy in the shape of Mr Croome-Nichols triumphant. He opened his mouth at Norah in saturnine good humour, and she smiled back. Didn't she play chess? Good for the mind. Do her mind all the good in the world. Didn't her father ever teach her? A pity. There was no way of making up for lack of parental tuition. Same with formal education. If you didn't get the best, well, you missed it; and that was something you could never make up. Not that it was quite the same these days. All these free scholarships and things . . .

'They may be the salvation of England,' said Althea as she fitted the chessmen into their little felt compartments. 'To create a peaceful revolution.'

Mr Croome-Nichols sniffed, twisting his long nose at her. 'No doubt they have their uses. In exceptional cases, that is. But like everything else these days, it's carried too far. Exaggeration: spirit of the age. Met a man last month – son of a butcher – been up to St John's for next to nothing, and just been given a fat living. Son of a butcher. Couldn't do it in my day. It's turning the world upside down, and – er – hm . . .'

'You're a little out of date, Rupert. It seems . . .'

'And a good thing too. Who wants to be up to date in this modern world? Look what that fellow Carew was telling us only last night . . .'

Norah glanced at her watch. In half an hour that fellow Carew would be waiting to meet her outside the conservatory door. Would she go? Did she keep night trysts like a love-sick servant girl? But he had worded his note cunningly.

She shifted in her chair and watched Mr Croome-Nichols making his nightly preparations to retire: the book, the glasses, the change of slippers, the winding of the watch, then unfolding himself from his chair like a rusty jack-knife. Be honest (because if you can't be honest with yourself . . .), if you go to meet Christopher it may partly be to discover what he has to tell you about the Symes, but it will also be curiosity to explore your own feelings. A sophisticated man, good-looking, well orientated, making a dead set. He was obviously very much at home with women, very expert. Great charm. Given encouragement, any sort of encouragement, he'd take charge. Would you be willing?

Surely not so soon, surely not after the hurting break with Robert. Life didn't arrange things very well. That lack of perspective that she had recently regretted was inevitable here. How *could* one begin again so soon and know anything for certain, what was truth, what was emotion on the rebound?

Everyone retired to bed, conveniently, at ten-fifteen. Christopher had estimated their movements well. She went up to her room, lit the lamp there, peered in at her sitting-room; nothing moved. She shut the door, sat on the bed for ten minutes, then kicked off her one good pair of Parisian evening shoes – cream lace court shoes – and put on a pair of suede shoes, swung a cardigan round her shoulders, took up a pocket torch and went down to the library. The conservatory opened off a short passage beyond.

All the lights in the house had been put out except for two small lamps which stayed on all night as pilot lights in the main hall and on the main landing. Once in the library she flickered the torch from wall to wall, anxious not to surprise or be surprised by Doole and Alice again. The room was quite empty except for chairs. It smelt dusty and old.

She went through the passage into the conservatory. The sky had split open, and a thickening slice of moon low down above the mountains peered between monuments of cloud. She reached to pull the bolt back and saw it was already drawn. Careless. But then what tramp or burglar would wander here? They'd be too scared. She stepped into the garden.

This side of the house you were protected from the breeze and it was not cold. A scent of late roses was in the air. All the same the garden was a place of secrets tonight, in which harmless and mundane shrubs took on a mysterious humped significance. She wondered what it would be like down by the lake. Of course Marion might now just be on her way up with dripping hair and staring eyes to ride the rocking-horse in her nursery. Perhaps that was why they left the door unlocked. (But had she not died in Cardigan Bay?)

Something moved not far away, and she started before she knew he was already there waiting.

'Good,' he said, 'you're dead on time. Hullo.'

Because her heart had bumped she was angry both

with him and with herself. As he loomed up, tall and grey in the half dark, she said: 'This – this jumping from behind stones is rather trying.'

'You let me down this afternoon. I waited two hours.'

'Sorry . . . we went to Aberystwyth. I couldn't let you know. Anyway, it was not . . .' She stopped.

'Important? Well, it was to me. But I've made use of the extra time with another session at the Dyfri Arms.'

'What's that?'

'The little pub at Llandathery. I told you. I go there sometimes to pass an idle hour, and this time the hour hasn't been wasted. Look, can we sit somewhere?'

'There's a bench by that tree. But I mustn't stop long. Supposing Doole came round and locked me out.'

'Maybe that would be a good thing.' He waited until she was seated and then sat down close beside her. 'It would force a decision.'

'A decision for what?'

'Well, you could come back with me to my cottage now and fetch your things away from here in the morning.'

'Tonight? But why? What's wrong?'

He groped for and found her hand. She let her hand be taken but was slightly restive at the possessiveness with which it was done. 'That first day I was half joking, saying this house wasn't for you. I meant it was stuffy, old, depressing, not your style. Now I mean it in a more positive way.'

She said: 'I'm perfectly capable of looking after

myself, Christopher. I can't see why everyone's so concerned for my safety. Just because you . . .'

'*Everyone?*' He bit on the word. 'Who else is concerned?'

'Did I say everyone? Well, you seem to be, anyhow.'

'Who else?'

She was reluctant to speak now. 'Oh . . . Simon last night – said something – when I went after him. It probably meant nothing.' She told him a few of the less vague of Simon's statements. To her annoyance Christopher was silent for a while, as if impressed. She didn't particularly want people to be impressed.

He said: 'Simon's the key, isn't he?'

'If there is one.'

'It's him I've come to talk to you about . . . Last night, of course, was the first time I'd met him, and as soon as I saw him I thought there was something pretty devious about the whole thing. First of all, he was lying about having been to America. Several questions I asked him he didn't know the answers to.'

'America's a big country.'

'But there are some things anyone who's been there knows.' The moon went behind a cloud and the garden was dark. A night bird was crying down by the lake.

'So?'

'So I asked about him at the Dyfri Arms. It's not much fun at first, going in there, because they all speak Welsh, and when they condescend to speak English and then switch back to their own language you never know whether they're going on talking about you and making jokes at your expense. But they come to know you after a while, and I met an old chap last night who has farmed round here for forty years and knows most of what goes on, so I asked him about the Symes.'

'What did you ask him?'

'Are you cold?'

'No, no.'

He seemed about to put his arm round her shoulder, but just refrained. She was not yet amenable.

'I've known the Symes three years, but it never really occurred to me to ask about them outside. One more or less takes a household for granted. I didn't like them as individuals but wasn't sufficiently interested to enquire, Until you arrived . . .'

'Well?'

'He was reluctant at first to say much, this chap – to display his prejudices to an Englishman. Obviously he thinks they were a pretty unscrupulous lot in the old days – made claims to land they'd no right to – that sort of thing – and the house has a bad name; one of the maids died here and the locals have fought shy of it for a long time.'

'So you told me.'

'Soon after Simon's parents died the house was closed, because the two children, Simon and Marion, were away – it was during the war. Then Simon was invalided out of the RAF and came back to recuperate. Then Marion came down with another RAF pilot she'd fallen in love with and they were married here. Apparently Simon objected.'

'Yes, I heard that this afternoon. I persuaded Gregory to tell me.'

'Did he tell you why Simon objected?'

'He seems to have been over-fond of his sister.'

'Yes – obviously – after last night. But he had another reason. Richard Healy, the bridegroom, was going to desert.'

'Desert – from the RAF?'

'Yes. He was Irish – Southern Irish – he'd flown on goodness knows how many bombing missions, and now he'd fallen in love and wanted to opt out. Apparently he argued that since he was a volunteer he ought to be able to leave when he chose. He was a high-spirited, irresponsible sort of chap, according to old Evans. He thought Simon, who had been invalided out, would understand. Simon didn't. They quarrelled. But Simon couldn't stop the wedding. They were married at Llandathery, went on to Shrewsbury for three days' legitimate honeymoon and then came back here before leaving for Ireland. Healy argued they could lie low there until the war was over. Simon had to go along with the idea, though he said that Healy would be a wanted man for years and that they would know no peace.'

'Your farmer seems to know a lot.'

'Well, his cousin used to work here, Abigail John; she died last year. She was here through it all – the only one.'

'And what has this to do with me?'

'Well, apparently it was pretty nasty here when they

got back from their three days' honeymoon. Simon had always been a bit neurotic and had been brooding on the marriage while they were away. There was only Abigail in the house besides them. She said Simon would not speak to either his sister or Richard Healy during the day they spent getting ready to leave. But he consented to drive them to the coast. Sometime during the following month, after they had left, that is, he tried to commit suicide.'

'Simon . . . ?'

'Yes. But they found him in time. The news had just come through that the boat the honeymooners were in had been lost at sea. Simon was breaking up and Mrs Syme came down to look after him.'

'Breaking up? In what way?'

'Well, I was right, he hasn't been to America. He. was put away. He spent the first year in the Redesdale, which, as you know, is a mental institution. Then he was transferred to the Conran Nursing Home in Norwich. I'm not sure of course exactly what type of illness Simon's is, but I rang a man this afternoon and he says the Conran specializes in cases of schizophrenia.'

CHAPTER SEVEN

I

HE KISSED her before he left, his hands holding her pleasurably, taking no liberties but promising what might come. She had been unable not to respond. It would have been ungenerous to seem cold, and for her quite out of character, but, perversely she had *wanted* not to respond, partly like the burnt child and because she hoped to keep their relationship unchanged for a while longer, partly because some other and perhaps deeper layer of her emotions was in a state of shock from what he had told her. She felt sick with the news.

He had again made the suggestion that she might be happier leaving tonight and coming to his cottage, but she had scotched the idea, arguing that there was no reason at all to suppose she wasn't perfectly safe and secure at Morb House, yet fully aware that she was withholding from him the one vital fact which would have given a fair and valid reason for persuading her to leave. He did not know of her likeness to Marion.

So why had she not told him?

She had closed the conservatory door on him when he left, but it now felt so stuffy and airless in the passage that she was reluctant to go up at once to her bedroom and lie between the sheets and try to sleep. So she went back into the conservatory and thence into the garden again, taking slow breaths of the cool scented air.

Why had she not told him? Because without that fair and valid reason his fears for her safety looked a trifle disingenuous. If she went with him to his cottage tonight, however much he might succeed in persuading himself or in persuading her that it was really for her protection, they were likely to end by sleeping together. And if she deluded herself or him into supposing she thought different, she too was being disingenuous. If she went she couldn't avoid it, and it was unlikely from her present feelings, that she would *want* to avoid it. So don't go. Just at present don't go. They had met three times. Something had flared between them. She didn't know yet whether it was important or unimportant. But she didn't at this juncture of her life want a casual love affair, however passionate. That it would be passionate she had no doubt at all; but she was being rushed by events; she needed longer, to think, to breathe in between, to consider, to take her time. She was sure of nothing and wanted to be sure.

But also, even if there were some very small element of risk in her remaining here, she still wasn't at all ready to leave. She had decided that this morning and saw no reason yet to change her mind. Too much had happened and too little was explained. Whatever the tragedy of seven years ago, this didn't explain what was happening now. Even if Simon should be a schizophrenic, no one had suggested he had ever been violent. (Why, then, had he mentioned danger himself? Was it danger from some other source?)

The moon had come out again and the garden was luminous with it. Where the light fell the shrubs were a snowy green; where the shadows lay it was azure-grey. Deep glooms existed as if whole areas had fallen away into some fathomless pit. Night animals stirred. She began to walk down towards the lake.

A night like this perhaps seven years ago. Only a breeze stirring in the valley, but gales forecast around the coasts. The front door of the house open, shaded lights flickering, a big car at the door, an elderly maid standing, three figures going out: the young man she had seen in the photo in her room, with him a girl, Marion, slim, medium to tall, brown hair; they were carrying suitcases; at the wheel a tall fair man sitting angrily silent. In the car, the door shut, the motor started, dimmed headlights switched on and away. Over the mountains, winding through the night. The house silent, the maid abed. Then the following day the big car returning with Simon alone. Driving up to the door, climbing wearily out, back into the empty house . . .

She stopped and looked back at the house. It was all in darkness except for one bedroom. She had never mastered its geography and had no idea who was not yet asleep. The animal bulk of Cader Morb blocked out all the sky to the north, the rock face here and there iridescent in the moonlight. It was about another fifty yards to the edge of the lake. She walked down, noticing that as she went lower so the tip of the crescent moon began to touch the nearest mountain.

Why had Simon drawn a woman's body floating in this lake? It was something else she had not told Christopher. The painting had quite deceived her, leading her to believe that Marion had been drowned here. Marion was too far away to come back every night from the Welsh coast to ride her rocking-horse again. What silly fancies came to one's mind with the barest encouragement!

Another silly fancy came to her mind at that moment and stopped her in her tracks. She could not give *that* thought room, otherwise there might really be danger, and it would be danger for her . . .

By the edge of the lake there was less protection from the breeze, and the rushes whispered among themselves. There was a bit of an island in the middle on which Mrs Syme had planted something called *gunnera manicata*. In this light the giant leaves did not so much look like rhubarb as like the scales of an extinct lizard of enormous proportions squatting on the bank with its head turned towards her.

She stood for a while, holding the cardigan to her throat, looking across the water, taking deep breaths, letting the breeze cool her heated face, willing her mind to empty itself of alarmist thoughts. It was curious how one could hypnotize oneself into terror with an absolute conviction of evil. Once when she was twenty she had thought herself gravely ill; every symptom corresponded precisely with the symptoms of the disease; she had the lot. A visit to a doctor blew it all away. Every symptom except one had a rational and healthy explanation, and that one was easy to cure. The ominous, the incontrovertible build-up was in her own mind.

So now.

The moon was in shipwreck. Half was sunk behind the mountain. She decided to wait until it had quite gone and then walk up to the house to see if she could catch a piece of its sinking over again. There was a rustling behind her and she would not turn, knowing it was the wind among the drying leaves of a tall pampas.

What had Simon said last night when she had followed him into the drawing-room? Many strange things, but one among them stranger and nastier than the rest. But if he was mentally ill, then possibly nothing at all that he said should be taken seriously. Yet, if he had been released, the doctors must be satisfied that he was cured. But cured of what – of mental illness or of guilt . . . ?

The pampas rustled again, and she thought she heard a footstep. What was it Keats had written? 'The sedge has withered from the lake and no birds sing.' Was she alone and palely loitering? Perhaps Christopher was still around, had come back to try to persuade her over again . . .

She turned and a man stood right behind her. But it was not Christopher.

II

SIMON SAID: 'It's you. I wondered who could be here so late.'

The moon had almost gone. Its last light showed up his narrow taut face, the pale skin which had seen so little sun, the intense preoccupied eyes. She swallowed her heart and said: 'I – came for a walk. The house – was stifling.'

'Yes . . . in more ways than one.' He put his head a little on one side, peering at her in the encroaching dark. 'I come this way most nights. I always loved the lake – before it was cleared and ruined.'

'Is that why the conservatory door was unbolted?' Her voice, from the shock, was wavering, unsteady.

'Why?'

'You came out that way?'

'Oh, yes, Doole is a great one for locking doors. It's a habit that grows on one.'

She shivered, half involuntarily, half put on. 'Well, I think I'll go in now the moon has set.'

' "The sedge has withered from the lake and no birds sing." Wasn't that what you were saying?'

She stared. 'Did I say it aloud?'

'The barest whisper.'

'You – must have been . . .'

'I was standing immediately behind you.'

'Yes . . . well, it just occurred to me.' She moved to pass him.

He said: 'Don't go. Not for a minute or so. The garden becomes more exciting in the dark.' She stopped. 'In the dark, I think, boundaries become frayed, one is more able to merge with inanimate things.'

She did not speak but stood beside him while the last

of the moonlight died and only the spiralling monument of cloud was lit.

'Do you ever think of it?'

'What?' she asked.

'The separativeness of self-consciousness. Without it, all things seem to live and to be an equal part of creation. Perhaps if one pondered it sufficiently it would be an answer to the mystery of life and death.'

'I don't – follow.'

'Well, isn't it a question of accepting the complete oneness and absolute sentience of all creation? Sometimes I wonder that. You see, man, because of his defective sight and hearing, imagines himself a distinct and highly individual – and indeed superior – part of the universe; whereas if he didn't or couldn't use his eyes and his ears he'd perhaps come to realize that he is, in mind, in body and in spirit, a part of an eternal pattern – d'you see what I mean? – one with it, woven into it, of the same texture throughout.'

She moved a step or two and he moved with her.

'It's out of doors,' he said, 'that you come to realize that sentience isn't confined to those categories of matter, those compositions of the carbon atoms, such as ourselves. Look at these stones.' He kicked one. 'Or that rock or those mountains – and of course in the sap of the tree, which pulses as surely as blood in the veins, the grass, the thrusting spear of grass, even the soft ground we tread on – in them all there's an identity with human kind . . . So that nothing is lost. Nothing is ever lost. D'you follow?'

'I think I do.'

'Well, even death is only a change. Isn't it? A change from what perhaps we see as beautiful to what we see as horrible. But that's a defect of sight and a failure of knowledge. I'm not sure that we *need* immortality. Because we're all part of the eternal mind and cannot escape even if we would. Corruption is another form of creation. It's a continuing process of development and change.'

She said: 'I've just lost my father. I wish I could feel more comfort in such a theory.'

'*Have* you? I didn't know. I'm sorry.' He touched her arm and then dropped his hand. 'After – after Marion had died, when I thought Marion had died, I went through hell. Torments of bereavement and remorse. It was only after a couple of years that I realized . . .'

She said: 'Tell me more about your theory.'

'It's not so much a theory as a slow *realization*. It's not as *cerebral* as a theory. Let me put it this way.' He was silent for a while as they took a few more paces up from the lake. 'D'you know I never painted anything for years . . . ? I suppose – look, you ask me to explain, but the moment I try to explain I have to put it into words – which, being made by men, are limited in their capacity of expression – and I have to *theorize*, which is contradiction of, or a rationalization of, what I feel here.' He touched his heart.

'I'm sorry, but I thought what you said might comfort me.'

'It's strange – and pleasant – to be thought capable

of comforting *anyone*. I'm usually looked on as the disturber.'

'It's the loss of personality that I find so hard to accept. So much lost and wasted.'

He stopped. 'Possibly Dylan Thomas said it all. It's art speaking for life, isn't it? "And death shall have no dominion. Dead men naked they shall be one with the man in the wind and the west moon." How does it go on? "They shall have stars at elbow and foot. Though they go mad they shall be sane ... *Though they sink through the sea they shall rise again.* Though lovers be lost love shall not ... And – and death shall have no – no dominion ..."' His voice shook as if he were near to tears.

Moved by his emotion she almost lost her fear. 'Simon, you feel too much, too intensely.'

'Ah,' he said quickly, 'that was what Marion used to say. You're so much like Marion. She would have said just that.'

'But I'm not Marion.'

'Well, you help to release feeling within me – as she did. Don't suppose – one of my problems these last few years, as it was early in my life, was a – an inability to feel deeply on a – a personal level. I was – too far away. Sometimes I almost became – someone else. Only Marion could release pleasure and grief. "Green pleasure and grey grief" – who said that? And I believe you can – by being so much like her – not only in looks but in personality – release in the same way green pleasure and grey grief.'

They began to walk on again, until they were halfway back to the house.

'Though lovers be lost,' he said, 'love shall not. That's the defiant cry of humanity, imprisoned within the walls of its defective hearing and sight.'

She said: 'You must feel deeply to be able to paint.'

'Oh, yes. That's why there have been times in my life – long spells – when I haven't been able to paint at all. When background and foreground become interchangeable, then creativeness suffers a sort of "heat death".'

After a few paces more she asked: 'Have you ever exhibited?'

'What? My paintings? No . . . oh, no. They are not for the world to see.'

'But if they give you pleasure – at least the pleasure of self-expression, might they not give pleasure to those who see them?'

'To a few, perhaps. But – exhibition; doesn't the word explain itself? Exhibitions are for exhibitionists. I don't wish to show off my soul – to hang it up for all to see. It would be like undressing in public.'

They walked through the dark in silence. Here and there the path was narrow and he stepped back for her to go ahead of him. When this happened her skin prickled, body taking over from cooler brain.

As they neared the door he said: 'I don't remember talking so much as this to anyone – certainly not for years.'

'Perhaps it's easier to talk in the darkness.'

'No . . . it's easier to talk to you.'

'I think you should let "a few" people see your paintings, Simon.'

'Why?'

'Well, if you believe in the – the interrelation of one part of life with another, can't emotions also be inter-related – and therefore shared? And if they are shared, isn't that some comfort? Surely one of the most valuable things in friendship, or in marriage, or in blood relation-ship, is to be able to share happiness and – and sorrow – to laugh together and if necessary to cry together. Therefore a creative person such as yourself who maybe can express what most of us can only *feel* . . . perhaps it is part of his – his responsibility to try to communicate his emotions to the world.'

He opened the door of the conservatory and they went in. She switched on her torch.

'We might be burglars,' he said, 'in my own house.' He struck a match but then shook it out again. Briefly his face appeared, lit by the smoky light. 'No, it's better in the dark . . . You're such a *kind* girl, Norah. And an intelligent one. I wonder if you'd be as headstrong as Marion. You deserve well of life . . . But then so, of course, did she.'

They went through into the dimly lit hall and he followed her up the first flight of stairs. At the top he turned to go down the long passage leading to his bedroom but hesitated. He said: 'You encourage me to hope,' and then went on.

Up in her own bedroom Norah slowly undressed. The fear and the tension were slowly draining out of her, to be replaced by feelings of courage and resolve. She lay in bed and did not sleep, tossing and turning, wrestling with the personal decisions she had to make; uncertain whether to allow the conflicting forces in the house to whirl around her and remain herself a play of them, or whether to strike out herself.

Once in the middle of the night she thought she heard the tapping in the next room, but she would not get up to see.

CHAPTER EIGHT

I

IT WAS the day for Mrs Syme to speak at her luncheon in Shrewsbury and she clearly took it that Norah would go with her. Norah went. It was an interesting meeting: the Townswomen's Guild; about sixty at the luncheon; after it Althea spoke for half an hour. Her subject was the virtues and the failings of the Welfare State, and she held the audience's attention throughout. It was a lucid survey, dealing with individual cases but never losing sight of the general picture. She pulled no punches yet never took political sides; and she ended by stressing the duty of every woman to help to make this great scheme work, by co-operating, by turning it to full advantage without abuse, by understanding the true intentions of the designers and by seeing themselves as important units in one of the greatest democratic experiments of all time. 'Make no mistake,' she ended; 'the eyes of the civilized nations are on us. If we fail to make it work we shall earn only derision: if we succeed we shall be the envy of the world.'

They drove home in fitful sunshine. As Norah had half expected, Althea was in a relaxed mood and expansive, having drunk a fair amount of wine at lunch and having enjoyed the added intoxication of delivering a successful address. All day the girl had hidden her resentment, exerted herself to resume the relationship of earlier times. Now she listened to her friend, putting in the occasional question, the required comment. It was easy while the talk was of generalities.

Then, with only half an hour to go and the mountains already closing around them, Althea broached the subject Norah had been thinking of all day.

'How are you getting along with Simon?'

'Very well, thank you. We had a long talk last night.'

'He told me yesterday he'd quite got over the shock of thinking you like his sister.'

'*Did* he?'

'You sound surprised,' Althea said.

'I am. I thought it still bothered him.'

'Has he said something more to you about it?'

'Yes . . . I didn't know he'd been ill? Althea. Seriously ill, I mean.'

'Did he tell you that?'

'Oh, not in so many words. But we were talking by the lake. He said he'd lost his memory.'

Althea Syme glanced at Timson's square head and bristling hair under its peaked cap. The partition was raised, so he could hear nothing. 'He had a sort of breakdown. It was quite short but it was quite bad while it lasted.'

'After Marion's death?'

'Yes. It was the last straw, I suppose. He'd hardly recovered from his war experiences, and his sister's death . . . well . . .'

'He said he blamed himself for what happened.'

'I must say he's been confiding in you, pet. Usually you can hardly get a word out of him.'

'But he wouldn't say more than that. I wonder why?'

'Why what?'

'Well, it's natural to be upset – but not to blame oneself.'

There was a pause. Althea said: 'Simon was frightfully possessive towards his sister. He couldn't *bear* her to go out with other men. When she married he absolutely opposed it. Her husband and Simon had been in the Air Force together. After their honeymoon Marion and Richard returned to Morb House before leaving for Ireland. It was wartime and there was only Simon – they of course had no chauffeur. So he drove them to the boat – and left them there – and came back. No one ever saw them again. He feels, I'm sure mistakenly . . .'

'Why?'

'Why what?'

'Why did no one ever see them again? If they were on board a ship that went down, weren't there any survivors? Did no one see them drown? Were they torpedoed? How did it happen?'

'No, oh, no, it wasn't that way at all. It was Richard's idea to sail across himself.'

'D'you mean in a small boat?'

'Yes. He was Irish, you know, and I think he had persuaded one of the fishermen in Aberdovey to hire him a boat. Or he may have bought it – I don't know. But the weather apparently was good. There seemed no

119

risk. Simon drove them to this boat and then came back.'

'You've said that before,' Norah observed.

Althea smiled thinly. 'Why shouldn't I say it again?'

The car slowed for a flock of sheep which were meandering across the road. There was a cacophony of bleating all round them, an orchestra tuning up without a conductor.

Norah said: 'So why does he blame himself?'

'Because he thinks he should have stopped the marriage – certainly that he should have stopped the foolhardy adventure that led to their death.'

'But how could he have? Anyway, that hardly seems an adequate reason for feeling guilt.'

'Who mentioned guilt?'

'He did. Althea, why is Simon so preoccupied with the lake? The lake in your garden, I mean.'

'Is he? You must appreciate it is his first time home for some time. He likes – has always liked to wander.'

The sheep had reluctantly parted, and Timson accelerated the big car away.

Norah said: 'I suppose he's enjoying his freedom.'

'What freedom?'

'Well, I understood – I thought he'd been in some sort of nursing home.'

'Did he tell you that too?'

'I got that impression.'

'Well, so he has. But it was of his own free will. He went there because he wished to and stayed there because he wished to. No one compelled him . . .'

'I didn't know. I'm glad to know that.'

After a minute Mrs Syme said: 'Naturally all this is something we don't exactly boast about outside the family. That's why I've been a little secretive to you. Perhaps it was a mistake not to tell you everything from the first.'

'Perhaps it was.'

The older woman raised her eyebrows but did not reply. Then she went on: 'Simon was a frightfully difficult boy. His mother had great trouble in rearing him. He'd sit silent for hours refusing to move or speak. At school he was very backward, not because he was stupid but because he wouldn't use his brain. Often he wouldn't eat or drink for half a day. The doctor said they were withdrawal symptoms. After school his parents tried to get him articled to a solicitor and eventually he passed the exams, but by then war had broken out and he joined the Air Force. He was in quite a lot of bombing raids before he was shot down and he was six hours in the North Sea. When he recovered he spent some weeks in hospital before being discharged. When Marion died in this useless foolish way it seemed, as I've told you, to distress him over afresh and he went back for more treatment. Since then, until recently, he hasn't chosen to come out. I visited him every quarter. He seemed content in his own way to live a pointless, wasted life . . . It was good news when we knew he was able and willing to face the world again.'

Norah said: 'I've seen some of his paintings. It seems to me very positive, strong. Surely that's a good enough way of living, isn't it? After all . . .'

'What were you going to say?'

She was going to say, after all your own son, but refrained. 'Well, many artists are a bit eccentric, aren't they? Without, I mean, being thought – schizoid . . .' The word was out. She hurried on: 'By nature they don't conform. Half of them would be considered dunces at school, in ordinary subjects. Their standards are different. They live what to a normal person would seem a lax, unconventional life, yet . . .'

'And Van Gogh cut off his own ear,' said Althea.

That seemed to end the conversation, but as they neared the house she added: 'Simon hasn't had a really depressive state for two years. He is coming out into the light. We must all try to help him.'

Norah said: 'I think he has the impression that someone was drowned in your lake. He has painted a body floating, in one of his pictures.'

They drew up at the door.

'That,' said Althea, 'was a maid. It happened in 1923, when Simon was a little boy. I suppose it made rather an impression on him. The girl became pregnant – in those days and in these parts it was the ultimate disgrace – she couldn't face it. I'm sorry that he has painted that. It shows that his preoccupation is still worrying him.'

II

WHEN THEY got in Althea went straight up to her bedroom to change, and Norah took the case containing the notes of her speech to the study. When she opened the door she found Gregory sitting at the desk with a number of ledgers open before him. He rose sharply and bent to gather some papers from the floor.

'You're back early,' he said. 'I always forget Timson drives so fast.'

When he straightened up his face was flushed.

'Your mother's just changing. Have you had tea?'

'I have. But I expect there'll be some in the small drawing-room.'

She saw that the door of the safe was open. It was a combination lock. She put the satchel in a drawer, picked up a sheet she had mistyped that morning and screwed it up, dropped it into the wastepaper basket. He stood watching her.

She said: 'It was a fine lecture. Your mother was a great success.'

He nodded. 'Oh, yes. Oh, yes, she's very good at that.'

'Do you ever go with her?'

'No.'

'I think she'd appreciate it sometimes.'

'Yes. Maybe.'

'Did you get your book?'

'Which book?'

'The one on heredity. You ordered it in Aberystwyth.'

'Not *yet*. Anyway, I think maybe I've got enough to study here.'

She was not sure how he meant this, but she could see he was in no mood to explain.

'It was beginning to rain when we came in.'

'That's the forecast.'

He waited until she walked away. As she opened the door to go out he moved to put the ledgers back in the safe.

III

AT THE mouth of the passageway leading to his bedroom Simon was talking to Doole.

'They just don't *disappear*, man. They were on my dressing-table this morning where I always keep them!'

'Alice hasn't taken them,' Doole said sullenly. 'I've asked her again. And I've looked all over the floor.'

'It was a bottle of twenty. I take two a day. It's Sunday tomorrow and I can't get into a chemist's to renew the prescription. Apart from . . .'

'Those pills on the dressing-table . . .'

'Are not mine, I assure you. They're peach-coloured instead of pink and they're not the right shape . . .'

'The bottle says . . .'

'The bottle is wrong – at least, it looks the same sort of bottle . . .'

'With your name on it, sir . . .'

'That's a *mistake*. Someone has made a mistake over that. Who I don't know. The point is that my pills have been removed or taken or mislaid. And I tell you, Doole, I will not be supervised, watched over, my life controlled or interfered with! No one has any right to do that. It was bad enough . . .'

He caught sight of Norah and his face lightened.

She said: 'Can I help? Can I look for you? If they've dropped on the floor . . .'

He said quietly: 'Thank you, I think we've all scoured the bedroom. Before we resort to more drastic measures I'll ask Althea; she may have put them somewhere for safety.'

But at tea he made no mention of his loss.

IV

SHE HAD thought there might have been time to take a stroll after tea in case Christopher were still anywhere in the neighbourhood; but it rained heavily. However at six there was a ring at the door and presently he came in with some photographs he had promised for Mrs Syme. He was particularly talkative, and stayed for drinks but refused dinner. This made dinner late. Norah saw him to the door; it was their only moment together standing on the top step looking at his little four-seater waiting in the steely rain.

She told him of her conversation with Althea on the way home today but did not mention her meeting with Simon at the lake last night.

He said: 'I was in the pub again at lunch time, but nothing fresh. Look I don't want to over-persuade you, but you've given this place nearly a week and you can't pretend you like it.'

'No . . .'

'Well, I'm going back to London at the end of next week, but I'd make it earlier if you felt like throwing this job up and coming with me. Maybe there's not a thing wrong with Simon now – personally I like the chap; you tell me he's got a lot of talent and certainly he's got a lot of charm. But it's not your scene, Norah. Honestly, I mean it.'

'Why not?'

'Well, you're too pretty – too *normal* to become involved. I think it will depress you – in a sense it may engulf you. Don't you find the house enormously *pervasive*? I don't think I'm specially sensitive to atmosphere, but I certainly feel it here. Look at it, it's out of its century. Most old houses come to terms with the times they're living in – this one hasn't.'

'Didn't you say the first time we met that I should probably grow a hump and a beard?'

'That was a bit of good clean fun. But I'm serious now. I think you should get out while the going's good.'

'And leave everything just as it is, unexplained, unsolved . . . *nasty*?'

'Nasty is the word. What is it all to you? Look at Doole – he's more like a keeper than a butler. Sure he isn't here to look after Simon?'

'No, no . . . They did come together – in the same car, I remember. But Doole had been on holiday.'

'I bet he'd been to fetch him.'

'I don't know about that. But I do know for certain that Doole has been the butler for over two years. So it can't be the way you think.'

'Even Timson looks more like a male nurse than a chauffeur.'

'Oh, now you *are* imagining things! Christopher, I think I should go now. They'll be waiting dinner . . .'

'Let them wait one minute more. Norah, you know I'm very taken with you. I think – I hope – you like me. If you come back to London maybe we could get together. I promise I'd play by the rules – your rules, whatever they are. If things went as I think they would, we could get married . . .'

She hesitated before answering and then said: 'I don't want to seem tactless, Christopher, but wouldn't this be number three?'

'Oh, so old Althea has been gossiping, has she? All right, I've made mistakes. I agree, it's not too much of a recommendation. But a wise man *learns*. Maybe the man who has had two motor accidents is a better man to be with than a beginner who hardly knows his left side from his right.'

Norah looked up at the sky. It was a vaporous evening. The downpour was thundery, the air warm and steamy; clouds hung over the mountains like white shrouds; no wind, nothing stirred, everything dripped.

She said: 'And shouldn't a man who has had two motor accidents – isn't it better for him to drive a bit more slowly for a time?'

'Not in an emergency.'

'And this is an emergency?'

'I think so, yes.'

She looked at the rain bouncing like steam off the steps. 'So that's a proposal, is it?'

'It's a proposition with, I trust, a proposal at the end of it.'

'You're very honest, Christopher. I like that.'

'I hope that's not all you like.'

'No, not all. Not by any means. But I . . .'

'But? Never say but!'

'I have to. At least, I think I have. Perhaps I've got to think for us both.'

'Why?'

'Well, you see – I've had a car accident too.'

'What – you've been married?'

'No – nothing as grave as that. Only dented one wing a bit. But it hurts. And it does make me – a little accident-shy.'

He stared at her. 'Is it over?'

'Oh, yes . . . Oh, yes. But I'm still feeling traces of concussion.'

He stirred with his foot the moisture accumulating on the top step. 'I think it may be a mistake, after one accident, to be too shaken to drive at all.'

She nodded. 'That could be true.'

'Yes . . . Well, as I said, we'll go at your speed. If necessary in a thoroughly decorous way. That's up to you.'

She glanced back into the house. 'I haven't an answer absolutely ready – not even to that. I still have to think. And I believe there's something here that I want to see out. But thank you.'

He shrugged impatiently. 'Don't *thank* me. If you're in love with a girl a marriage proposal is the most selfish of acts.'

'And you're sure you're in love with me?'

'Yes. And being very selfish, I want you to myself.'

She said: 'You'll be here a week yet?'

'Eight days, if I stay my full time.'

'I think I should know by then. I ought to.'

'Then we must meet more regularly. This hole-in-the-corner business is no good.'

'Christopher, I'm not sure about even that. It might be better if we even saw *less* of each other for the next day or so.'

'Whatever makes you say that?'

'Just a hunch, a feeling. It would sort of – help perspective, I think.'

'Who cares about perspective?'

She laughed. 'Well, I do – in the peculiar circumstances. And seriously, I *want* to stay here another few days. I want to let things work themselves out.'

'So be it. You're the boss. Though I don t promise to keep away, if that's what you're suggesting. Anyway, if you should want me urgently . . .'

'Is it likely?'

'Who knows? Give me a ring. Llandathery four one. Is there another telephone in the house except in Althea's study?'

'No. But there'll be no problem about that.'

He kissed her, a little less certainly this time; it was as if he lost confidence the deeper he found himself involved. 'Don't let's argue. That's a bargain. If you should want me – for any reason – I'll make an excuse and call.'

'Thank you . . . All right. I must go now. Goodbye.'

As she shut the door and moved towards the dining-room she heard the whirr of his self-starter.

129

She felt her face was flushed, but there was no time to cool it before she went in.

'Ah, there you are, pet,' said Althea pleasantly, eyes going appreciatively over her. 'We took the liberty of starting.'

But Simon stared at her angrily. As she sipped her soup it crossed her mind to hope that he was not thinking of her as another Marion who was involving herself with a man against his will.

CHAPTER NINE

I

SUNDAY WAS fine but sulphurous. Unusual weather for October. The summer had lasted all through and now was breaking up. Marble-coloured clouds spiralled on dark foundations. Rain moved over the mountains and the sky showed faded flags of green and blue. It was still warm.

In the morning Norah went down towards the lake but stopped short when she saw Simon there painting. She halted by a mespilus whose leaves were turning a brilliant orange-brown. From here the clouds over the mountains looked as tangible as the mountains themselves. The lake reflected alpine ranges.

She turned and went back into the house and through it and began to walk down the valley the opposite way from the way she met Christopher. She had three or four days to sort herself out before coming to a decision, and taking a long walk was as good a way as any of doing this.

She wondered what her friends would say if they heard that, having broken so comprehensively from Robert, she suddenly dashed off with a man she had only known a week. (Not that it mattered. Not that

that was the important thing.) 'I'll play it by your rules,' Christopher had said. But what *were* her rules? She really hadn't any to fit the situation. (Was Christopher even free to marry her if they decided on that? Presumably, since he had asked her.)

Really, all this was peripheral to the central question. Did she love him? And if so, to what extent? If she loved him everything followed, and it wasn't so important in what order it came. If she didn't love him, then surely nothing followed, nothing ought to follow for someone like herself who didn't seem able in her nature to give or receive lightly.

She stopped at a turn in the valley and stared back at the house. It looked bigger than ever from here. There were a lot of other rooms she had not yet seen. The uncurtained windows nearer the cliff looked like eyes gone blind with age.

So she didn't love him – was that it? She was attracted, more physically attracted than she had yet admitted to herself. She could see herself being completely bowled over by him, by his maleness, by his charm and – to do him justice – by the sincerity of his own emotions. But a certain amount of fear added to her hesitation – fear that once they were committed to each other he might tire and be able to disengage while she by then could not. The other two wives flickered about in her mind.

A spot of rain fell on her hand. It was an isolated spot but large and spread across her knuckles. Another spot fell on the leaf of a sapling sycamore, a third on the ground at her feet. They were like shells from a battery finding its range. She was half a mile from the house and clouds were congregating overhead. She turned and began to walk back.

Well, all marriage, all love, was a risk. You either had the courage or you did not. As she walked she tried to dredge up from her subconscious the one other very definite element contributing to her reluctance to commit herself. It was something to do with Cader Morb or Morb House or the people living there. She wanted something *resolved*. There were questions in her mind that had to be answered – and they were not only in her mind but in her heart. They *had* to be resolved before she could move to the resolution of her feelings for Christopher.

It was to do with Simon, really. No one else in the house but only Simon. Sometimes he seemed to be more in her thoughts than Christopher. He was the crux. She realized that now.

In some way now she was involved personally – almost as if she were Marion come back from the dead – or as if Marion, or a part of Marion, now inhabited her. She wondered if the wayward spirit that came to sit upon her old rocking-horse had found a new home, in the person of the woman who was inhabiting her room and so closely resembled her. Had Simon recognized more than a resemblance when they first met? Had he wanted her to leave, perceiving already the extent of the possession?

She kicked impatiently at a stone. Old wives' talk. She was free to leave tomorrow, unencumbered by any entanglement here. The only involvement was her own curiosity. Apart from Simon. The only compulsion was her own determination and choice. Apart from Simon.

On the way back an occasional great drop splashed on her head or shoulders. She was wearing a fine cardigan, and the drops went through it and were cold on her skin. Yet as she neared the house she felt again a reluctance to go in. In spite of all scepticism, it was as if here outside she were mistress of her own thoughts, once indoors the heavy atmosphere of the house closed on her like a damp cloud about a hill, cloying, misting, distorting, putting the most familiar object out of shape, leaving the simplest judgment in doubt.

Althea was waiting for her on the front doorstep, just as she had been when she first arrived.

'Hullo, pet. Been a walk?' She looped at her handsome hair. 'I wasn't looking for you, though it's nice to see you. I've *such* a headache. I suppose it may be the weather.'

'Would you like me to get you something?'

'Thank you. There are aspirins in my bedroom. In the first drawer of the dressing-table. If it's not too much trouble.'

'Of course not.'

'Did you see a man on a bicycle down the valley? It's time the Sunday papers were here.'

II

BY LUNCH the day was so dark that they had the lamps lit. Simon, they said, was painting in his room. Mr

Croome-Nichols retired soon after for his usual siesta, and Gregory began to practise Schubert. Althea Syme was surrounded by Sunday papers, so Norah slipped away into the hall.

Doole was there, lighting a lamp.

'Oh, Doole,' she said, 'where do these doors lead?' pointing to two at the opposite side behind the stairs.

He looked up, bold eyes carefully impersonal. 'It's a part of the house that's not used, miss. Madam finds it too big to keep it all up.'

She went to one of the doors and tried to open it. It was locked.

'Do you have the key?'

'Well, yes, miss. But there's nothing to see, like. It's all dusty.'

'I'd like to explore.'

'Did Madam . . . ?'

'Yes.'

Reluctantly he came across with a bunch of keys, stepped past her. He smelt of after-shave lotion.

'There, miss. Do you want a light?'

'No . . . It seems lighter in here.'

'Careful of the floorboards, miss. Some of 'em are a bit shaky.'

'Thank you, Doole. Don't bother to wait. I'll find my own way out.'

It was in fact lighter in here because of the lack of curtains. She was in a hall similar to the one she had left. It was unfurnished and uncarpeted. She went across to the other side and opened a door into a large sitting-room, also empty, though one or two pictures hung on the walls. It smelt stale and dusty and mildewed, and she wondered whether, if she owned Morb House, she would be happy to have these rooms left untended. Wood beetle? Damp? Dry rot? Better to pull it down.

This window looked out at the back, and she peered through the dirty pane at the weather. It had not rained at all. Every hour or so the great scattered drops would fall, staining leaf and stone like thin blood, but then it would pass away. The white and grey cauliflowers of cloud still grew one on another and manoeuvred for position; the mountains were hardly to be seen; thunder rumbled distantly but never came nearer. It was all like the overture to a piece of grand opera on which the curtain failed to rise. Just at present the light was a sulphur yellow, such as Norah associated with the tall chimneys of industry rather than the open countryside.

She looked in another room, but there was nothing much to see. Dust on her fingers, she went up the bony uncarpeted stairs. At the top she tried to remember how the occupied part of the house was laid out and reverse it. There was the same broad landing, with three bedroom doors and a flight of steps down to the bathrooms, but only one passage leading off. She stumbled into a derelict boxroom, found two doors locked, went along the passage and looked out of another room towards the front. There was a flicker of lightning – the first in all the day. As a child she had been scared to death by her mother's story of the girl who watched a thunderstorm out of a window and when she was struck by lightning the impression of her face was left on the glass. The story had remained with her all her life. One thing, if she ever had children she would never stain their minds with unnecessary fears. As she moved away from the window she saw the other flight of stairs going up, corresponding to her own flight in the next house. Perhaps there were corresponding rooms up here – how silly never to have looked when she was out of doors. But had she not glanced up more than once and seen no other windows except her own?

It was dark going up, and halfway she saw why. The heavy oaken door at the top was shut. She climbed the rest of the stairs and pushed at the door. It was locked and there was no key. A tap was dripping somewhere. Bad that that should be left – didn't they ever get frost?

She pushed at the door again, very curious now to see more. But nothing would budge it. She decided tomorrow when the light was better to get the key from Doole and see what was up here.

She descended to the first landing but as she was about to go down again she stopped and looked at the upper stairs. There was dust here and there, but the handrail looked free of it.

Thunder leaned and thumped over the house and she was suddenly scared. She turned and pattered down the next flight, chose the wrong door to leave the empty house and found it locked, thought for a moment Doole had locked her in, and then saw the right door.

She slipped through. Gregory was still playing Schubert.

III

IT WAS still only three o'clock. Althea was nowhere about, and Norah picked over the Sunday papers for ten minutes. The heaviness of the weather had given her a headache too. She decided to go up to her room and lie on the bed for a while, maybe take an aspirin. She borrowed one of the less staid of the Sunday papers and went upstairs, conscious that she was now repeating something she had done half an hour ago in the other part of the house.

It was lighter in her room than downstairs and vaguely less airless. She took the aspirin and lay down, rustling quickly through the paper. It was the usual dredging up of the week's bad news, a couple of scandals the paper was supposed to be unearthing, football results. She dropped the paper over the edge of the bed and closed her eyes. Almost at once she went to sleep.

She dreamed she was in this bed and just waking out of a deep sleep. She climbed reluctantly out of bed and went to the long mirror to comb her hair. But in the mirror she saw Marion, who was just like herself except that she wore a trench coat and brown felt hat, from the brim of which rain was dripping. They stared at each other and then Marion said: 'We never left the house that night. We never went to the sea. We never left the house that night at all.' And then it looked as if the splashes of rain from her hat were like the splashes of rain that had fallen this morning, so big and so heavy that they looked like thin blood. Norah was looking at Marion but at the same time looking into a room that was not her own. The door opened behind Marion and a man came in carrying a heavy iron bar . . .

She jerked awake, started up, looked round.

All was as it had been before – her own room, the familiar chairs and table and mirror, her frock hung over the back of a chair, her slippers by the bed, the newspaper in a ruffled pyramid where she had dropped it. A distant rumble said the thunder was not all spent. She looked at her watch. Twenty minutes to four. She listened but it was ticking. She could only have been asleep ten minutes.

There might be nothing to old-fashioned beliefs in possession, but there was plenty in theories of suggestion – particularly auto-suggestion. At this rate she was going to hypnotize herself into a state where she believed she *was* Marion, had lived here all her life, that this was her bedroom, next door her playroom, Simon her brother.

She lay back, breathed out, then trailed a hand over the bed for the newspaper. There was trouble in the Berlin corridor, elections in Italy, meat prices were rising, there had been riots at a film star's funeral. She dropped the paper again and closed her eyes. And then she heard the tapping.

It was the first time it had ever happened in the daytime, and she tried to believe it was still part of the dream. Not so. She lay there listening.

It stopped and then began again. Someone trying to attract her attention? Or Something? Her heart began to beat.

She got up slowly, put her feet in her slippers, remained seated on the edge of the bed. The sound definitely came from her sitting-room. She stood up, picked her frock from the back of the chair, stepped into it, zipped it up.

The zip stuck. In her haste she had caught a piece of the lining. She struggled with fumbling fingers, could not move it up or down. The tapping had stopped. She went to the mirror, craned her neck to look at her back, half afraid of seeing Marion. It was only a tiny piece of material. She forced the zip down, pulled it up more carefully. As she changed hands to finish the zip the tapping began again.

She took a deep breath, stared at herself taking the breath. Norah Faulkner. Not Marion Syme. Norah Faulkner, born in Twickenham twenty-three years ago. Educated here and there during the war. Came to this house less than a week ago. Never seen it before. Never heard of Marion Syme. Quite separate. This is *my* identity, no one else's. I am sane, healthy and sceptical. I do not believe in ghosts, hauntings, possessions, old houses that carry the impress of long-dead people or rooms where evil things roam.

So there is *nothing* in my sitting-room, and if there is a noise, I must go in and find the cause, which must be a *natural* cause.

It was so dark that she turned to light the lamp, but then she checked herself. Not such a coward. It wasn't *that* dark. She could see perfectly well across the room. She would be able to see the whole of the sitting-room without the aid of a lamp.

She went to the closed door, turned the handle and pushed it open, went sharply in.

It *was* darker in here because the window was smaller. As she entered the room the tapping stopped, but the sound had definitely come from the wall behind the rocking-horse. In the yellow-grey light from the window the room looked like a painting by Sickert, seedy, dark-shadowed, indefinably neglected and sad. A still life in which only one thing moved. And this time there was no lamp in hand to give her the illusion that the fault might be hers. The rocking-horse was moving.

At least an inch each way. At least an inch. With dry throat she forced herself to go towards it. A grey dusty old horse, with straggling mane and thin grey tail, the saddle worn with use, the paint rubbed off the rump, the stirrups tarnished, the rockers kicked and scarred. But no one rode it. No one visible rode it.

She put a cold hand out and touched the head. The movement stopped. She stood watching. It did not restart. She waited. The horse was absolutely still, as quiet as the rest of the room, as still as the day. There was no more knocking. She had stopped it. She had interrupted the children's play.

She took another breath. She couldn't leave it like this. Not *again*. The wall behind the rocking-horse was the farthest from her bedroom, possibly backed on to the locked rooms in the other part of the house. The wallpaper, as she had noticed before, was a slightly

different pattern from the rest of the room, a piece of it
bulged as if the wall behind had warped.

She went up and felt it. The paper was a little loose
but the wall firm behind.

She went back into her bedroom and fetched a pair
of nail scissors. With these she began to pick at the
paper. It cut easily enough and she pulled it away in
strips. There was another older paper behind it. She
stabbed at this and it also came away, revealing the
cracked plaster and the brick behind. There seemed no
advantage but she nervily went on, tearing the paper
down in strips so that the wall soon was striped like a
faded zebra.

Presently she paused for breath and stood back. You
couldn't attack a brick wall. If anything was behind
that wall it was beyond her reach. Short of a pick-axe.
She knelt down and began to gather up the shreds of
torn wallpaper, rolling them into a dry crackling pile.
Then she noticed that the skirting board here had come
loose, perhaps with damp. She put her fingers behind it
and it squeaked slowly away. Behind it was more brick,
but here the brick was loose.

In the tiny firegrate was a poker. She fetched it and
began to work on the nearest brick. But work was an
overstatement. It came away easily into her hand and
left a gap. She put her hand in but there was no brick
beyond, only a slight draught. Whatever was beyond
was a single partition away.

Half a dozen bricks came easily. Either the mortar
had dried too soon or the mixture had been wrong. It
crumbled like crusty sand. Another dozen came and she

rebuilt them in a pyramid behind her and looked speculatively at the wall. Her knees were sore and she stood up and dusted her stockings. One was laddered. The air coming through the gap she had made was even dustier and staler than the room she was in.

There was a flicker of lightning over the hills. Her throat was very dry and she had no saliva to swallow. She went back to the wall.

Once the paper was stripped off you could almost lift the bricks away. Even those she had supposed firm were only really held by the pressure of those around. To save the risk of a fall she worked more narrowly upwards. Soon she could peer in.

It was a room, almost in darkness, and the floorboards ran through continuously from her own sitting-room. It seemed to be furnished. There was a big square object in the middle, and piled boards against the walls. But no window, or no visible window. There was another door at the opposite side, and through the cracks in this a few thin glints of light penetrated.

She worked until there was a space about four feet high by three feet wide. Not caring about the dust and the dirt, she crawled cautiously through, feeling with her hands along the floor to make sure the floorboards were secure. When she was almost through her hand came into contact with some hair.

Disbelief sometimes interposes itself between the recognizing sense and the recognition. It did now. Her mind took every evasive action of supposing it some kind of wool, of tissue, of meshed cotton. Then still incredulous, groping, conviction rising like bile, she extended her hand and felt the shape of the head, the cold brow . . .

She gave a choking scream and scrambled to her feet in the dark sour attic, banging her shoulder as she straightened up. Blood beating, draining, she clawed at the wall and the opening behind her to try to escape.

But then the door of the dark attic opened and light flooded in. A man stood on the threshold, silhouetted in the grey afternoon light. She did not need to be told it was Simon.

He came a step into the room.

'Marion! So you have dropped the – the pretence at last . . .'

CHAPTER TEN

I

DON'T FAINT. Can't faint. Must not look down. Not look at what is on the floor. Keep away. Get out. Back out. But one has to bend, to squeeze –

He was beside her. 'Marion! Are you not well? Oh, my love, my love.'

His hands were on her, arms around her. She could not fight, her knees like water. He put his hands on either side of her face and kissed her. It was a long, slow, loving kiss, exploring her lips, and she gasped and could not move.

Suddenly she was standing alone, reeling against the wall. He had jerked away, released her as if he had been shot.

'Oh, dear Christ, what am I thinking of?' he said. 'Why've you come to torment me like this?'

Her senses were going now. She *must* not. 'Simon, leave me, let me – go.'

'You should have gone when I warned you!' he shouted. 'The devil himself couldn't have thought up a nastier trick! What's the matter? Damn you, are you ill? Why have you broken through like this?'

She sagged, head reeling, into his arms, though she

dreaded them more than anything; yet unable to stand; he half led, half carried her; but *away* from her own room, towards the next room beyond the attic, the way he had come. She tried to resist, to get back to her own room, to escape, but presently she was lying on a couch in this second room, hair hanging, lips white, eyes smudged with horror.

'Here, drink this, it's only water, but . . .'

She sipped something he had brought, liquid spilling down her chin. He wiped it from her neck. The room kept coming and going, like adjusting a telescope.

He lifted her feet and put them on the couch. Presently the room began to steady. Head back, she looked at him peering down at her. It was an artist's studio, the light from big fanlights high up. The fanlights showed a copper sky and diamond stars of rain.

Abruptly he turned away, put his hands to his eyes. 'My God, you are her and not her! It's been a torture ever since I came. Now . . . now, not content with that, you break through the damned wall! What's the matter with you? Are you mad?'

She choked and stared at him and said nothing. His expression was sour, his face heart-shaped with anger, lines drawn in parenthesis.

'For God's sake, why are you trembling? What's the matter with you?'

'Let me go,' she said. Her lips wouldn't frame the words.

'What d'you say? What is it?'

'Let me go.'

'I'm not stopping you! I didn't invite you here! I asked you to leave two days ago.'

She tried to take another sip of water. Perhaps her trembling fingers convinced him, for he said more quietly:

'Is it the thunder? I know it affects some people.'

She shook her head. He put the glass down. 'For that matter I don't like it myself. Altogether I suppose it's been a trying day.' He moved a little away. 'I stay up here as much as I can to get away from the others and to be near *her*. It's as near to her now as I shall ever get . . .'

On the walls a dozen paintings, most of them of a girl. Marion – herself – like her yet unlike. Resemblances, differences. Did he use *her* as a model next door in that dark attic, propping *her* up against the wall, imagining *her* as she had once been, not seeing the horror in front of him?

Sickness welled up.

'In a moment I'll go,' she whispered, trying to think of the soothing words that would persuade him to let her escape. If he once came to realize what she had seen. 'It was just the shock. I – didn't know what to think when I saw you . . .'

'Nor I when I saw *you*. But people who break down walls must expect shocks! Did my aunt put you up to this?'

'No, oh, no!'

'It's all been part of a design, hasn't it? In which you play the innocent! God, I've been a fool! Of course at the beginning I thought . . . But you seemed so natural, so fresh, so *genuine*. I was charmed, taken in. I have to tell you I've thought of you a great deal. But this – you were put up to this – weren't you? Come, tell me the truth!'

She whispered: 'Please let me go. Oh, Simon, I'm so upset. Please let me go.'

'I've told you, go and be damned!' He gulped in his throat. 'When you like. As soon as you can walk – it will suit me!'

'Not that way.'

'Why ever not? – That's the way you came. The other way leads through the empty part of the house.'

'Not that way.'

'Well, for God's sake, please yourself. Only just leave me alone.'

She tried to sit up, staring at him and his matter-of-fact tone, trying to subdue the nausea just long enough to get down the stairs and away.

He struck a match and lit a lamp on the desk beside her. He shook out the match and replaced the glass, slowly turned up the flame. The light glowed about his hands, spread across the room. His back was to her now and she glanced assessingly at the other door.

He said: 'I hope you broke nothing coming through. I prime and stretch all my canvases in there. It leaves me more room.' With horror she watched him go to the open door of the attic and hold the lamp aloft to peer in.

She stood up, took a step away from him.

He said: 'Oh, you've knocked over Marion's doll. I hope you haven't broken it.'

II

HE HAD gone into the attic. Yet now she could not move to escape. What he had said stiffened her with a new sense of shock.

As he came out of the attic she stared at him.

He said again: 'What's the matter with you? What are you staring at?'

She didn't answer. He put down the lamp.

'Go this way,' he said. 'The other way I'd have to come down and unlock the door. I'll not *follow* you. Indeed, I'll get someone to rebuild the wall, if that's what's worrying you.'

She went to the door of the attic, held on to the door, half fearfully peered in.

'Marion's *doll*?' she said.

'Yes, didn't you see it? You must have fallen over it. I keep it here along with a few other of her personal things to remind me of her. It's all there is left . . .'

'Her – doll?'

He sighed. 'What else?'

'I suppose I did – fall over it. It – added to the shock. It's so *enormous*.'

He smiled painfully. 'When I was twelve and Marion was eight our parents took us to Italy on a holiday. We spent a couple of nights in Milan and Marion saw this doll in a shop in one of the arcades. All through the holiday she talked of nothing else, so on the way home my father bought it for her. When we brought it back to England one of the passport officials asked my father why the other child wasn't entered on his passport . . .'

'May I – see it close to?'

He brought it out for her, a doll three feet six inches tall, long flaxen hair still silky and lifelike, blue eyes that closed, legs that stepped forward when you led her along.

Norah put her hands up to her face. 'Simon, I don't know what to say!'

The sharpness had now altogether gone from his voice. 'Haven't we already said all there is to say?'

'I think I have more to explain . . .'

'As to why you didn't leave when I asked you? But that's plain enough. Your arrangements with Althea . . .'

'I have *no* arrangements with Althea! I'll leave tomorrow. But – there are other things I have to say. About the wall . . .'

'I'll get it built up.'

'It's not that. I want to explain why I broke it *down* . . . ! In my room I was always being disturbed by tapping. Usually at night about eleven o'clock. I couldn't sleep for it. It – worried me. But then this afternoon. It was like someone tapping to attract my attention . . .'

'Oh . . . that was me. I'm afraid it never occurred to me the sound would carry. I often work at night. I was simply tapping the stretcher to get the canvas taut – or working on a frame.'

'And then – ' she looked at him – 'often when I went into my sitting-room to look, the rocking-horse was rocking backwards and forwards as if . . .'

'What rocking-horse?'

'The grey one. Marion's, I suppose . . .'

'Is that still there? No, it was mine. Marion didn't like it. Rocking? How could it be?'

'I don't know. Just moving gently, as if someone had just been using it.'

'Some other trick of Althea's? No, it couldn't be. Wait. I wonder. Come and try.'

She followed him slowly into the attic room, looking around it now with new eyes. It was stacked with finished canvases, with a few old dolls, a doll's house; on hangers were three frocks, a school bag, a pair of high-heeled dance shoes, a tennis racket, a hockey stick.

'Look,' Simon said. 'You see these two rooms – your sitting-room, as you call it, and this attic were one room in the old days sixty years ago. The floorboards run right under the dividing wall. Well, see, this board, and these two, are loose. Probably when I walked round here working on the stretchers I trod on this end and it moved the one under the rocking-horse and set it swaying. Would you like to go and see if I can do it now to set your mind at rest?'

'No,' said Norah, wearily. 'I – think not. But thanks.'

'You look exhausted. Did you think the house was haunted?'

151

'I – didn't know. I got upset. I suppose it was the weather. Please forgive me.'

He looked at her closely. 'Then you really aren't – in this with my aunt?'

'I don't know what I'm supposed to *be* in – but I swear I came here only as her secretary and without any knowledge of this house or anyone in it.'

'Perhaps,' he said gently, 'if this – this breaking down of a wall – is the means of our coming to understand each other a little better it will have served a useful purpose.'

'I wish we *could* understand each other better,' Norah said, almost in tears.

'Then will you stay a little while and talk to me? I come up here to be alone – but all the same sometimes it becomes – isolated, lonely.'

III

THEY TALKED for an hour. Mainly he talked and she listened. She sat on the creaking sofa where she had first lain. He straddled a cane-bottomed chair.

It came slowly at first. He said, as he had said in the garden, that he was unused to talking and particularly unused to talking about himself. She believed it. He said confiding in someone else was like having to climb a wall. Or perhaps breaking one down, he amended with a smile. But somehow confiding in her was different.

Everything she had heard about him was true, but it all seemed altered when explained by him. Yes, he had been a difficult child. He had had meningitis when he was seven, and for a while he could not go to school. He had had periods when he seemed unable to communicate his feelings and so would not speak to anyone. He used to fancy himself living on a draughtboard with only the white squares safe and frightful chasms gaping in the black. Sometimes by rubbing his knuckles together he could make all the people in a room dwindle until they looked like toys and disappeared into the black holes. Sometimes he was able to withdraw from himself and look down upon himself sitting there, shivering and alone. He became someone else and yet lived his own life at the same time. Loneliness was the greatest fear of all; other people inhabited their different world and could not understand his.

After a while he began to recover; his improvement was begun and continued by the discovery of what he could do with chalk and paint. As his sister grew up she also could communicate with him, and he with her, in a way no one else could; and there grew up an affinity as deep as between twins.

'I don't think I was specially difficult in my teens. Of course I didn't work at the ordinary school curriculum, but that was because I wanted to spend all my time painting. What I wanted to read I'd read all night – poetry particularly, biographies of artists, any notes or personal letters they had left – things like the Journals of Delacroix and Constable's letters. I didn't do well because it was an orthodox school. If it had been somewhere like Dartington Hall I would probably have been a star pupil. Maybe not for achievement – I can't assess that – but at least for effort. Anyway, that's the way it was until I was about eighteen and Marion was fifteen. She was away at school as well and we just met during the holidays. And then . . .' Simon blinked his eyes as if they hurt or as if he were shutting out some hurtful picture. '. . . And then one time I came back from school – it must have been the Christmas, because I was due to leave in the following July – and I saw Marion in the dining-room in a new frock. And suddenly she was no longer just a schoolgirl. I saw her with absolutely *new* eyes, as if I'd never seen her ever before, and I fell in love with her. It was like a – a revelation.'

The lamp had been burning low since he lit it to look in the attic; now he rose and turned up the wick. The diamonds of rain were spreading more thickly on the darkening window lights.

'Does that shock you?'

'Not particularly.'

'It shouldn't. We're brought up, of course, to look on it as unnatural, because it's undesirable biologically. Otherwise it's the most natural thing. When it happens as it happened to us it's – it's a *benign* thing.'

Feeling a sudden need to move, she got up and stood looking at one of the paintings of the girl they were talking of. A fresh lively young woman in a yellow frock, hair curling loosely. That struck a chord of memory.

'Don't go,' he said.

'I'm not going.'

She looked at the other paintings. There were two nudes of the girl; another one in a low black frock, unfinished, the arms and hands barely sketched in; one in a tennis frock, one lying on a sofa reading.

'She looks very young,' Norah said.

'She was very young in all those paintings; eighteen or nineteen. In the last years I only painted her twice – there wasn't the opportunity. And those two I destroyed.'

'Destroyed?'

'Yes. They were quite good but they reflected something – alien in her. Alien in her after she had been away.'

He sat down on his chair again. He had picked up a dry paintbrush and was running his fingers up and down the handle.

'Affinity between human beings is always hard to achieve. It's one of the great problems of making a successful marriage, isn't it? People are drawn together by a sexual attraction and urge. Once the first impulses are spent they have to accustom themselves to living in amity with a strange man or woman who for the first twenty-odd years of their lives have grown up with different backgrounds, different likes and dislikes, different prejudices, different ways of judging things. Sometimes it works, often it doesn't. With a sister, *everything* is shared. All the common memories of childhood, the background, the understanding, the – the affinity of thought. When to these are joined the love of a man and a woman I believe there can hardly be a greater joy.'

She did not speak, waiting for him to finish what he had to tell.

'Did I say joy? Well, joy and also torture. Because it is, I suppose, doomed from the outset . . . That holiday I'd come home determined to ask my father to relieve me of the undertaking to go in for law and to let me have three years at an art school instead. But this feeling for Marion – which she seemed to return – swamped everything else. It was a – a blinding four weeks. I hardly thought of anything else. When I left I'd only mentioned my career to my father once. Of course there'd been a conditional refusal. One might have expected it. Qualify first, he said. Get your articles. Then, if you want, take a year or so off to paint. Once you're qualified no one can take it away from you – you've a career at your finger-tips . . . Those were bad years, you know. Two million unemployed. He had enough money to live comfortably but all the rest was tied up in property which in those days showed little return. He didn't know he was going to die so soon. He wanted me to be secure . . .'

She went to the door leading to the attic, then stared down at the great doll which had been left sitting on the threshold. Its blue eyes were staring wide, blank, innocent, mindless.

'And then?'

'And then . . . ?' He seemed to have lost the thread, as if he had been wandering down dark corridors of memory and regret.

'She – Marion – she loved you in the same way?'

'I think so. Yes. Yes. In those days. In those days it was total commitment on both sides. You know, Norah, she was so lovely. Not perhaps quite so much so as you . . .'

'Oh, that's . . .'

'The contours of her face, the planes of expression were less right in their proportion. And there was not so much light in the darkness of her hair. But she had the exquisite charm of youth. The untouched, unsullied beauty of a woman discovering herself before my eyes. Nothing can ever replace or repeat the freshness of first love . . .'

After a minute or so Norah came back from the door and sat on the couch again. He put his hand quietly over hers and then withdrew it.

'If the tragedy of childish love is that there can be no fulfilment, so the tragedy of our love was that it had no future. But we didn't pay much heed to that. Sufficient for the day, sufficient for the hour . . . I always thought, hoped, when I allowed myself to think, that some day we could come together permanently even if the physical tie had to remain hidden. So it went on, at intervals, for some years. But then things came up that separated us. My father and mother died within a year of each other. Marion had left school and gone to London to study theatre design. That year, it was the year I qualified, the war came. In 1940 I joined the Air Force. Marion went into the Ministry of Defence working on camouflage. We saw each other sometimes, but rarely, so very rarely. Of course it was no worse for us than for millions of others. We wrote, usually twice a week. We met when I was on leave. I became a navigator in Lancasters. By the end of 1943 I had flown more than thirty bombing missions. I was very lucky but in the end the inevitable happened. One night we bought it and had to ditch the plane off the Norfolk coast.'

The hand that had tentatively lain on hers hesitated as it re-grasped the brush. 'Strange . . . the water was more difficult for me to endure than the flak. Perhaps enmity is always easier to suffer than indifference . . . I watched my friends as the sea impersonally drowned them . . . Against all probability I was picked up . . . So I came to hospital.'

'And then?'

'Then the old trouble. After I'd got over the minor injuries and the exposure – I suppose I'd been living on too tight a rein. And no painting, which always served as a catharsis. I was in hospital for months, most of the time trying to reinhabit my body. Couldn't sleep, couldn't think properly, couldn't eat. I couldn't sleep because just at the moment of sleep I'd withdraw and look at myself down there: thin, fair-haired, eyes closed, sheet awry, hands half relaxed; and I'd know that I was not sleeping, only watching. For the same reasons I couldn't read or write or even paint. This is boring to you: I'll skip quickly over it.'

'No. Try to tell me. You talk too quickly, Simon, say too much in a breath. Tell me everything.'

He looked at her. 'I can't. It would take too long. A lifetime.'

'Not that long.'

He said: 'Well, I recovered; but they said my nerves

were too bad for active service. I was discharged, sent home. Do you smoke?'

'Not often.'

'I smoked sixty a day at that time. Then I gave it up. No reasons of restraint or determination. The taste just went bad on me. I've never smoked since.' He smiled, suddenly at ease for the first time. 'So I'm afraid I can't offer you one.'

'I've said – I don't often.'

'Indeed, all I've offered you is a glass of water. It's pretty poor hospitality, but I wasn't expecting – a guest. Until you came I was alone with my thoughts.'

'Why should they be so unpleasant?'

'Who said they were unpleasant?'

'You did.'

'Not altogether. When I think of Marion now it's – it's with less sense of responsibility. Heaven knows, I suppose one grows a sort of skin. Even over the rawest spots . . .'

'But why the responsibility at all?'

'Don't you think I should feel any?'

'I don't think that much.'

'When I was discharged from hospital she came back for a few weeks to look after me. But she was changed. She had some sort of a grudge against me. Eventually it came out. While she was in London she had had an affair with another man. It hadn't lasted. For her it hadn't worked. She blamed me. I'd spoiled it for her.'

'I see.'

'Yes. It was a difficult time. Gradually she settled

back into the old ways, though never entirely. And her leave from the Ministry of Defence was only temporary. She prepared to go back. I couldn't stop her. Indeed I couldn't attempt to. One day she left – promising she would see her chief in London and talk it over with him, see if she could be released permanently. Perhaps I over-persuaded her. Anyhow she stayed away, telephoning to say she couldn't get back. Then three weeks later she wrote to tell me that she was going to marry Richard Healy.'

The rain had stopped again, still reluctant ever to commit itself to a downpour.

He said: 'I'd first introduced them. Healy was a gunner in Lancasters. We'd flown together several times. Totally unsuitable for her in every way. Utterly charming but drank too much and prattled *endlessly*. In a year she would be unable to stand him, bored to death with his talk, its shallowness, its uncouthness, its lack of originality. He was marvellous company – but with beer and skittles so to speak. I – I tried, tactfully at first, to dissuade her. She would have none of it. She said she would be down next month and they would be married from her father's house. She asked me to be best man . . .

'I went up to London to plead with her. It was no use. We argued – bitterly – long into the night. I told her that, for better or worse, she was committed to me. Anything else would be second best. Always. She took me by the shoulders and shouted at me: "But don't you understand – there can't be anything for us together – it's accursed! I'm breaking free. This is my *chance*!

Richard has given it to me! I must seize it! I must look ahead and never, never again look back!" She shouted. It was something she could never have done before, it wasn't in her, it just wasn't in her.'

He sat back for a minute, as if the memory of her vehemence had exhausted him. He looked pale and tired, his face in half shadow like the thin moon that had sunk over the mountains last night.

Norah said: 'But Simon, I suppose she had realized . . .'

'Yes, oh yes, she had realized. And of course I was not blind. I too realized. And that made me give way. Against every instinctive judgment I gave way to perfidious reason. So they came down to Morb. And then they told me he was going to desert, to return to Ireland, to lie hidden till the end of the war . . .' Simon made a hopeless gesture. 'It was the last straw. I told them I would have none of it. It was a lunatic scheme. He had sworn allegiance to the British Crown. His own government wouldn't help him or offer him asylum. He said he didn't intend to ask it. Friends and relatives in Ireland would give them all the cover they needed. The war could not last more than another year. But in that time he might be expected to fly forty more bombing missions. He wasn't prepared to take the risk. Looking at Marion, he said that his life had suddenly become important and precious. He'd done his bit for a country that wasn't his own anyway. Let others carry on and finish the war. Not he.

'I gave way. I blame myself for being so weak. They were married in Llandathery Church just over the hill.

Later they came back here and packed and I agreed to drive them to Aberdovey, where he had hired a boat. It was a gusty evening with more wind threatening, and I made a last plea to delay for a day or two. But they wouldn't listen. His leave was up. They had to get away, he said, before he was posted. He had sailed all his life, and they had a good engine. In a few hours they would be across. I blame myself for being so weak. I drove them to the coast and left them there in the harbour. I waited for a while and presently I thought I saw them leaving. But it was a dark night, and of course they sailed without lights. I know the throb of their engine was clear, and then it disappeared into the gusty night. It was the last I saw of them – anyone saw of them.'

He passed a hand across his eyes. 'You can't imagine the remorse.'

'But why, Simon, *why*? *How* could you have stopped them? And why should you have?'

'It was as if they were bent on self-destruction,' he said. 'The whole crazy plan. By marrying him at all Marion was running headlong into disaster. They were utterly unsuited. But that at least was only a disaster of personality. The attempt to run to Ireland was a disaster of an irretrievable kind. In trying to preserve his life Richard lost it – and with his own my sister's too ... I could have stopped that. I could have put my car out of commission, I could have telephoned his commanding officer; I could have done a dozen things to make their escape impossible. Instead, I let them go.'

'And then ... this drove you to ...'

'To what? Oh, to a clumsy attempt at suicide.

Looking back now I don't know even if I was altogether in earnest. When I learned they had never reached Ireland, and I came to realize that Marion was dead, my life ceased to be of any further use or importance. It was hardly worth trying to destroy myself because there was nothing left worth the effort to destroy.'

He seemed to have come to the end of all he had to say.

She said: 'It's – good of you to have told me all this.'

He got up and dropped the brush into a pile of others, went over to the easel, which had a canvas on it splashed with preliminary whites and greens.

'When I was in the nursing home,' he said, 'they were always persuading me to talk. But I never would. Never could perhaps. In the end you get out of the way of it. Some people – most people – think while they're talking; in their minds they prepare the next sentence while speaking the one before. I can never do that. I lack the confidence. I have to listen to myself. And when there is no real sympathy between the speaker and the listener I dry up altogether. So you are the first person I've told this to. You have the quality of sympathy. And of course the likeness.'

'I hope now you believe I knew nothing about that.'

'I do now. But some day it may look as if your coming here was a good thing after all. It will to me, if not to you.'

She found herself colouring. 'Thank you.'

'This place will always be haunted for me. Maybe I'll leave Althea in peace and go right away again. Perhaps I shouldn't have come back.'

'But you're *better*, aren't you? So much better. I mean . . .'

'Oh, yes. This last twelve months utterly different. I never want to look back – to the apathy, the separateness, the self-recrimination. I've – grown a skin – of protection, of callousness, if you like. Events this last week have done their best to rub it raw. They've failed.'

'They should never have happened.'

He said: 'When you came in this afternoon, just for a moment the past and present came together in your face. I thought I was lost. And then I kissed you. And then I knew . . .'

'That I was not Marion.'

'That Marion will not mean quite so much to me ever again.'

CHAPTER ELEVEN

I

THE RAIN came at last with the dark. It fell in solid
pale sheets drumming on roof and soil and window and
wall, pale in the masked moonlight, heavy as surf.
Gutters spouted and little rivers ran. Here and there the
house dripped, here and there the test was too severe
for the old slates and they let water in. There was a
damp spot on the rocking-horse and another by her
bed.

At seven she rang Christopher.

'No,' she said, 'everything's pretty well all right. I'm
beginning to understand a bit more ... I think it's all
probably going to work out.'

'For us?'

'I didn't mean – For the moment I wasn't thinking in
that sense; I was thinking of the situation here. But give
me perhaps two more days.'

'For which purpose?'

'Both ...'

'What about tomorrow?'

'I think I need that. I'll ring you again about this
time.'

'I'd rather see you.'

'I know, but . . .'

'When shall I come? In the morning?'

'No, I have to type for Althea. I'll ring you about six. I'd rather.'

'Why are you being secretive?'

'I'm not. But, dear Christopher, I'm the one who was invited here, and I want to know before I leave *exactly why*. And I think I'm the only one who can do it.'

'Vanity is a dangerous guide.'

'I know. And I'm not going to rise to that. If I come a cropper it won't be a very serious one, and you can reprove me then.'

'Reproof is not in me. Only the usual word of warning: take care.'

'I will.'

'And,' he said as he rang off, 'I reserve my own freedom of action.'

When she had hung up she felt suddenly very isolated, as if she had been in contact with the normal, level-headed, sophisticated outside world. Now she was back in the ingrown world of Morb House. But this was where she belonged.

'Leave the wall,' he had said. 'I'll build it up this side as best I can when you're through. Then tomorrow I'll make a bit of mortar in the garage and block it up properly, if only to restore your privacy.' 'Don't bother, I'm leaving tomorrow.' 'Tomorrow? Must you? Can't you stay longer?' 'Why? I thought I was . . .' 'Not now. The very opposite, after this afternoon.'

Up in her rooms she saw he had done his best to put the bricks back. She had moved the rocking-horse into the centre of the sitting-room, and there it was just a shabby toy without capacity for movement or menace.

As she made up her face it looked yellow in the yellowing light; more like Marion's than ever. But Marion's ghost was laid. The terror of this afternoon followed by the tremendous relief had left her shaken and exhausted; but out of this exhaustion new emotions had already sprung. One was the liberating realization of her complex accord with Simon. Another was bitter anger against Althea Syme.

Impulse would have taken her down right away to face her friend and demand an explanation, for she could not be entirely innocent of Simon's private history. Or if she was it was time she was acquainted with it. It was hard to believe that there could be any real *design* on Althea's part – for what had she to gain? This surely was one remaining sign of Simon's illness, to suspect a plan where there had only been callous indifference. But such indifference, such callousness was intolerable. Certainly she, Norah, could not tolerate the situation in which she found herself, and she must leave at the earliest opportunity. But *Simon* now cautioned some delay. *Simon* now badly wanted her to stay 'a day or two more', and she necessarily went along with him.

Necessarily? It seemed so. She must support him as his sister had supported him, and not let him down as his sister had once let him down.

After leaving him this afternoon she had got out Marion's exercise book and looked again at the writings and the drawings. Now she picked it up again and leafed through it. 'Marion Mary Syme, Morb House,

Llandathery, Montgomeryshire, Wales, Great Britain, Europe, The World.' Marion Norah Faulkner Syme, Morb House, Llandathery . . .

He had said this afternoon: 'After I came out of the nursing home in September, I didn't come straight back here, I spent three weeks in Ireland. It was a last despairing thought. Supposing, just supposing, they had landed after all. Supposing they had made landfall safely and just – disappeared – without getting in touch with any of his relatives. I spent three weeks, asking, asking everywhere. I tried all his relatives, but they all knew they were dead. I've no doubt in my mind now. Perhaps I never had. Perhaps we were always too close, she and I, for the other not to know . . .'

The drawings of the boy of fifteen with the mop of fair hair. They were Simon, she saw quite distinctly now. She felt she had known him all her life. Were *her* feelings towards him sisterly? How could they be? Was *she* the girl climbing the tree with the boy clutching her ankle? What had Marion's first feelings for Simon been, and when had they changed? The untouched, unsullied beauty of a woman discovering herself before your eyes . . . It was total commitment on both sides . . .

She dropped the book on the bed. How and when had *her* commitment begun? This afternoon or earlier? She did not know. All she knew now was that she was deeply and emotionally involved.

Before they separated they had spent a time looking more closely at his portraits of his sister. 'I still want to paint her. Perhaps you think it's all part of my morbid preoccupation with a dead girl. The classic *idée fixe*.

But it's not quite that. It's something to do with my creative life as well ... If you stayed long enough, I wish you'd let me paint you.'

'... I believe I like this one best – the unfinished one in the black frock. She has more character in her face.'

'That was the best and the last. I mean the last before the war separated us. I still have the frock in there. It was one she wore when I took her to a dance in Bristol.'

'You never tried to finish the hands and arms?'

'I'd not the talent, without a model, and not the heart, without her ... I remember my mother didn't like the frock. She thought it was too grown-up for a girl not yet twenty – black velvet. And too low-cut.'

'I expect that was what appealed to her.'

Simon smiled. 'Yes. She told me so.'

So they had talked, friendship stirring between them. The first tensions past, there seemed no bar. Affinity grew in the reaction from fear.

At the very last he had said: 'If you'd only wait a day or two – I'd have to make business arrangements with Althea first – but if you'd wait a day or two, maybe I could come with you when you leave.'

She had stared at him, startled. They had looked at each other very carefully for a moment or two.

She said: 'If you think that's the right thing – for you, I mean.'

'I'm sure it would be the right thing for me. I believe you could help me to forget the past.'

'But how can I when I am so much like her?'

'That's why, Norah, that's why. One can't *destroy* the past with some radical change – one can't cut it away. But one can forget it with a perpetual merging. Your likeness to her is no longer a threat. It could be a promise.'

'A promise of what?'

He had replied, his eyes deeply engaging her: 'For me perhaps a new life. For you as much or as little as you care to give.'

II

AT DINNER Althea asked Norah if she were feeling well, as she was looking rather pale and seemed quieter than usual. Norah said she was fine. Trivialities passed the meal, but Simon excused himself as soon as he had finished.

In the drawing-room over coffee Norah said: 'Althea, you knew Marion. D'you think I'm really like her?'

The older woman's glasses were misted with the coffee steam as she looked up. 'Simon hasn't been worrying you about it *again*, has he? Because . . .'

'I've been thinking . . .'

'What?'

'You put me in her room, didn't you?'

'Well, it was her room once – when she was a girl. But that was long years ago.'

'I found some of her old drawing-books today, and a few of her belongings – slippers, etc. in that cupboard. The memories of her are still there.'

Althea frowned. 'Sorry about that. I'll have them cleared out.'

'I'd like to know if you think I'm at all like her. Not in looks – I know that – but in temperament, voice, character . . . personality, if you like.'

'Voice – a little. I was struck by a resemblance on the tape. Temperament – a little. Quick, volatile, easily roused – perhaps emotional? Personality – I hope not.'

'Didn't you like her?'

'I don't say that. But she didn't have your warmth. She could be very calculating, very hard. She didn't show that side very much to those she cared for, but it was always there – like a stone in a peach – sooner or later you knew it was there.'

Silence fell. Norah quietly studied her friend. Whether or not the afternoon had lent her new eyes, she seemed to see defects she hadn't noticed before. Or perhaps it was the thunder, the headache, the heavy day that had brought Mrs Syme to dinner with her lipstick off one corner of her mouth, the face powder crusted, the excellent lace of her cuff stained with something blue. There seemed also to be an element of shallowness, of meretriciousness in the affection in her voice. Did growing distaste produce a new perception or did new perception produce a growing distaste?

She said: 'It's a very odd feeling; coming to a house where there's been someone so much like yourself – and your age when she died. I wonder you didn't think of that when you invited me.'

'You know exactly why I invited you, my pet. Because I'm very fond of you, because I love your company, and because I get the distinct impression that you have a certain affection for me. If Simon bothers you I can't get rid of him. But if being up in these rooms makes you feel spooky, just say the word and you can come down.'

Norah sipped her coffee. 'I have the oddest feelings sometimes when I look in the mirror – as if I might see Marion there instead of myself. Or as if there's another person beside me trying to share my thoughts.'

'Good grief, you are in a strange mood! Whatever has got into you?'

'That's what I ask myself. Exactly. What has got into me?'

Although resolved not to force an issue tonight, she had been unable to keep off what was uppermost in her mind, and if she couldn't challenge Althea with the enormity she wanted to, she could at least nag at the fringes of the subject. So although all her fears had now been dissipated, she perversely chose this moment to thrust them at Althea, to display them, as another challenge or as a taunt, like someone showing the spent bullets of a fusillade they have narrowly escaped. Yet in the moment of speaking it crossed her mind to wonder whether all the bullets were quite spent. Marion's ghost was laid. But was she really looking forward to going up to those rooms to sleep tonight? Was she absolutely free of compulsions not quite her own?

Althea said: 'I said you looked tired, Norah. I expect you've been overstrained – before you came here, I mean – by your father's death and the unfortunate end to your friendship with Robert Jenkin. It's easy, then, if you're tensed up about something, to allow something quite different, quite trivial, to upset you. I'm very sorry there has been this – coincidence. But don't worry about it, *please*. I'll arrange tomorrow for you to come down to the first-floor bedroom that Miss Harris had.'

'No, thank you. I'll stay.'

'It's a *nice* one, looking over the front. Only it hasn't got a bathroom.'

'I'll stay,' said Norah. 'I think it's – *right* for me up there.'

Gregory came into the room and his mother asked him to play the piano. After a while Norah left them and went into the library. She wished she had refused to listen to Simon's pleas for delay. It was foreign to her nature to hide her true feelings and to put up with a situation that had now become insupportable.

Yet she saw his point of view; and for the moment at least she simply could not desert him. For me, he had said it could be the promise of a new life. For you as much or as little as you care to give. Was this, she wondered, an egotistical demand or a loving supplication? And to which would she be most likely to accede? After the barrenness, the emptiness of only a week ago, now, after only a week, not one man but two were making demands on her – though of a radically different nature. Christopher spoke from strength, Simon from weakness.

But it might be a bad misjudgment to suppose that there was no weakness in one or strength in the other. Confidence was not an absolute, insecurity not a measurable liability. Everyone's personality was a succession of Chinese boxes, one within the other, each contradictory of the one before.

As she went back through the main hall Simon came from among the shadows on the other side. He had changed since dinner and was in a polo sweater and old flannel trousers, his hands grey. He smiled at her.

'I thought I'd do the mortaring tonight. The wall's almost as good as new.'

'Already? You shouldn't have bothered,'

'Afraid we have some wallpapering to do. You didn't spare the decorations. Does Alice come up to your room?'

'I make my own bed. But somebody's sure to go up soon. Simon, I *can't* keep quiet about this – the whole thing is so monstrous that I feel I must ask her for an explanation!'

'Do you think you'll get it?'

'I don't know. But I can try. And then leave. It's the only way!'

He was staring at her thoughtfully. 'D'you know what occurred to me when I was up in the studio just now plastering up the hole? D'you know what I thought?'

'What?'

'That unfinished portrait of Marion – the one you admired. I wish you'd sit for it – let me finish it before you go. Before I go.'

She stared back at him. 'What, d'you mean sit – for Marion . . . in her place?' When he nodded. 'But that's impossible!'

'What's impossible about it?'

She struggled to find the right words. The wise, the tactful ones. 'What you said this afternoon . . .'

'D'you mean about separating her from you? I made

that stupid mistake when you first burst in – but it was over as soon as I touched you. That's the difference. It's the chasm that exists between a human being and a ghost – between warm flesh and a cold memory. Painting you in her clothes would I think achieve the ultimate separation.'

'In her clothes?' She stared at him. 'But how *could* it? Anyway, I wouldn't want to.'

'If you don't want to, that's an end to it.'

'But why should *you* want to?'

He frowned. 'I think Marion would have liked me to finish it.'

'Must we – must you consider what Marion would have liked?'

'Not of itself, no. Of course not. But you're right about that painting – it's the best thing I've done, and not merely of her. Among the many self-recriminations I've suffered over the last years has been the regret – *my* regret that I didn't finish it. The regret grew, I think, with my recovery. My ego was beginning to emerge from its eclipse.' He gave a wry smile. 'So in a way, helping me to complete the hands and arms and shoulders would be helping me in an artistic way, and that was something I thought you might want.'

There was a splash of water from a choked gutter over the front door.

'But, Simon, if you painted me as Marion, I should feel that I *was* Marion! Sometimes I think even now up in that room . . .'

He shook his head. 'The mistake can never be made again – certainly not by me, least of all by you.'

'At times I get an extraordinary sensation . . .'

'You could sit for me perhaps two mornings. Then it would be done with. Over. A door closed. But anyway – whether you do or not, when I leave this house I shall buy a studio somewhere and start painting in earnest. Until now I've lacked the courage to see myself as a full-time artist. You've given me that courage today.'

CHAPTER TWELVE

I

IT POURED all night. Norah dozed fitfully, waking often to hear the tom-tom drums of the rain. Simon had made a good job of the wall. Only the damp mortar and the pile of stripped wallpaper on the floor remained to betray the breakthrough. She had promised him nothing for tomorrow. Her mind was in a condition in which emotion constantly upended rational thought. As day began to split the thin line of the curtains she sat up and mentally listed the problems before her.

(1) Sometime soon, whether at a politic time or not, her true feelings for Althea would betray themselves. Last night restraints had just held, but they must give way any time. If Althea's reasons for inviting her here were solely those she had already given, then she stood condemned as the all-time monster of blundering insensitivity. If there were other reasons then they could hardly be less than sinister.

(2) Sometime soon, two men would expect her to make some sort of choice between them. Although they might seem to be asking fundamentally different things, they were asking in essence for something from her that she could only give to one.

(3) Sometime soon . . .

And there she stopped. For all the minor problems and decisions of her life hinged upon the decisions she came to over the first two. Such other decisions as she might have to make, such as when she should leave the house and with what purpose, simply waited upon these. If she argued in her mind that she could escape from or delay the important choices for the unimportant she was simply deceiving herself. She lay back and shut her eyes again and tried to empty her mind of thought. For in the end thought was not going to have the ultimate voice.

Surprisingly, she dozed again and woke in full daylight. The rain had stopped but the weather was still heavy. Shards of broken sunlight fell through clouds as grey and heavy as a sepulchre. At ten-thirty Christopher rang. They talked for five minutes but she gave nothing away. She *could* give nothing until she could be completely frank. He complained that he had not seen her at all yesterday, and she said: 'Tomorrow. Come over sometime tomorrow.' Put off until you are surer. Delay, delay just a little while. After yesterday's fears and shocks perhaps one quiet day will allow emotions to settle, to sediment. But a quiet day? Will it be a quiet day?

She saw Simon at eleven as she was going into Mrs Syme's study. He was looking cheerful.

'Have you decided?' he asked.

'Decided – what?' She was startled, as if he had read her thoughts.

'About today.'

'Oh ... about today. I'm – just going to do some work for your aunt.'

'How long will it take?'

'She's dictating an article. Most of the morning, I'd think.'

'Well, if you're free this afternoon I think I could finish all I need to do in one sitting. I'll leave the door to the other house unlocked so you can come up. If you don't come I shall know you've decided against it.'

'I already have.'

'What – decided against it?' He looked disappointed.

'Yes. It's – unhealthy. Playing with fire.'

'Long-dead ashes ... In one sense you're right, of course. Anything that brings that time back ... But in another, not so. Don't you think, artistically, it will decide something?'

She looked at him. 'Yes.'

There was a long tense silence between them. She turned to put her hand uncertainly on the study door.

He said with a change of tone: 'I rang the chemist's in Aberystwyth about my pills. They'll have some by this afternoon.'

'Then ...'

'Timson will go in and fetch them.'

'D'you feel any different without them?'

'A little ... As if I'd been without sleep. But much happier.'

'Happier?'

He nodded: 'It stands to reason. Wouldn't anyone be? I feel like someone at the end of a long tunnel seeing the daylight again.'

II

WHEN THE article was finished it was nearly one, and Althea said: 'Thank Heaven that's done! My head! You've been so patient with me. What a wonderful nurse you'd make, Norah. Have you ever thought of taking it up?'

Yet in spite of the generous words it had not been an equable two hours. Friction had come into their relationship; it surfaced now and again like some conger eel of discord moving through apparently clear water. When Althea put her arm round Norah as they walked towards the dining-room, Norah willed herself not to edge away, yet she thought Althea detected the movement that had been stillborn.

When Gregory came to lunch he had broken his glasses. He had pushed the pebble out when polishing them, and it would need an expert to fix the thick lens in place again. Timson had been told to take them in when he went for the pills. In the meantime the boy managed with a spare pair that were short of one side piece and were anchored grotesquely on his nose by the left ear only. Thunder eructated over the house on different cloud levels, but in the west the sky was bright like a piece of torn touch paper.

Simon had been out walking in the fitful sunlight. His face was warmed by the exercise. He said he had been to the top of Cader Morb and then beyond it as far as the Dwynt Valley.

'The clouds are like fog up there. You can walk into

one suddenly and as suddenly out the other side. They're like ideas passing through a man's head. It often happens at this time of year, when a season is breaking . . .'

'Did you talk to Cader Morb while you were up there?' Althea asked, with a hint of malice.

'No, dear aunt, nobody should need to ask questions of Cader Morb – only of themselves. What we can't answer ourselves no mountain can answer for us.'

'In other words,' said Gregory, peering, 'the wisdom of the ages resides in the id.'

'That's a very clever remark in one so young,' Althea said, smiling.

'I had a funny dream last night,' Gregory said. 'I dreamed I was dead, and Heaven was a sort of great hall where everybody was gathering to hear me play a concerto. And wherever I looked, whichever way I looked there was a piano, destroyed, broken in pieces, all the wires hanging out.'

'I had a habit of repeating stupid dreams at breakfast,' said Mr Croome-Nichols, 'when I was a boy. My father soon cured me of it. Every dream I told I was compelled to learn ten verses of Samuel by heart. Very good discipline.'

By the time lunch was over it was raining again. Norah had not finished all her typing but she went up to her room and washed some stockings and combed her hair and examined her finger nails. All the arguments for and against had long since been through her mind; now it was a matter of instinct, of intuition, possibly of some inner compulsion. Yesterday she had been in a panic of apprehension, of fear for her own life. Now that was gone and in its place an apprehension of another sort. To allay it she must do which? Go or stay?

'Don't you think,' he had said, 'artistically it will decide something?' She thought it would decide something for her, perhaps the second of the two questions she had debated this morning. But it was not an artistic one.

She went downstairs. No one in the hall. Across to the other door. It opened today, as he had promised. The empty part of the house struck damp and a little chill. Up the stairs. Only yesterday she had come this way for the first time, idly peering into rooms, half scared, yet still relatively uninvolved. Now, although entirely aware of what she was doing, she was conscious of a curious elision of time; as if she had thought herself here rather than walked here; as if she dreamed what she did and yet knew it to be real.

The big door was latched back. He must have heard her footstep, for he met her at the studio door. He didn't say anything but smiled his pleasure as if sure she would come, took her hand, led her in.

The picture was out of its frame and back on the easel. She looked at it, seeing no resemblance now to herself in the girl pictured there. The face had a defiant expression, the rather heavy eyelids lifted, smiling.

'Your hair's longer than hers,' Simon said. 'But it doesn't matter. That part's almost done. The frock's in there when you feel like changing.'

They hesitated, as if suddenly strangers to each other again, seeking some final agreement.

She said: 'Simon, are you sure this is sensible?'

'If by sensible you mean what can be appreciated by the senses, then, yes is the answer. Sensible, you know, means what can give pleasure or pain. In other words, what is alive.' He was arranging his brushes. 'And I am alive again – through you.'

She went into the other attic, only half shut the door to allow some light in. The repaired wall showed more rough mortar this side, and the paper that she had broken through drooped like dead vegetation. The big doll sat on unwinking guard beside it.

The frock was out on a chair. She touched it. Good velvet, and it had kept well. All these years while he was away ... Smell of lavender; something else, a little acrid. Shoes too. Black high-heeled, dated. She kicked off a shoe and tried one experimentally. Her feet were bigger; she could just get them on but they pinched. That wouldn't do. She thankfully edged back into her own. And the frock?

She held it up to herself, peered in the half dark at the reflection in the mirror on the Victorian wash stand. It was the right length anyway. She unzipped her dress, stepped out of it, put it over the chair beside the other; stood hesitating a moment then unfastened her brassiere and took that off also. She stared a second at herself in the dusty mirror then picked up the evening frock again.

Marion might have taken a size smaller shoe but she was an inch bigger in the hips. Slight satisfaction. It seemed about right round the bust. There was no zip, but buttons, and contortions were needed to fasten

183

them. It was off the shoulders but had small puff sleeves part-way down the upper arm. Low-cut it certainly was.

As soon as she had got the frock on she knew why some part of her primitive self had wanted all along to do this. Because it was an emotional challenge, a sexual challenge, perhaps even a psychic challenge. The feelings of involvement of the last few days were deeply reinforced. She stared in the mirror, frowning, excited, oppressed.

Well, now it was done. The gauntlet taken up. She was contending not only for Simon but for herself. Shrugging off the oppression, shaking it away from her like a clammy shroud, she stepped out into the studio.

Rain purred like a heavy cat on the fanlight.

Simon looked at her, then passed a hand across his eyes. 'It's a complete triumph, isn't it,' he said in a voice carefully matter-of-fact. 'A triumph of matter over mind, of flesh over spirit, of life over death, of beauty over the beast.'

In the same casual voice Norah said: 'Where do I sit? Here?'

'Just there. You can't see the picture now, but you remember how she was sitting. Wait a minute. Let me move this pier-glass. Then you can see her still.'

She sat absolutely motionless while he moved the mirror. Then she could see the painting again. She put her left arm on her knee, the right along the back of the chair.

'Head up,' he said.

'But you're not painting my head.'

'No, but it gives the right curve to the neck.'

He began to paint. She thought, what's wrong with me? Is the frock too tight or is something else making my breath come short? Her rational mind, when it was allowed to function, thought, what *is* this resolving? I must talk to him, remind him that these are my hands and arms, not hers. That's the whole point, the *reasonable* point of my coming here, to convince him, or to enable him to convince himself, once and for all. But is he in doubt? Not by a word or a look does *he* suggest what *I* fear. That was as far as reason went. Thereafter it was only unreason – which after all dominated her movements this afternoon – and unreason saw the defiance of the half-smiling, brown-haired, white-shouldered girl who looked back at her. Marion looked back at her, like a third individual in the room, for it was the painting that was reflected, not the sitter. And the hand and the artist's brush. And the brush was making slow firm lines of darkness around the left arm. So the arm, from being a sketch, began to take shape and colour. It was forte growing out of a void, substance created – or recreated. Living arms grafted on a dead person.

She suddenly tried not to shiver.

'Are you cold?' he said sharply.

'No . . .'

'I've brought coffee up in a Thermos for later.'

'Simon, I've never sat before. I may not – take to it too well.'

'About an hour will do.'

'Maybe – not that . . .'

He said: 'My hand's so cursedly unsteady.'

'Then let's stop.'

'No . . .'

She moistened her lips. 'I believe this may be doing the opposite of what I intended – we intended. Isn't it? Surely this is – is trying to bring Marion back to life.'

'Far from it. This will lay Marion to rest.'

The painting went on.

He said: 'Your arm isn't quite right. Can you see what I mean?' He stepped from behind the easel. 'If you could move it farther back.' He came up to her and turned her hand. 'Like that.' He looked at her deeply, his eyes searching hers. Then he lowered his head and kissed her on the upper part of her breast, his lips pressing firmly on her skin. She looked at his hair, the side of his face, took a breath.'

He said against her: 'Do you know the story that a man once lay with a woman on a mountain top. And when he took her he cried: "At this moment – at this moment there is no other God but me!"'

He rubbed a hand over his eyes, went back to the easel. 'Art should never imitate life, for life will always win.' He picked up his brush. 'Yet the solution surely lies not so much in outright victory as in the emergence of truth.'

'I think,' she said, 'we should stop.'

'Yes. But now we cannot. So give me twenty minutes more to establish what has been begun. Then it will be the end of it – the complete and utter end.'

The frock did not fit her at all well. Even round the hips it seemed to be pulling, as if caught up. She shifted a little to sit more easily and he made no comment on the move. She took another slow difficult breath and saw the other arm growing on the canvas. In his peculiar way he was again not so much painting it as creating it out of the background. Now the hand. She watched, for a moment fascination getting the better of unease.

Then she thought she saw a movement behind the canvas. Through the pier-glass she could see the other end of the room and the door leading to the stairs. And the door had moved. She stared at it, pulse beating. The wind? But there was no wind. Only the waterfall roar of the rain.

Then while she watched a hand came round the door, holding on to the door. It was a girl's hand. It was not unlike her own hand, the one he was painting. And it was wet.

It stayed there quite still, and to her it was as if in re-creating Marion's hand on the canvas he had begun to re-animate some long-drowned hand come back from the sea to claim him.

She swung round with a jerk of head, arm, spine; cushion falling, almost oversetting the couch.

'What is it!' he said. 'What are you doing?'

She pointed at the hand on the door.

Simon stared, screwed up his eyes, dropped the brush.

'Who is it?' he called.

There was no reply.

He lurched to the door, pulled it wide.

Gregory stood there, taking in what he saw. His hair was plastered with rain and his suit dank with it.

'What d'you want?' Simon demanded.

'I came to tell you. But then I heard voices, so I didn't like to come in.'

He was staring past Simon at Norah in her frock.

'What is it? What have you come to tell me?'

'I thought I ought to. Timson's back. He couldn't get through. There's floods. The road beyond Llanidloes is flooded. So he couldn't go to Aberystwyth. He turned back. I've just been out to look at the car. There's yellow mud up to the windows.'

Norah stood up, straightening her frock, stared at the boy's hands, then down at her own. Then she shook her head as if trying to disperse the miasma that had gathered about her.

'So,' said Simon to the boy. 'What of it?'

'Mother sent me to tell you. Because you won't be able to get your medicine now, not until tomorrow.'

CHAPTER THIRTEEN

I

'THESE PILLS,' she said. 'How long have you been without them?'

'Two days. A bit more.'

The boy had gone. Refusing adamantly to sit again, she had changed back into her own clothes, glad now to get the others off. She was sitting sharing his Thermos of coffee. The spell, the mood, whatever had built up between them had been shattered – the commonplace had returned. But the memory of the mood remained. And the mood itself was not far away. Normality had to be firmly grasped and persisted with.

'You had plenty left?'

He was staring at the painting. 'What?'

'The pills, I mean.'

'Oh . . . yes, more than a dozen.'

'They're important to you?'

'Not as important as what has happened to me in the last two days.'

After a moment she said: 'Were you told to keep on with them?'

'What? Oh, yes. Essential, they said.' He looked down and reluctantly replaced a brush in its jar. 'They're

French, you know. Quite experimental. I think in the first place they did more for me than anything else at all. A tremendous lightening of depression. After only a few weeks I began to belong to the ordinary world ... And yet – so far so good.' With a rag he wiped a spot off his hand. 'It could be a good thing provided it goes on all right. Because the essential thing is that I shall have learned how to live – and love – without them.'

She stared again at the painting, which he had almost completed in broad design: half Marion, half herself. He could finish it, if he chose to, without her. Gregory's interruption had come either too soon or too late; she wasn't sure.

'That boy,' she said. 'He has a girl's hands.'

'What boy?'

'Gregory. He makes me shiver.'

'Sometimes one feels sorry for him.'

'Was he always like this?'

Simon frowned. 'I wish he hadn't come in then. He broke ... In another half hour ... You won't sit, even like that?'

'No. I'm sorry. No.'

'When I last saw him he was nine. Certainly he was more – understandable then. I've tried once or twice these last few days.'

'You're not alone. Of course I think his eyes ...'

'Bad eyes are in the family. There were three brothers: my father, the eldest, Gregory's the youngest. In between was Claude, who died young. He was half blind.'

'You're – an introvert family,' Norah said.

He smiled. 'That of itself is no drawback. Ultimately the introverts – the balanced introverts – make up most of what is worthwhile in the world.'

She said: 'I've got to leave tomorrow, Simon, at the latest. This afternoon makes it more necessary than ever. Gregory is sure to go straight to his mother.'

'Does that matter?'

'Only that she won't like it – and she may say something, and if she does . . .'

'. . . I realize that. I'll see her myself tomorrow.'

'D'you mean you'll leave?'

'Yes. I'll leave.'

She looked up at the fanlight. If the floods go down!

'Oh, the road to Morb Lane is always open. And the trains will run.'

She got up to go, and then something he had just said impinged on her mind.

'Simon . . . your father . . .'

His eyes flickered back from the painting. 'I don't think I can leave that behind,' he said. 'All the rest, yes, but not that because it – it's part of you both.'

'Your father, Simon. You said he was the eldest. Is that – are you sure?'

He smiled. 'I ought to know.'

'Well . . . it stands to reason when one thinks of it. But I never have thought of it. I understood Althea's husband was the eldest. Thomas Syme.'

'Hubert, Claude, Thomas, that's how it went. Four years between each.'

191

'Then how did this house come to belong to Althea?'

'It doesn't. It never has.'

II

'LLANDATHERY FOUR one,' she said into the telephone.

'Llandathery four one. Trying to connect you.'

She stared down at the heap of typing, some yet unfinished. She felt responsible slightly that she had not completed it that afternoon. 'But why did you not tell me before?' she had asked. 'Tell you what: that the property belonged to me?' 'Yes, of course.' 'It didn't occur to me that you didn't know. Anyway, does it matter?' 'It could matter a great deal. Of course it could matter.'

Burr-burr. Burr-burr. It was earlier than she had said, and probably he was out. But in this weather?

'Sorry, there's no reply.'

'Oh, keep ringing, will you?'

Burr-burr. Burr-burr.

In spite of its frustrate ending, the afternoon had helped, and was still helping, to bring all the strands together, all the tensions to a head. And out of the fear, the nausea, the pleasure, had come some decision. 'D'you mean you'll leave?' she had asked. 'Yes, I'll leave,' he said. But he would have to come back. And surely she must do the same. Unless . . .

'Sorry, there's no reply. Shall I give 'em a ring in ten minutes and ring you back?'

'No – er . . .'

'Hullo?'

'*Christopher!* I thought you were out.'

'I was. This downpour's flooded my kitchen. I was trying to unblock the gutter. What is it? Are you all right?'

'Yes . . . I rang early. I thought it might be easier now.'

'Some developments?'

'Yes . . . Everything's *much* clearer. But I can't explain now. Could you come tomorrow about eleven?'

'I was coming anyway.'

'Yes, well . . . I think I shall be having a quarrel with Althea – and Simon is involved and . . .'

'Will you leave then?'

'I think so. But I'll need your support.'

'You'll have it, moral and physical.'

'Well, it depends how things turn out.'

'Are you all right tonight?'

Was she? 'Perfectly, thanks.'

'You sound a long way away.'

'Is that better?'

'I don't mean just in distance. In something else.'

Perceptive. 'I'm – no different.'

'Well, take care. I don't trust that lot.'

'It's all right.'

'Norah!'

'Yes?'

'Shall I come round now?'

Should he come round now? 'Thanks, but there's simply no point. Everything's better kept till tomorrow . . .' She thought she heard a footstep. 'I must go now. I hope you get your kitchen dry.'

'The rain has even put the fire out.'

She laughed. 'I think you have more problems than I have.'

'Don't joke. All I need is a woman's tender care.'

'Oh? Well, that's another matter, isn't it?'

'No, absolutely one and the same. All our problems can be jointly solved, I assure you.'

When she hung up she got the same feeling of isolation that she had felt yesterday. Yet she was more secure in herself than she had been then.

As she came out of the study Mr Croome-Nichols was passing, and he opened his mouth at her in acknowledgement. They exchanged a few words about the flooded roads. She thought that Mr Croome-Nichols for some reason had come to approve of her – perhaps because her father had been to the right university. Yet of all those in the house (apart from Simon) his was the only integrity she felt she could rely on.

She went upstairs to wait until dinner.

III

So AT dinner – the last dinner they were likely to eat together – Alice served grapefruit and everyone behaved as if they were acting out a part in which it was necessary to carry on a tradition of conduct already established. Gregory, overheated in a thick suit, his spectacles ludicrously awry, picked and peered at his plate as if suspicious of being cheated. Rupert Croome-Nichols forked food into a corner of his mouth and turned up his eyes in search of revelation. Althea, in brown velvet, her bare plump arms appearing and disappearing through the slit sleeves, bore the burden of the conversation as usual, but more heavily, words sometimes halting on her lips, like swimmers hesitating to dive. Simon had changed his suit and looked smart and well and more composed than Norah had previously seen him.

If Gregory had carried the story of the afternoon to his mother she gave no sign. Over the pre-dinner sherry she complained of her headache still; but there was something more than sherry on her breath when she did so. Once or twice at dinner Norah caught Gregory peering at his mother, as if anxious for her.

They talked of the flooded road, of a letter Althea had written to *The Times* yesterday on the population explosion, of a painter called Kokoschka Simon was interested in, of the frugal food Mr Croome-Nichols had had when a boy and how it had done him no harm at all and how all the young today were overfed.

'It's a possibility,' said Althea, 'that the young do get too much. It makes them develop much earlier. What we shall not know for another thirty years is whether it will lead to a premature senescence.'

'By then,' said Gregory, 'they'll have life pills. To slow it all down.'

'And maybe death pills too,' said Mr Croome-Nichols, opening his mouth wide at the joke. 'Euthanasia is not a Christian ethic but it's going to become a moral necessity if the population keeps increasing. Or else we shall be standing shoulder to shoulder inhaling air through a pipe.'

'I really have no use for *any* pills,' Althea said. 'Almost everything is controlled by what one *eats*. Just like a plant. If plants were fed as unsuitably as human beings they'd all turn yellow and die. If . . .'

'Perhaps that's what we are doing,' Simon said cheerfully. 'Turning yellow, at least. Crawling with bacteria. Withering at the roots. And preparing to die.'

'It's wrong to be morbid, Simon,' Mrs Syme said. 'You of all people should think of . . .'

'As for pills, my dear aunt, theoretically I share your distaste for them; practically, there are hundreds and thousands of people who wouldn't be alive today without them. I think I am one of them.'

'Oh, I have no doubt they have their uses in exceptional cases. The antibiotics, for instance . . .'

'Bomber crews were kept going on Benzedrine. Didn't you know? Even drugs I suppose you would admit are acceptable in so good a cause. Even the drug that I was taking and which so mysteriously disappeared.'

'My dear Simon, you had it on your dressing-table! No one has touched it.'

'Well, I shall have to do without it for another day shan't I?'

'The floods will be down by morning: you see.

Timson nearly lost the car! He was only just hauled out in time.'

It's all a sham, Norah thought. We're all thinking our own secret elemental thoughts and behaving like the civilized human beings we are not. But it's only till morning. In the morning we can drop this pretence and tear at each other with tooth and claw. Will it come to that? It hardly seems possible. Yet how else, with what other result, could the whole thing be dragged out into the light of day?

Towards the end of dinner Simon smiled at Norah and excused himself and left. He hardly seemed to grasp – or even to want to grasp – the significance of what he had told her about his father. He didn't care. It was not so much that material considerations were not important to him as that other things in life were more so. It was not a view with which in other circumstances Norah would have been inclined to quarrel. But this was not the occasion to be altruistic or unpractical. She had to think for Simon, and indeed for them both.

After dinner, Althea poured herself a brandy to go with her coffee, but Norah refused coffee and left them to it. Once out, she doubled back through the larger drawing-room and so into the study. With any luck no one now would stir for twenty minutes. The small risk was worth taking for Simon's sake. There was just a chance that his pills were here, and to face the unpleasant scene that was inevitable tomorrow he might particularly need them.

The Aladdin lamp was out, so she lit it, watching the flame go blue and the yellow light blanch as she turned up the wick. The study came into view. She carried the lamp to the desk and began to go quickly and lightly through the drawers, trying to disturb as little as possible. An unnamed portrait watched her censoriously from over the fireplace. Three brothers, he had said, Hubert, Claude, Thomas; four years between them, that's how it went. Claude had been the blind one. Thomas always the ne'er do well.

'Tell me,' she had said this afternoon. 'What made you paint someone drowned in the lake? A woman? That picture you were doing the first morning. It made me think . . .'

'Oh – that. I suppose I am preoccupied with drowning, but at first the woman seemed to add something. You remember what you were saying the other night – about *La Belle dame sans merci*. Something of that sort. It's over there, back to the wall, if you want to look. But I never went on with it. It became too Burne-Jonesish and Victorian.'

'So nobody was ever drowned in the lake?'

'Oh, yes. A girl; a maid. She disappeared one day and was found a couple of days later. She was unmarried and pregnant. I saw them bringing her up. I was about seven at the time. It made a great impression.'

'Althea told me but I never know whether to believe what she says.'

. . . Nothing here. She left the drawers and went to the cupboard in which was kept a miscellany of objects: papers, clippings, photographs, glue, plant labels, rulers, pencils, catalogues.

Probably this was a useless waste of time.

'Are you looking for something, Norah?'

Althea in the doorway, voice soft and friendly but sharpness in the eyes.

So this – this might be the crisis, before she was quite ready for it; tonight instead of tomorrow. Lie, lie. It's easy still to evade – a smooth excuse – not convincing but delaying. All that was necessary. But the anger burned. Anger and pride. Why *should* she evade?

'I was looking for Simon's pills.'

'Simon's pills? But why here?'

'Why not? He needs them.'

'My dear, he *has* them. They were where he had left them.'

'They were not the same. The bottle was similar but the pills were not the same shape.'

'Norah, d'you really believe that?'

'Yes.'

Althea sighed and came farther into the room, leaving the door ajar. Her bulk was formidable but her tone was still light. 'My pet, it's all part of his persecution complex. Didn't you hear him at dinner?'

'I heard him very well.'

'Anyway, he'll have more tomorrow . . . But you still haven't answered why you expected to find them here.'

'I thought they might just have got here by accident.'

Althea Syme closed the cupboard, brushing against Norah to do so. A breath of brandy went with her. 'That's not a very polite remark. I know you came here as my special, personal friend but there are liberties one shouldn't take. Ransacking my study on such a flimsy excuse, for instance.'

'I *thought* I came as your personal friend. Not as an understudy for Simon's sister.'

Althea laughed. 'You're looking at everything in such a distorted way tonight. Perhaps it's the thundery weather. I know I . . .'

'The weather has nothing to do with it.'

'But you accept everything Simon tells you as the literal truth. You forget that he has been mentally disturbed.'

'Did you forget that he had been mentally disturbed when you invited me here?'

'I've *told* you. I told you when you mentioned it last week. Do I have to repeat it yet again?'

'Not unless you wish to.'

A hand on her arm. 'Please, dear. You know we've been quite fond of each other, haven't we? So you really must believe me in this. I've said it over and over.'

They looked at each other, Norah assailed by a sudden weak wish to believe her friend, Althea warmly affectionate, fractionally glassy, her eyes bloodshot. Enmity could still be kept out of sight, with a few evasions could perhaps be prevented from ever surfacing. Much easier to keep it all in, to feel it, not to express it. Dear Althea who had invited her here, with her quick wit, her youthful brain. Let it all remain as a suspicion, a doubt. Let them separate tomorrow and . . .

'The resemblance to Marion is really so slight. I've told you so often before, pet. No one could possibly mistake you for her. No one *in his right mind*, that is. My fault, my only fault, lay in supposing Simon was cured and would not pick a chance likeness to make so much of it.'

'I wonder,' Norah said, 'why on the evening he came you persuaded me to change the style of my hair so that it should be more in the fashion that Marion used to do it.'

'Oh, *Norah*.' That squeeze on her arm again. 'You do think badly of me, don't you? I didn't suggest you should change your hair to a style more like Marion's but *less* like hers! The way you did it before *was* rather similar to hers.'

Norah listened to the rain. 'But,' she said, 'you've said repeatedly that you'd forgotten all about my likeness to Marion and that it never occurred to you that Simon would be upset.'

Althea withdrew her hand. 'No, I didn't say quite that.'

'Oh, yes, you did.'

'You're trying to trap me into a fancied contradiction, pet.'

'That isn't difficult, is it, all the way along?'

'I don't understand what you mean.'

'Besides, you must know; I expect Gregory's told you: I've been up to Simon's studio and seen all the portraits he did of Marion. The likeness is obvious.'

'Gregory told me he went up with a message this afternoon and found you sitting there half naked. It's not something I would personally be proud of.'

It was all sliding now, sliding with every sentence spoken, down the road to open war.

'My likeness to Marion made an impression on you when we first met. Didn't it? So when you knew Simon was going to come out you got rid of your other secretary and offered me the job in the hope that confronting him with me every day would upset his new balance. Everything's been to that end, hasn't it: your sending Doole to meet him as if he couldn't be trusted to come alone, the sort of supervision you've imposed on him here; the tape with Marion's voice "accidentally" on it, mislaying his pills, which are so vital to him; every little contrivance! My part in it was to be passive, wasn't it: it didn't much matter what happened to me – whether I might find myself embarrassed or – or humiliated or even put in danger. That was all unimportant so long as it worked your way. From the beginning your pretending to be fond of me was a sham!'

'Never a sham, Norah, never a sham! That's absolutely untrue.'

'Then what do you call it?'

Althea seemed to struggle for a moment with an inability to express herself. 'You can leave tomorrow, Norah. I'm grieved – bitterly upset – but I won't have these insults thrown . . . Do you think, do you seriously believe that I'd have made so much of you for petty personal advantage?'

'Yes, I do! And the advantage isn't petty, is it . . . ?'

'Well, it's not true! My fondness went deeper, far deeper than that. You must have known. This sort of hysteria is something I hadn't expected . . .'

'What *had* you expected? Just tell me, please.'

'Some loyalty, some affection felt for *me*! But you

can leave. You can leave first thing tomorrow, Norah, and that's the end of it.'

'I'll leave,' Norah said, 'and take Simon with me!'

The rain had stopped at last. Its silence emphasized the silence in the room. She wished now she hadn't said it, but it was out.

'What did you say?'

'Simon is coming with me. When I leave he leaves. I want to see he gets a fair deal. So long as he needs me I'll stay with him.'

They had moved farther apart, like adversaries sparring, but she was still near enough to see the mottled pink of Althea's arms, looking more naked for their half concealment, the flush under the heavily powdered cheek, the yellowing tinge that drink had brought to the eyes.

'This – romantic attachment – this shallow little love affair with my nephew ... Perhaps you'll tell me what you intend to do.'

'Romantic ... My romantic attachment simply means getting him out of this house and to a place where he won't be subjected to petty annoyances and persecutions. Especially to a lawyer who'll see that his rights are safeguarded.'

'What rights are those?'

'You'll know them – and he'll know them – better than I do.'

'If you call in the law, dear, it can be a two-edged weapon. Never forget that.'

'I shan't be concerned in it except to help Simon if he needs me.'

'You already are concerned in it. Aren't you? By interfering in my private affairs, by prying . . .'

'You've *thrust* me into your private affairs . . . !'

'By prying, by questioning my maids and my butler, by – by pursuing Simon up to his studio in the other house this afternoon, and by offering yourself to him. Gregory says the way you were sitting . . .'

'Gregory's an ignorant boy . . .'

'The law, I think, wouldn't quite approve of the way you've thrown yourself at every man in the house since you came – even Doole – or the way you were caught tonight pilfering my study . . . It wouldn't – be a pretty picture, would it?'

Venom now, spilling from plump lips. Worse, more virulent, wounding more because there *had* been this physical attraction between them – innocent enough, at least on Norah's part, yet sincerely felt – quite aside from any obvious contrivance or need. Unctuous, angry, hurt, Althea was no doubt uttering the first threats that entered her head. But don't underestimate. She could count on her staff, certainly Doole and Timson, to back up any slanderous counter-attack. Her influence in Morb House was still strong. She was a fighter; no holds barred.

Norah walked away to the other side of the room, partly to put more distance between them, partly to have time to think. A quarrel like this . . . She stood with her fingers white on the back of a chair listening to her friend.

And her friend was changing tack again. 'I *don't*

understand you, Norah. All these wild accusations. And based on what? The words of a poor unfortunate half crazy man you've known less than a week. Why do you have to believe everything he tells you and nothing I do?'

'Because I've already detected you in so many lies,' Norah said quietly.

'You insolent little . . .' The words were bitten off.

'Honestly I wonder . . . I wonder, Althea, how much insanity there is in the Syme family, and whether Simon is not the only sane one . . .'

Anger was alive now, genuine, sickening, rough as tinder. It was as if they stood defenceless before each other, defenceless and armed with knives.

'You'd better go to your room. I'll see that you are sent away first thing in the morning.'

'I'll go to my room when I choose.'

They stared at each other, words halted.

Althea swung round and pressed the bell. They both waited. Norah was short of breath. Like violent exercise: heart and head pounded. Her friend's dignified brown back was towards her, ominous and silent.

Doole appeared.

His mistress made a horizontal cut with her hand. 'Will you please show Miss Faulkner to her room?'

One eyebrow moved ironically, otherwise the expression was correct.

'Yes, madam.' He held the door open and waited to follow the girl out.

Norah did not move.

'Doole is waiting,' Althea said.

'I have no intention of going to my room,' Norah said; and then fatally added: 'So you may *go*, Doole.'

Mrs Syme's back stiffened as if it had been struck.

'Doole!'

'Yes, madam.'

'I have found Miss Faulkner ransacking my desk. It is not a pleasant thing to discover that one's secretary is dishonest and a thief. She will leave this house first thing tomorrow morning. In the meantime, lest we have something else stolen, you will see that she is confined to her room. What method you employ is in your hands.'

She swept out. They heard her padding heavily away.

Norah blew out a slow breath, thought: nothing can happen. I've called her bluff. A pity this had to be tonight . . . But what if it isn't bluff . . . ?

She turned down the lamp, which was smoking. Well, he can't lay hands on me. But can he? He'll get hurt if he tries . . . but so will I. Well, he *can't*. Simon would hear or Mr Croome-Nichols, or . . . It's *fantastic*, nobody would attempt physical force. It can't be.

'Thank you, Doole, I'll stay here.'

'I'm sorry, miss.'

She's probably standing in the hall waiting for the noise of a struggle . . . If he touches me I'll sue them . . . But sueing won't stop anything tonight. And if Simon's in his room at the other end of the house, where are the witnesses? Who's to say I was mauled by this man? Who's to stop him now? Better to give way . . . I'm damned if I will. But it makes sense, to go. It's playing into their hands, this refusal.

'Miss Faulkner, please.' Deadpan face, but in his eyes a tiny flame. He thought he was going to enjoy this. He'd discover his mistake. But he'd win in the end. To be carried struggling up to bed like a naughty child – it was what Doole was anticipating. Either she must satisfy Althea by obeying or satisfy him by refusing. Did they propose to *lock* her in her room? It wasn't possible!

Her eyes strayed to the hearth. A poker. But she was as far from it as he was.

Doole smiled. 'Now come along. Don't try any tricks. You'd only get hurt, and I don't want to hurt you . . .'

And then he stopped, head up listening. Someone was knocking. They both listened. The rain had started again.

Gregory put his head round the door, eyes askew. 'There's someone at the front door, Doole. Mother told me to tell you. Alice is answering it.'

CHAPTER FOURTEEN

I

'STAY WHERE you are,' Doole said. 'Please, miss.'

In silence they listened to the sound of voices. He went out.

Gregory peered scrutinizingly at Norah and then followed. She went slowly and shakily to the threshold of the study. Only when the crisis is over do you realize the cost.

Voices. Several voices. Too far away to hear. Like an invalid just out of bed she went towards the front door.

Mrs Syme: 'But of course you must all come in. What a terrible night. You must all be soaked.'

A man's voice: 'I counted on it. I said your hospitality was famous. "I was a stranger and ye took me in." I always think of that as particularly applying to this house and to you.'

Only one person surely would be capable of opening a conversation with such a *double entendre*. Relief in a great wave threatened to upset her; she wanted to burst into tears.

Althea in the hall, Christopher Carew and three people in rough walking clothes, just pulling off plastic macks. A running fire of explanations and apologies.

Had started out from Eisteddfa Gurig this morning to walk to Plynlimon – been overtaken by mist on the mountain and then this rain, and then the dark. Had reached Mr Carew's cottage an hour ago. Had tried to dry out there. 'But my kitchen was almost awash and the coal was damp and wouldn't burn. When the rain eased off I put them in the car and brought them here. Hope you don't mind.'

'Oh, it wasn't so bad; we were glad of any shelter till morning, but Mr Carew seemed to think . . .'

Two young men and a girl; late twenties, she blonde but plain; the men brothers called Repple; she Ann Dawson.

'Nice to see you again, Norah. A violet by a mossy stone.' She smiled her relief at him. The smile must have been more emotional than she had intended for his eyes showed their surprise. His hair was lank with rain.

They were soon all in the big drawing-room, Althea not betraying by any sign that they were unwelcome. The fire was stoked up, Doole sent for hot coffee, Mr Croome-Nichols standing beside his chair, having unfolded himself, keeping the place in his book with one finger, plucking at his bottom lip; Gregory the other side, scowling crooked heliograph messages as he peered at the newcomers.

'My cottage,' Christopher said, 'is in a bad way. My bedroom's dry, and the boxroom, but nothing I could do stopped the rain flooding over the step into the kitchen . . .'

'Oh,' said one of the Repples, 'yes, it was a bit damp, but I can tell you we were glad to see that light.' To

Althea: 'It's very good of you, honestly. We wouldn't've bothered you but . . . We took a bus to this Gurig place, we came over from Aberystwyth. Maybe later we can get a lift back . . .'

'I told Ted,' the girl said. 'The weather was threatening when we set out. But he said it was always like this in Wales. I dunno . . .'

Norah exchanged another glance across the room but made no attempt to get a private word. Whether this was an accidental arrival or not, it seemed at the moment important that he should not appear to be involved with her at all. Althea certainly showed no suspicion in her manner. Hair falling in charming disarray, she was being kind and hospitable and considerate, living up to the reputation Christopher had given her. And then coffee was brought and served by the man who ten minutes ago had been looking forward to the pleasure of laying hands on a young woman and carrying her kicking up the stairs. Two worlds. As if so much fresh air had been let into a chamber of lethal gas. People laughed and chatted and apologized and got up and down from chairs and sipped the hot coffee and looked self-conscious and smoothed damp hair and stretched a foot gratefully towards the fire.

She wondered where Simon was, whether he would suddenly appear among this group, whether he had gone to bed or back to his studio, trying to work by the light of a lamp. And how long would these people stay?

Ann Dawson's clothes were dark-edged with damp so Norah offered to fit her up with a pair of slacks and a jumper and cardigan. It enabled her to get away from the others for a few minutes and exchange agreeable platitudes with a normal girl of her own age. The house itself was so much less forbidding with these ordinary people in it. Ann was engaged to Ted Repple. They were from Birmingham and were having a late holiday because Ann's father had been ill and had just died. Fellow feeling. Mum's like a baby, so lost; you see, he did everything. You'd have always thought to see them together that she was the boss; but when it came to being without him you suddenly realized. Ann's older sister was coping while she was away, but she was expecting her third and it was all rather difficult. At present Mum just couldn't bear to be left, but she'd simply have to get used to it sometime. Ann wanted to get married in the spring – and then what? Does this look all right? I mean, I'm a bit fatter than you round the seat. Really? OK, then. I mean, you must be longer in the leg. But I expect this tuck won't show.

So down the two flights of stairs. Bit spooky, isn't it? You been here long? Don't think I could do without the electric. All these pictures. Family are they? Ever so nice of you to have us in like this. Mrs Sykes – Mrs Syme, is it, dear old lady. You don't see many like her about nowadays.

At the foot of the second flight Simon. He looked in surprise at Ann Dawson and then glanced enquiringly at Norah, who introduced them and explained what had happened.

'Oh, I never heard them. I was in the other house. Bad luck. Of course they'll stay the night?'

'Oh, I dunno about that. You see . . .'

'I hope they will,' said Norah 'You should, you know!'

'Tell my aunt they're to stay,' Simon said.

He passed on and then turned back. Norah allowed the other girl to get a few paces ahead.

'Simon, I've had a frightful row with Althea.'

'You have?'

'It's happened as I rather thought it would. A lot of what I felt slipped out. So it's absolutely impossible for me to stay.'

'You'll leave in the morning?'

'Yes.'

'Then I'll come with you. Whenever you say.'

'I'm *glad*.' She smiled at him. 'I may need your support as well as . . .'

'I need yours even more, and for always.'

As he still hesitated she said: 'Are you coming in tonight? Everybody's talking and drinking coffee.'

'No. I'm not really one for parties yet. Good night, Norah.'

'Good night.'

She rejoined Ann Dawson who was waiting by the door.

'What a nice man,' Ann said. 'Is he sweet on you?'

II

WHEN THEY went in Althea Syme had just done what Simon had suggested. With the road to Aberystwyth closed, there remained only the station and to get to

Aberystwyth by rail from here meant a long detour. So she could hardly do less, as Christopher probably assumed when he brought them.

'I'll tell Alice and Shirley to make up the beds. And you, Mr Carew? We have ample room.'

'Thank you, my dear. You're very kind; but I think I must go back to my cot, make sure it's not altogether washed away.' He caught Norah's eye, and she willed him to change his mind; but he went on: 'I'm anxious about some of my equipment. I'd like to make sure it's not floating out of the door. But I'll be round in the morning to see how things have gone on. Can I have some more of your delectable coffee then?'

All the same he stayed on a while talking to one or another of them; and it was eleven before he left. She had two minutes alone with him as he went for his coat.

'If this was to help me, thank you. It couldn't have come at a better moment.'

'Too good a chance to miss.' He looked at her closely. '*More* trouble since you rang?'

'Afraid so. A really nasty time with Althea.'

'Nasty?'

'Just a quarrel – but *really* nasty all the same. All that you said about her . . .'

'*Are* you all right tonight?'

'Yes. Now.'

'You'll leave with me tomorrow?'

'It isn't just that simple.'

'Why not?'

'Christopher, there's a lot I'm going to have to explain to you.'

'About what?'

'I'll tell you tomorrow.'

'I don't like the sound of that. Tell me now.'

'There's no time . . .'

'Well,' he said, 'so long as we're of the same mind.'

'I'm not – sure . . .'

'Your coat, sir,' said Doole.

'Thanks. Thank you. Goodbye, Mrs Syme, Mr Croome-Nichols, Gregory. 'Bye Ann, Ted, Leslie. I leave you in good hands.'

They all chorused good night and presently the front door closed on him and the house was much quieter for his going.

'The moon is out,' Althea said, sipping another brandy. 'I think the storm is over.'

III

THE ARRIVAL of the three walkers had broken the tension altogether. There need be no more trouble now. A few hours of a single night to be negotiated, then she would leave with Christopher and Simon. Beyond the act of leaving there were no plans. Christopher would help them. Simon was still perplexed on one or two points, not because he couldn't reason straight but because he didn't have the facts and had never been interested enough to ask. It would be necessary to obtain those facts before making the next move. A good lawyer could do that for them.

Seeing the hikers trying to hide their yawns, she

forestalled them by wishing them good night and leaving first.

'I'll walk with you as far as the stairs, dear,' said Althea. With a nasty feeling in her stomach Norah felt her come up behind her, felt the breath of the brandy again on her cheek.

She linked her arm as affectionately as if they were mother and daughter. 'I believe I lost my temper with you after dinner, Norah. And you lost your temper with me. Very harsh things were said on both sides.'

'Yes . . .'

'Whatever you think now – however harshly you may misjudge me – never fall into the error of supposing I wasn't fond of you. You have a very charming side to your nature, and I saw only that to begin with. Indeed, my – my fondness could have grown into something more. Of course, it's all finished now.'

'I'm sorry it ever began.'

'The other side – the other side *is* like Marion. Did I tell you once, d'you remember I told you – like a peach; you couldn't avoid the stone. It's exactly the same with you – I don't wonder Robert Jenkin cried off.'

Her hand was gripping Norah's arm.

'I'll go to bed,' said Norah. 'Good night.'

'My fondness could have grown into something more. And my affection is *worth having*, if only you knew. Together we could have . . . stormed many citadels. But you have to throw it all away for the prattling complaints of a sick young man who half the time mistakes you for his sister. What misjudgment! The peach will never prosper in *his* company. Nor in the company of the twice married Mr Christopher Carew, if I may say so.'

Norah tried to free her arm but the grip tightened. Short of making another scene, for the Repples were now in the hall, she could not break away.

'Mr Christopher Carew would find the stone in the peach a lot quicker than my unfortunate nephew. For he has had no sister to upset him. His – his judgment is better.'

'I'm leaving in the morning,' Norah said. 'Good night.'

'I don't wonder Robert Jenkin cried off. You're hard – you see. No doubt he discovered that. But I was very fond of you. You have a very charming side to your nature, and that at first is what everyone sees.'

They were at the foot of the stairs.

'I'll tell Timson to have the car ready for you at nine. I'm very disappointed in you. I am indeed. Together, you know, we could have stormed many a citadel. But it's this fundamental lack of judgment – lack of balance – that's so deplorable. Instability. One perceives the hysteria behind it all. Robert Jenkin – he saw it too, he just bowed out in time. So would the others if they but knew. Oh, yes, they would, I know they would . . . I'll tell Timson to have the car ready. Flood or no flood, you can leave at nine.'

Norah said nothing.

'I shall not see you again; I shall not be up by then; I shall have a morning of rest, for this has upset me very much. So this is goodbye. Just one word of warning, if I may offer it to you, if an old friend may offer it to you, who now sees the defects in your nature all too clearly. Take my advice and when you leave this house forget all about us – including Simon. It will be for your own good, I assure you.'

CHAPTER FIFTEEN

I

WELL, THAT was it. She sat heavily on the edge of the bed and let out a deep breath. She was still shaky. An ugly evening! It left a taste in the mouth like some acid, corrupting the mind and the tongue.

Guile, that was what she needed and had always lacked. A little guile, a few lies, would have saved it all. Searching for the pills hadn't helped Simon – anyway he seemed to be getting on well enough without them – then by refusing to back down when discovered she'd precipitated all the rest of the horrible scene. So *simple* to lie, that was the maddening thing; the study was where she typed; she could have been looking for more carbon paper, anything. But no. Blunt little Snow White had to blurt out the truth.

Couldn't be helped now. But Christopher's arrival with the hikers had averted the worst crisis . . . In spite of what she might feel for Simon, Christopher was her lifeline to stability and the outside world.

The moon was bright now, though clouds still hung about the sky like discarded scenery. She rubbed her forearm where three little pink crescents still showed the imprint of Althea's nails. They didn't go.

She remained perched on the edge of the bed for about twenty minutes, turning over the pages of a novel, trying to empty her mind of the events of the day. The effort was not a success. The marks Althea had left on her arm were duplicated in her mind. Soft lips moving in a gentle whisper, trying to sting, to stain. The brain behind them seeking any crevice, any chink. Odd that one could come to detest so much what one had once admired. At close quarters in the shadowy light of the hall the face had looked coarse, the make-up smeared and sticky, the hair as powerful as Medusa's.

Well, there was no sleep this way. She threw the book down, walked about the room a few times, then picked up the lamp and went into her sitting-room.

The heap of stripped wallpaper still lay beside the repaired wall. She stood lightly on the carpet where the rocking-horse used to stand and felt the loose floorboard move under her weight. All this afternoon she had been on the other side of the wall, helping Simon – she hoped – but also obeying her own secret impulses. There was no question but that, under the rational distaste and reluctance, she had *wanted* to go. She had wanted to prove something to Simon about herself. And she had wanted to defeat Marion.

She touched the rocking-horse and watched its shadow move on the wall behind. Although it held no terrors for her now she felt a sensation of distaste. Well, tomorrow, thank Heaven – whatever happened tomorrow – all this would be behind her. Not to be forgotten, for Simon would be with her, but seen in perspective: Althea brought down to her true proportions as a clever, scheming, misguided woman, this house like any other old house, full of creaks and whispers and memories that were food for the over-active imagination. A new life to begin.

But she wouldn't sleep tonight. Too fatigued to relax, more so even than yesterday. She went back to her pretty chintzy bedroom; and as she got there she heard a tapping . . .

For a distraught second she felt that all the relieving discoveries of the last two days were an illusion and that it was beginning over again. Then she knew that the tapping was on her door.

It was so gentle and secret that she hesitated before opening it. Through a two-inch slit she saw a man.

'Christopher?'

'May I come in?'

She stepped back, and he slid in, fingering the door lightly shut behind him. His mackintosh was over his arm.

In the same whisper she said: 'What is it? Why are you here again?'

'I had to go back, I thought some of my photographic stuff might get wet. But as soon as I stopped worrying about that I started worrying about you.'

'Oh, it's all right. I'm all right . . .'

'Why did you never tell me you were like Simon's sister?'

'It didn't seem important. Who told you?'

'Old Croome-Nichols let it out while I was talking to him. It *must* be important. And this nasty time you had with Althea. Why be so mysterious about having to explain something to me?'

'Sorry, but I . . . How did you get in?'

'Any fool could. Doole wastes his time locking doors with window catches like these.'

After a moment she said: 'You're kind to be worried, Christopher. But really I'm all right. It could have waited.'

He looked round the room with an ironical eye. 'May I sit down?'

She indicated a chair and herself sat on the edge of the bed. Perversely she half wished now he hadn't come.

'Will anyone hear us up here?' he asked.

'Not if we keep our voices low.'

'Mind if I smoke?'

She shook her head.

He offered her a cigarette but she refused. He didn't take out his pipe.

'Where's your car?' she asked.

'Where nobody will see it.'

'Did you bring Ann Dawson and the Repples purposely – I mean, because of me?'

'Of course. After you rang I couldn't make up my mind whether to take you at your word or barge in on some excuse this evening. It already seemed too long since I'd seen you. And knowing you a bit, I felt pretty certain that you were playing down any crisis that had come up. Then my three hikers arrived. They took some moving again, I can tell you . . . Norah, now what's been happening? I want to hear it all.'

'It's – a long story.'

'We've all night.'

'Well . . .'

'Oh, in due course I'll leave. Have no fear.'

She said quietly, '*I* have no fear.'

'OK, it was a figure of speech. But we've got an hour – or as long as you need. In the morning there'll be others around us and I'd be expected to play it by ear. Tell me everything now.'

When it came to the point she didn't know how to start. Nor did she even want to. It was another confrontation she would have preferred to avoid tonight. She didn't know how he would react at all; in this he was almost as much an unknown quantity as anyone else. But she forced herself to begin to speak. She began with the terrors of yesterday afternoon, her meeting with Simon and the long personal conversation that followed. He didn't say very much, but now and then his long face tightened at some expression she used or at some tone that crept into her voice. He finished one cigarette and lit another.

She came to today, her decision to sit for the portrait, what had come from it. In the middle of this he got up and walked a few paces about; but the creaking floorboards drove him to his chair.

'And all this happened before you rang?' He looked at her uneasily. 'What since then?'

So into battle with Althea Syme. But this was easier, for Simon was not part of it.

Christopher said: 'You didn't actually accuse her of mismanaging Simon's affairs?'

'No, I thought it better to leave it until we were on firmer ground. You see, I don't know how much Simon has consented to any of this.'

'My God, that woman . . . ! And you're sure Doole would have laid hands on you?'

'I think so. And if I'd later sued him for assault, can't you see the counter-charges? I wouldn't have stood a chance of getting any satisfaction.'

'Well . . .' He blew out a breath. 'The sooner you're out of this place the better. And the sooner you forget the Symes ever existed the healthier you'll be.'

This was the point of embarkation.

'Christopher . . . I can't go without Simon.'

'D'you mean he wants to leave with us?'

'Yes.'

He shrugged. 'Fine. It might be a good thing if he comes with us as far as Bristol or somewhere and stays there until the whole legal position is cleared up. If he's as completely recovered as he seems, then he'll be perfectly capable of managing his affairs on his own.'

It was the same sort of choice as there had been when facing Althea Syme. A discreet silence now would suffice. But this time was no excuse at all for compromise.

'I don't want him to be on his own.'

He looked at her, his face long and serious again. 'Can you explain that?'

'Explain it? I wish I could, my dear, I wish I could tell you in so many words just what I mean. I'm . . .' she hesitated, 'I'm . . .'

'Are you trying to tell me – no, you can't be.'

'I don't know what I'm trying to tell you except that I want – I hope to be with Simon for some time to come . . . to help him, to give him the support that – I think – only I can give him . . .'

There was silence. At last the question came. 'Are you trying to tell me that you're in love with him?'

'I – I think so.'

There was a longer silence. A third cigarette smouldered in the china ashtray.

'It's impossible!'

'No, Christopher. No, it's not.'

'But he's – ill, sick. Sick in the mind, surely.'

'Not any longer. You don't write off a man just because he once suffered from TB.'

'No, but this is different.'

'Only different because it's a different part of the body. Anyway – one doesn't always reason with one's feelings.'

'No, that's true. You haven't forgotten,' he said, 'that I'm in love with you?'

'I've never forgotten it for a moment.'

'So you'll see that you telling me this, it comes as quite a shock.'

'Yes, I know. I wish . . .'

'When – first of all, when did you begin to feel as you say you do?'

'I don't know. Quite early. But it was mixed up with fear and anxiety and . . .'

'But these last two days you've become sure.'

'. . . Yes.'

'I'm sorry I ever left you alone here so long! I had misgivings at the time. But not these misgivings.'

'I had to stay. For every reason. This amongst them.'

'And how does he feel?'

'I think he cares.'

'For you or for Marion?'

'I think I've taken her place.'

'In other words he's still in love with his sister and you provide the substitute.'

'Not quite. But his sister was so much the centre of his life that he never looked at another woman. Now he has – he does. But not as a substitute.'

'Even though you are so much like her?'

'In spite of it. Over the last few years he has made a gradual recovery, so that he has come to accept the loss of Marion and all that goes with it. His complete recovery is in his discovery that he can live – and love – again.'

He got up and sat on a chair nearer to her. 'How do you know this is true?'

'I feel it.'

'How do I know this isn't something born of this strange lunatic house, so that you're hoodwinking your-self into a state of mind where – where Marion comes alive in you and you – you almost cease to be the person you were?'

'That's fanciful. But – yes, I've felt it myself. But that's all past, Christopher. The world goes on. Simon is only thirty-four, and it's his one chance to start again.'

In saying this, in trying to explain to him how she felt she was for the first time formulating explanations to herself. She groped for words and found them and they helped her to understand.

He took her hand. 'Dear love, you've got to think of this very carefully. If possible you've got to try and detach yourself from your feelings and take a good cold look at them.'

'I've tried.'

'I'm sure you have. But I believe there's the risk of your doing a Florence Nightingale on yourself. That's the risk. You may truly believe you're in love with him but really be in love with the idea of helping him – helping him to recover, to fulfil himself, to become a whole man for the first time in his life. I don't say that's a bad thing at all. He seems to me a man infinitely worth helping – and someone whose paintings might eventually come to count for something. But you've got to look at your wish to help him and recognize it for what it is. It may not be what you think it is *at all*. It may be half mother-love, half a devotion to the idea of service.'

'I don't think you're right, Christopher, but of course I can't prove you're wrong. I can only try to explain to you why I feel this about him. It began almost as soon as we met but for a time I couldn't – or wouldn't – recognize it for what it was. You don't argue with a thing like that. You don't even try to rationalize it. If you did, then the explanation might be – might seem to imply what you suggest. But it isn't that really. I know it isn't that!'

'And what do you intend to do?'

She shook her head. 'I've no idea. None yet. It will depend altogether on what happens when we get away from here.'

'Shall you marry him?'

'Heaven knows. Don't ask me.'

'But if *he* does?'

'Then, yes, I suppose so. But don't press this too far. I'm – I'm trying to play fair with you, as well as with him. That's why I felt I had to tell you this when you came back – try to explain. You may feel now that this more or less lets you out and that you'd rather I tried to get along without you . . .'

'No, my dear, even I have my altruism . . .'

'Don't be offended, please.'

'I'm offended that you should think my interest in you so narrow . . .'

'Well, I had to say that, for it's true. But if you want to continue to help me, then you must be willing to help *us*.'

He was silent for a long minute. 'So be it.'

She frowned. 'I said – I began to say – that I'd rather you didn't press too hard at the moment. *Nothing* has been planned. It's all still more a matter of feeling than words. Once we're away from here things may change – bring us close together or thrust us farther apart. All I feel at the moment is that he loves me, and – and that I am committed to him. Beyond that everything is vague, unformulated. I'd really rather not have tried to explain. But I just couldn't – as it were – sail under false colours.'

The house was quiet. He released her hand, which had been entirely quiescent under his.

'I wish I'd kidnapped you on Saturday.'

'I was already involved then.'

'It's a bitter pill . . . Not that I'm yet wholly willing to swallow it. But I'll play it as you want.'

'Thank you.'

'As I said, perhaps he *is* rather worth salvaging. Certainly more so than I am.'

'You don't need – salvaging, as you call it. You're very self-reliant – and self-sufficient.'

'Don't be too sure. But I'll not base my appeal on that. Nor must you base your judgment on it. I think you've got to go very carefully from here on, Norah. There's a lot more to be considered – all sorts of questions I want to ask.'

'Don't ask them.'

'I won't. Not yet. But they'll have to be asked sometime. Meanwhile . . .'

She nodded. 'It's late.'

'Yes, I'll go.'

'Can you get out safely?'

'If you can be left safely.'

'Why ever not? What can happen?'

'I'm thinking of your physical safety now, the other having already gone by the board.'

She smiled. 'There are three hikers sleeping here and only a few hours till morning. I don't think Althea's that dangerous.'

'Well, there's a lot at stake for her. I trust her as far as I would a rattlesnake.'

'She'd never go beyond certain limits. She wouldn't endanger her own position.'

'She already has.'

Norah got up. 'Yes, I suppose so. But I think one mustn't *over*-rate her. D'you know, during this horrible quarrel I knew that she really *had* been fond of me, and this made her all the more angry and bitter and in a way confused.'

'And perhaps more desperate.' He got up too. 'So I'll be back early – by ten at the latest. Avoid her altogether till then.'

'I will. Good night, Christopher. And – I'm truly very sorry.'

'Don't be sorry. I'm still hoping.'

He kissed her.

'Especially,' he said, 'don't be sorry for this.'

She let him out, and after a moment turned to lower the wick of the lamp, which had been sending up a watch-spring of smoke. If she had felt un-sleepy before, this final meeting of the night had swept away the last vestiges of repose. She no longer had a brain but an overwound machine that would be nerve-powered throughout the night.

Yet she must rest, she must put out the light and lie quietly in bed, content with decisions taken, content that any hazards that had to be faced were tangible ones. The hauntings, the fear, the fear of Marion, of the unknown, were all past. Althea's enmity, though horrible, was easier to bear. She unzipped her frock, stepped out of it and hung it up. Then she began to take off her stockings. As she did so there was a tapping at her door.

Her dressing-gown was in the bathroom. She

sheltered behind the wardrobe door and called: 'Who is it?'

The door opened. It was Christopher.

'What d'you want?' she asked.

His grey eyes glanced briefly over what he could see of her. 'Your advice, chiefly. This big door out here . . .'

'Which one?'

'This great thing at the head of the stairs. It's locked and I think bolted.'

II

PRESENTLY, DRESSED again, she joined him. What he said was the truth.

'It's never even been closed since I came,' she said. 'It's always looped back on the chain. You didn't touch it when you came up?'

'Hardly. Why should I?'

'D'you think someone saw you coming up?'

'No.'

'There's no key. I've never seen a key. But there were bolts . . .'

'Which appear to have been shot.' He pulled at the big metal ring which lifted the latch. 'You could never break this down – at least not without making enough noise to wake the dead. It's oak – in fact it looks like a fair copy of the front door.'

'Yes . . . The other one – the one in the other house that matches this – has a key. Because that's the door that leads to Simon's studio. But he always keeps that locked. Even if we pulled part of the wall down you'd only be in the other attics.'

He rubbed his hair. 'I *don't* like it. I don't like to think someone saw me coming up here. But the alternative is no more likeable.'

'That they were locking me in?'

'Yes. I think that's it. I suppose Mrs Syme instructed Doole to do it, to keep you where you belong. But I can't understand why he didn't bolt the door before I came up – the house was dead when I ventured in.'

'She may have intended it as a gesture. She wants to make me out as untrustworthy, so she bolts me in until tomorrow morning when Doole will come up and say: "The car's waiting".'

Christopher walked back into the bedroom and drew back the curtains at the window. The moon was sinking, and a flicker of lightning moved among the bold, anthracite-coloured clouds.

'Nobody could get out of here without a fractured skull. It would be almost impossible even to get on the roof. So it looks as if you're lumbered with me for the rest of tonight.'

She said, still pursuing her own thoughts: 'It's – more complicated than ever now. You see, she may be reckoning that when I try to go down in the morning and find the door bolted I shall kick up such a fuss – hammering on the door etc. – that your three hikers will be excellent witnesses to my anti-social behaviour. If Doole is prepared to swear that I have been carrying on with Simon and even making approaches to *him*, my credibility as a witness to Simon's complaints won't be very high.'

'Still less now.'

'Yes,' she said, eyeing him, 'still less now.'

He threw his head back. 'Well, I'm sorry for that – if that's the idea. Otherwise I'm glad I'm here. In the meantime, can I sleep in your sitting-room? I won't make other suggestions – much as I should like to – because this clearly isn't the time or place.'

'Oh, Christopher. No.' She smiled at him. 'I feel you've been so kind, that it's not much fun to find yourself keeping company with a girl who has – suddenly – pledged herself elsewhere . . .'

He smiled back. 'Who knows what my fun will be yet?'

He kissed her again. He made it a long kiss, and she did not for some moments break away.

'Well, that's it,' he said. 'Good night again. And now for the rocking-horse.'

CHAPTER SIXTEEN

I

FOR AN apparently passive boy Gregory Syme had a very active brain. And for a short-sighted boy he saw a great deal.

He had few interests in life, but those few were diamond sharp, and one person he thought he understood better than she understood herself. His attitude towards his mother was a mixture of dependence, of affection, and of patronage. He relied upon her for so much – as he had always done since a child: she saw to his clothes, his food, his likes and dislikes, his health, his wealth and his well-being. He could hardly imagine life without her, and while he often found her love oppressive, especially as he grew into mid-adolescence, he mutely returned the love. Yet he had altogether too sharp an eye not to be aware of her faults, and in some ways he thought her a silly woman. He knew she was gifted both as a writer and as a speaker – far more gifted than he could ever be – but in almost every other respect he knew himself to be cleverer than she was. Like many young people, he tended to despise older people, as if their longer time on earth made them automatically less gifted, or as if youth were not a passing phase but a prize awarded for special virtue. Unsullied by knowledge but armed with certainties, he observed his mother closely and saw all her faults.

One certainty he carried close to his heart was that she had been abysmally silly about Morb House and about Simon. Of course it had all begun before he was old enough to understand; but since he became old enough he had listened and watched, and particularly attended to what his mother did and said, and he had arrived at something like a full understanding.

As a very small boy Gregory remembered visiting his Uncle Hubert and his Aunt Arabella at Morb House, and there meeting his cousins Simon and Marion. But they were so much older than he – fifteen years and more – that they had appeared totally grown up and aloof from him in every way; and it was not until Marion was drowned and Simon had had his breakdown that he had come more frequently with his mother and then had finally moved here so that his mother could look after her sick nephew.

Gregory remembered many things about those early years but only later was he able to piece them together. He remembered Simon's strangeness, his long bouts of depression, during which he was not himself allowed near his cousin. He remembered the frightful occasion when Simon had been found with a rope around his neck and the long discussion with doctors, from which he, Gregory, was carefully excluded. He did not know until much later of the power of attorney that Simon had willingly granted to his aunt before going to a mental home for treatment; nor of the renewal of this grant each year that followed. Still less in those early days did he appreciate the uses to which his mother occasionally put her privileges. Quite by chance, barely a year ago, he had tumbled to the combination of the little safe where many secrets lay hidden (his mother had chosen for the combination the day, month and year of his birth) so that the next time he was alone he was able to open it and look through all the ledgers and the correspondence.

He was startled by what he found. The creation of two new trusts, of which he was the benefactor, the shifting of monies and properties from trusts beneficial to Simon. He didn't understand the legal language but he saw the purpose.

He quite clearly remembered his life before he came here and he remembered the poverty of it. After his father – a Territorial who never saw active service – had driven home drunk from a dance and killed himself it had been worse; though even before that it was a sort of pretence life in which they shammed well-to-do and all the time existed under the shadow of the next writ. Though then so young, he remembered the terrible rows his father and mother had had, because he would hear them through the wall; and after them his mother would often come into his room and enlist his sympathy against the ill-behaviour and neglect she was suffering. Usually there was another woman mentioned, and although he didn't understand at that stage quite what was meant, he came to detest his father for making his mother so unhappy.

But when Captain Syme died, deep in debt, they had

had to leave their house and move into two rooms where even the pretence could be carried on no longer. His mother had been trying her hand at freelance journalism for some time, but paper shortages made it impossible as a livelihood, and she had had to depend on subsidies from relatives to keep going.

So the invitation to live at Morb House had changed their lives, and in a few years he had seen his mother blossom and expand, physically as well as mentally, and become a distinguished woman writer and speaker. Money and position had opened many doors, and they had lived happily here until the summer just past. Then he had become aware that his mother was worrying over something, and that something was Simon.

Gregory did not understand everything about Simon, but he had heard the word schizophrenia mentioned and he knew that schizophrenics by definition never got better. Gregory had read all about dementia praecox, and knew that people who suffered from it simply went from bad to worse until they eventually, after many years, fell into a stupor and died. Therefore Simon was never likely to return to Morb House or indeed to be free in the world again. Everyone believed that. It was sad, but as it turned out this made things very comfortable for them.

So, although his mother did not confide her worries to him, Gregory gradually began to suspect the truth, and one day, making his monthly inspection of the safe, he found a letter from the senior physician of the Conran Nursing Home saying that their new treatment had effected a complete cure and that Simon Syme was free to leave at any time he wished. In fact, the physician went on, as Mr Syme had been a voluntary patient throughout, this would have been true at any time; but he could assure Mrs Syme that Mr Syme was now perfectly able to face the world and, what was more, wished to do so.

This clearly presented a dilemma for his mother, since all her present positions depended on her remaining in control of Simon's affairs; but it was not until he had made another very careful examination of the papers in the safe that Gregory began to appreciate the risks his mother had been taking.

It was so *stupid*, Gregory thought. So like a woman to get confused over money and legal affairs. True, if Simon returned and showed no interest in their remaining, they would necessarily leave and be in poor circumstances again. But there was nothing to prove he should wish them to leave if they played their cards correctly. Much better to have done that than take the greater risk of misusing her position.

And all for *him*, Gregory; that was the most pathetic and lovable and stupid thing of all. Of course he had also read the copy of Simon's will, made shortly after his parents died, leaving everything to his sister and if she should predecease him without issue, then equally to the Slade School, the Tate Gallery and two French academies. So that his mother had seen the danger to her welfare as more likely to arise from Simon's death than from his recovery. And she had been trying to make provision against *that*, in order when the time came that he, Gregory, should have a substantial fortune of his own.

And Simon's recovery had caught her unawares, off guard, facing, as it were, the wrong way.

It was all very infuriating, and the measures his mother had taken to defend herself had been typically feminine and ill-considered. Now they *were* in a mess, up to their eyes, and he could see no way out. This girl his mother had brought here, for reasons he had only half appreciated, was going to be the worst complication of all. This evening, wandering out of the drawing-room and hearing voices from the study, he had drifted silently along and had heard pretty well the whole of Norah's quarrel with his mother. With a vindictive woman against them they'd hardly stand a chance. If his mother had tried she could hardly have managed it worse.

She had been drinking today, too, which was rare. He'd known it sometimes when he was a little boy, but her affluence had changed all that. Comfort, authority, position: they had been better for her than any bottle-bred stimulus.

Almost on top of her quarrel with the Faulkner woman the hikers had arrived, and Gregory had observed the tension and agitation under his mother's superficial calm. It was well done but it hadn't deceived him. So when they all finally drifted off to bed and the house settled down for the night he went along to his mother's bedroom to make sure she was all right. He found her in tears.

This was a new experience. Even in the bad days when she had come to his room after a scene with his father he had never known her cry. She was always so *strong*, so self-reliant, so *calm*. Even when she had been at the brandy. Even when she insisted on being stupid, when she did things that were not to his liking, even when she acted 'for the best' when his superior reasoning told him she was wrong, she had always been strong, self-reliant, calm. Intellectually he might rather despise her but emotionally he had always relied on her. Now, although he knew and understood her concern, why she cried, the sight of it upset him more than he could say. It aroused a new sensation within him – one he had not felt before for her or for anyone else – the feeling of pity. For a few moments he hated her for infecting his spirit with it.

Of course she blew her nose and lied to him about some trifling disagreements she had had with Miss Faulkner and told him to go to bed and not to worry; but he stayed a while, hands in pockets, looking at her through his crooked glasses, still wanting to make some affectionate gesture but inhibited by his age. Eventually, just as he was about to leave, she said:

'If there's any trouble, dearest, it is mine, not yours. And if I have made mistakes in my life with you it has been from too much love, not too little. Whatever happens in these next few weeks, there's one thing I know I shall be able to count on, and that is your loyalty and your trust.'

Emotional speeches always angered him, and his normal tendency was to shy away from them like a nervous horse from a snake; but this one, combined with the tear-streaked face that his mother turned towards him, moved him again, more detestably than ever, and he felt the tears welling up in his own eyes.

He muttered something, had an impulse to kiss her, resisted it, and then forced himself to do so – hating the stink of the brandy, and not even liking the feel of her tears on his lips; but glad now that he had overcome his restraint. His glasses swung by one ear, and he pulled them impatiently over his nose, muttered a grumpy good night, and with her murmured blessing in his ear went out of the room and back towards his own. As he was about to go he heard a footstep.

Choked with angry emotion, he stood quite still in the dark and saw a tall man moving stealthily along the landing. Gregory was short-sighted but he had come to recognize people by their shape and he instantly knew that this man was the man who had brought the three hikers here and was then supposed to have gone home.

The boy moved a step or two at a time and by the tiny light of the turned-down landing lamp saw Carew reach the foot of the second flight and go up. There was only one place that flight led to and that was the bedroom of Norah Faulkner.

After a moment Gregory advanced until he could look up the stairs. They were empty and dark. Step by careful step, avoiding the centre of the treads, he went up too until he was three steps from the top. There was a light under Norah Faulkner's door and the low murmur of voices.

So there was to be a repeat of this afternoon, was

there? – but with Carew this time and in far guiltier circumstances. This afternoon he had crept up the other stairs and listened at the door for some minutes before curiosity as to what Simon and the girl were doing inside induced him to push it open. But that had had at least the pretence of painting as an excuse. No such excuse here – and with another man. In the quarrel this evening his mother had done her best to cast doubts on the Faulkner woman's reputation – anything, he thought, to make her accusations less believable. But really it was one person's word against another. Not so here. Here was proof that the girl was a mischief maker and a cheap tart. If he could surprise them – maybe even find them in bed together ... It would altogether destroy her credibility.

But had he the courage to do it himself? Different this afternoon when he had a simple reason for going in. Best fetch his mother, and she could perhaps arouse Doole. He turned to go down, and there stopped. Supposing it wasn't all it seemed. These were deep waters and he might be assuming all the wrong things. Supposing Mr Carew had just gone up there for a minute to see Miss Faulkner. Supposing he too was in the plot to expose and disgrace his mother. Supposing he, Gregory, went down and roused the house, or some part of it, and they all went up to see what was to be seen, and in the meantime Carew had come down again and left. That would make him a fool and they would lose any advantage of the discovery.

Gregory hesitated and peered at the light again. Someone, he thought, moved in the room, because there

241

was some change in the light under the door. He hesitated, and then he mounted the remaining stairs and very cautiously unlatched the chain that held the big oak door in place. He was afraid the hinges would groan, but the door moved with scarcely a sound, and presently it was latched. He stretched up and bolted it top and bottom.

II

HIS FIRST intention was to go straight to his mother and tell her. When he left her he had been raging at his own impotence to help. Now, immediately, the opportunity had arisen. He was elated with what he had done but not absolutely sure of himself. He was playing for high stakes in an adult world where just possibly his reasoning might be wrong, his judgment at fault. He *thought* his mother would be pleased, but he wasn't sure how she could or would act on it. If she went up immediately she might not be able to do much except create a further row with even more disastrous results. Yet you could hardly wake the three hikers and ask them to be present as witnesses. Anyway, there was no *hurry*. If Carew wanted to come down and couldn't and raised the house, that couldn't be a bad thing. It would surely play into their hands. If he didn't find out until the early morning he would still be unable to get out. Maybe it would be better to leave it until the morning. Maybe it would be safer to have had nothing to do with it at all. The door had somehow got itself shut and bolted. What a pity. How unfortunate. Leave it alone and see what happened.

As soon as he thought this Gregory knew it was right. It left things to happen without his having to take any more on himself. If the locked door turned out well he would take the credit for it; if not he could disown it altogether.

He was not at all sure that his mother would approve of what he was going to do next, but he had been thinking of it for four hours, ever since they had found the Faulkner girl searching the study. The excuse that she was looking for Simon's pills was nonsense. She was searching through the papers there trying to find anything that would strengthen her case against them.

And there *were* things that would strengthen her case, if she came on them, for everything was not in the safe. A couple of months ago Gregory had found a sheet of paper in the desk covered with Simon Syme's name. Simon Syme, Simon Syme, Simon Syme. All over the page. It wasn't difficult to guess the purpose of the exercise. Then there were lawyers' letters, income tax returns, rent books, receipts and accounts, lists of property, bills of sale. He couldn't make all that much of them but the Faulkner woman probably could. Certainly Christopher Carew would.

It was another facet of his mother's stupidity, to keep so much. Of course some of these letters would be duplicated elsewhere, but not all. And not all available for anyone to pick up and see.

So after he had bolted the door upstairs he did not disturb his mother again but went along the corridor to his own bedroom where a small reading lamp burned. He sat on the bed for a few minutes swinging his feet and not sure whether to undress first or after. He decided to undress after.

He put matches in his pocket and slipped out again, back along the long corridor to the head of the stairs to where the eye of the night lamp glowed. Down to the hall, stumbling once. The big drawing-room had unfamiliar smells: coffee and cheap cigarettes; the remnants of a fire still glowed behind the mesh of the fireguard. The lid of his piano had been closed to accommodate a tray and some cups. He opened it again and propped it up, stared at the keyboard, tempted. Then on to his mother's study.

There were two lamps in the room, one with a mantel, and an old-fashioned one with a double wick and a container of pink glass so that you could see when it needed refilling. He chose this one; struck a match, took off the glass and lit both wicks, turned them down. The room edged into view. Somebody had moved a chair from its usual place and it was luck that he hadn't fallen over it.

He looked around, holding up his glasses as they wobbled. The enormity of what he was proposing to do struck him, and he almost funked it. It was one thing to take a private look at his mother's papers; it was another to destroy them. And yet . . . if he did not she certainly would not, and any day she might be called to account. Even tomorrow. Within a week there might be people in this room demanding to go through everything she had.

He knelt down by the safe. The fifteenth of April, 1936. You turned the knob four times to the right, stopping the fourth time it reached 15, then three times to the left, stopping the third time at 4, then twice again to the right, stopping at 36. *Click*, the handle turned and the door came open.

He carried the bundles of papers to the table in the centre of the room, moved the lamp nearer and turned it up. A vase of frayed gold chrysanthemums were dropping petals on the bank sheets as he began to go through them.

He was mad at his lack of practical experience in the business world. Some things certainly would be easy to replace, and probably bank sheets were in that category. But other things – particularly her own account books – would not. And some letters. And cheque stubs? And these long thin sheets of paper recording the transfer of shares? And rent books with covering letters from men employed to collect money from tenants.

To do the job properly someone should break into the offices of solicitors in Aberystwyth and Barmouth and Cardiff. At best this was a delaying action. Yet the very fact that his mother had employed such a variety of solicitors seemed to him a reason for hope. One firm might be reluctant to release information to another. It would all take time.

Presently he had done with the safe and he put back the things which were obviously harmless; then he turned his attention to the desk. Here there seemed even more value in what he was doing, for much of this was handwritten stuff which was not likely to have been copied. Mrs Syme did not keep a diary but she committed too many of her thoughts to paper. No wonder the Faulkner woman was searching the room. Had she taken anything away?

As he increased the pile he wondered whether he could in any way disguise what he was doing. If he opened the window and broke the catch and left a gaping safe it might look as if some marauding tramp was responsible. But the papers had to be burned – he could not safely hide them or bury them somewhere out of doors. There was a convenient grate in this room – seldom used because of the two radiators – it would do well enough.

He looked at the pile. Some of it, while having a bearing on the estate generally, probably had no relevance at all to his mother's contrivances, but it was better to err on the side of safety. It was a fine lot, and some of it on stiff paper might be difficult to burn, so he had better start right away.

And then he hesitated again, screwing up his courage, nerving himself for this act of destruction. 'If there's any trouble, dearest, it is mine, not yours. Whatever happens in these next few weeks, I know I shall be able to count on your loyalty and trust . . .'

He carried the first bundle to the fireplace, stuffed it in, struck a match and applied it to a couple of corners. He was right about the stiff papers; it was going to be slow. Trying not to think now, not to let doubts enter in, he concentrated on the practical mechanics of the task. It was like starting a bonfire out of doors; there was a technique: you fed the easily inflammable in and mixed it with the slow stuff.

The fire began to burn. A grey cloud of smoke eddied into the room, and he coughed. The chimney was cold and would take time to draw. More smoke than fire. Then he looked in the wastepaper basket and saw a bunch of carbon copies of his mother's speeches which she had been weeding out earlier in the day. The paper was flimsy and there were about fifty sheets. He crumpled these and fed them in.

More dense smoke for about fifty seconds, then a sudden satisfying yellow blaze. The whole small fireplace was alight.

He looked at his watch. One o'clock. More than ever scared and anxious to be done, he carried the rest of the papers and pushed them through the bars. The fire roared and blazed, and he was on tenterhooks when some of the paper fell out blazing into the hearth. There was no fender and he grabbed the nearest book and used it as a brush to sweep the sparks and the bits of burning paper off the carpet.

He squatted on his heels at a safe distance, the thick lenses protecting his eyes from the heat. The fire was making more noise than he had ever known, and he was worried that someone in the house might hear it and come down. The last thing he wanted was to be caught, but he couldn't leave for another few minutes until the paper burned down.

At present it wasn't burning down. Or rather, the flames were a little less but the noise was greater. It was a roar. It was making a noise like a vacuum cleaner only deeper. A couple of sheets of paper fell out, burning and twisting, and he could see the ink discolouring as he leaned forward to push them to safety. As he did so a shower of burning soot fell out and two or three sparks fell on his hand.

He leaped back, sucking his hand and stamping out the bits of soot with his foot. The damned chimney had caught fire.

Was it dangerous? He knew that in towns the fire engines were always called out when a chimney caught fire. This was roaring now like an angry furnace. Bits of burning soot kept spattering down into the grate and every now and then a larger lump came down and burst, sending showers on to the carpet.

Sweating with heat and with alarm, he stamped here and there among the smoke, putting out the bits of fire as they fell; but he was only wearing carpet slippers and one or two sparks caught and burned, and he singed his fingers trying to knock them off.

Cursing and panting, he worked to prevent any serious damage, but as the worst of the fire subsided in the grate the weight of burning soot increased. It was the accumulation of years. Three great masses came down at once, and the largest of the three struck the top bar of the firegrate and burst like a bomb. In a few seconds there were three separate fires on the carpet and the room was thick with smoke.

He stamped one out and the fire caught on his slipper. He kicked it off and then was powerless. Water. Something to quench it. He looked round. The vase of chrysanthemums was on the table beside the lamp. He jumped across, pulled out the flowers and snatched up the vase. As he pulled it off the table the bottom of the vase hit the lamp and toppled it on to the floor, where both the lamp glass and the glass container broke. For a moment all was darkness – then a new light came, yellow like the fire but paler, as the paraffin ran and spread across the carpet.

III

SOMEWHERE IN the smoky darkness Gregory lost his glasses. One moment they were precariously on his nose, one side piece secure, the other dangling. Then he darted at the flames and they fell and hung momentarily from his ear before vanishing in the yellow-lit smoke. He groped for them, panting noisily. Without them only colours were clear; outlines merged and he lived in a world of opaque brilliance.

Panic was very close now, real screaming panic, but he fought it down, not quite believing it could be as bad as it looked, knowing that his cool, detached mind could still deal with this minor emergency but not certain how.

With his one slipper-shod foot he stamped on the burning paraffin, but it always seemed to escape like some evil and miraculous snake which avoided the blow before it was struck. The room was so filled with smoke that he coughed and retched and tears filled his eyes.

He tried again, going on hands and knees, feeling

with ten outstretched fingers to find the frame that meant eyesight to him; but suddenly in the middle of it, his hand caught fire with pain. He stood up, holding his fingers in his mouth trying to stop the hurt. Then he bolted. It was out of his control now, but others would soon make short work of it. Doole with the fire extinguisher on the wall of the kitchen, Timson with a hose brought in from outside. It was a nasty mess but not difficult to deal with. In an old inflammable house like this there had to be ample fire precautions, and there were. (He could even pretend that he had *discovered* the fire and it was nothing to do with him. It might well be the perfect explanation.)

He ran from the room, found darkness outside, stopped short and groped down the passage, fingers on wall. The large drawing-room was dark and he stumbled across it, brushing his leg on a chair. The next passage and the dimly-lit hall. He could see so little that light was as much a hindrance as a help, increasing the deceptive colours. He weaved his way across, grasped a banister but almost missed the stairs because it was the right-hand banister and not the left as he had thought.

Up the stairs now. No problem here. The wide plateau landing at the top with his mother's room to the left near the bathrooms. Better to wake her because she would immediately and competently take charge. Doole was too far away, at least for *him* to find without his glasses. Besides, there was a bell in his mother's room which went direct to the butler's room.

Make up a story before you get there. Couldn't sleep, decided to go down for a book, smelt smoke, went in and found ... He hurried across the landing towards his mother's room, knowing exactly where the door was, then hesitated as to his sense of direction. But of course. He took another couple of steps, and walked into space.

A worm twisted in his stomach; he shouted and put out his hands. In a second's anticipation he realized where he had made his mistake; then the impact cut across his mind.

CHAPTER SEVENTEEN

I

ALTHEA SYME was dreaming. These last few days her rest had been disturbed by unpleasant fantasies halfway between waking and sleeping. She dreamed that Marion had returned and was turning her out of the house. Marion had always disliked her, and snubbed her when as a young widow she had come to stay here with Hubert and Arabella. Marion had seen through her flattery and her sycophancy and had had no room for her at all.

In the dream they were *all* young again. Marion, her hair flowing, and Gregory a little boy of eight, slim then, and his voice clear and bell-like. Marion was demanding to be told of all the transfers of properties which had been made in Simon's absence. 'But,' Althea said, 'it's all perfectly *legal*. Twice a year I've been up to see Simon in Norwich and got his signatures for the transfers.' 'Because he didn't care!' Marion said. 'He didn't care what happened in those days because he thought I was dead. But not later. In this last eighteen months since he began to recover, he's signed nothing since then. They're *forgeries*!' 'Not forgeries,' Althea pleaded. 'It was only implementing what had been arranged earlier. He *agreed* to it all earlier. He didn't want the property. He didn't want anything. He was happy to pass it on to Gregory.' But Marion said: 'You've been here long enough, battening on Simon and cheating him. Go back to your two-room flat and your unsuccessful journalism. Take your horrid little boy with you.' And *she* had replied: 'Why should I be turned out? And why should my boy go? He's a Syme on both sides: he's more entitled to this house than anyone else! Besides, you're *dead*! Didn't you realize it? You're dead and can't interfere any more!' Then another girl came into the room and it was Norah, and she was wearing only a flimsy nightdress that showed all her slim soft body through it, and she came across and leaned against Althea and whispered: 'Marion's dead but *I'm* here. I'll help you to lock Simon away. Listen to him knocking! Listen. I've locked him in! Listen to him knocking!'

Althea Syme raised her head from the pillow. A confused light was in the room. Someone was in the room holding a lamp, which wavered up and down.

'What is it?' she cried. 'Who is it?'

The elder Repple boy said: 'Sorry to wake you but I think there's a fire somewhere. The place is full of smoke!'

II

ABOUT TEN minutes later Norah woke to find Christopher standing by her bed with a lighted candle.

'The house,' he said, 'is burning under us. Get dressed

as quickly as you can while I try to break this door down.'

He was gone. Norah raised her head and looked about. There was no sign of fire but there was noise downstairs. Then she caught the whiff of smoke. He began hammering at the door with the poker he had snatched from the hearth.

She got up and dressed quickly, uncertain whether it was really serious and not sure that she was yet ready to face discovery with him. As she was fastening her stockings he came back. He was dressed except for a collar and tie. He showed the bent poker.

'That's the worst of these pieces of tin.'

'Is it bad? D'you think . . .?'

'Bad enough. If you doubt it, look out of the bath-room window.'

She was aware now, suddenly, now that she was dressed, that she was too warm. It was a very unpleasant discovery.

He picked up a chair and went out. As she lit the lamp she heard him smashing the chair to bits against the door. She followed him.

'Someone must hear that,' she said.

'I think, my dear, that we've been overlooked. Or you have. From the sound of it there was a bit of panic.'

She went into the bathroom and peered out through the tiny window.

From here you could only see the sloping roof, but all round from under the eaves, curling round the guttering, came billows of grey smoke. And farther away the moorland and nearby hills were as if fitfully sunlit. Above the uneven mass of hills in the direction of Plynlimon it was possible to see a faint, cool star. She withdrew her head, fear clutching at the pit of her stomach.

'Someone,' Christopher said beside her, 'may yet remember you. Meanwhile I can try the door again while you tie some sheets together.'

'They'll not nearly reach.'

At the rear of the house there was little sign of the fire except for some drifting smoke, but it was farther down this side because of the slope of the ground. And Mrs Syme's rockery lay immediately beneath.

She went back to watch him destroy another chair. A few dents were made in the door but otherwise there was no sign at all of breaking down the stout old wood. His face was streaming with sweat and he began to cough.

'Try this way,' she said, and led him into the sitting-room, where together they attacked the wall that Simon had rebuilt.

It came away easily and in a short time they were through to the attic. Here the smoke was thicker. They pushed through into Simon's studio, while Marion's doll sat and watched them with mindless eyes, past the easel and the paintings and the couch and the pier-glass, to the big oak door at the head of the other stairs. It was locked. Christopher rattled it and flung his weight against it, but it was like trying to force a stone wall.

'Anyway it's worse this side,' he said. 'I don't know where it started but the smoke's thicker here.'

They ran back to Norah's rooms. From the bathroom

the reflected light on the hills told its own tale, but because the long roof hid so much of the ground there was no one to be seen. She screamed shrilly twice into the open air and caught her breath and coughed.

'Don't do that,' he said. 'Soak your handkerchief in water and tie it round your face.'

'There must be *someone*. *Somebody* must know! There'll surely be ladders – or a fire brigade.'

'Can you help me with this sofa?'

They dragged it out. The heat in the rooms was increasing, and tiny wisps of smoke were creeping up under the rugs and through the floorboards. The house was going up like tinder, in one big roaring mass. All the old wood, the dry beams, the panelling, the heavy curtains. A great funeral pyre.

The smaller end of the sofa was the more effective because it was made of wood and not cushioned by stuffing. They crashed it into the door for two or three minutes and then fell back in frustration. The door had been made before panels were thought of, and the bolts held firm.

'It's no *good*!' Norah said. 'Why doesn't someone *come*?'

'Because if they know their business everyone will be out of the house by now.'

'But everyone will know I'm here – Doole, Gregory, Althea . . .' There she stopped.

'Well,' Christopher said, and coughed. 'I didn't believe even Althea Syme . . . But the door *was* bolted . . .'

They stared at each other. 'It's not possible,' she said.

He shrugged. 'Well, we've got to – face it – however it happened.'

He went back to the bathroom window, she following. They waited in a curtain of smoke until a light breeze temporarily lifted it. Then he put back his head and shouted and she with him. His voice, though cracked, was very powerful.

'There are people there!' she said. 'You can see their shadows. See – there and there!'

He withdrew his head. 'Well, the next move is to get on to the roof, but I'm afraid . . .' He stopped. 'D'you know, this has happened so quickly I can hardly believe it.'

'No . . . I'm sorry . . .'

'For what?'

'I brought you into this.'

'My own free will. But for God's sake! It can't happen . . .'

'It may.'

'Well, I can't regret anything . . .'

He spun round and turned on the two bath taps and then the two in the basin. 'Put the plugs in. Then tie the sheets and the curtains.'

She heard him go back to the door with a piece of iron he had picked up in Simon's attic, and she could hear the screech of it as he tried to get it into a hinge.

Curtains would only add a few feet and they tended to slip. The thin counterpane was good but the blankets almost useless. All the knots kept slipping. But she persisted, for a break in the lifeline was no worse than a failure of length. She tied the end of the first sheet to a leg of the bed and pushed the bed to the window. Then she pushed the sheets through the window. They fell about halfway to the ground. The heat in the room was now appalling. She had never thought that in a fire the heat would get there first. One wasn't going to be burnt, one was going to be *roasted* . . .

Shut up – that way lay panic.

She went back to find Christopher in the bathroom.

'Pipes have melted,' he told her. 'There was a gallon or two in the cistern.'

The bath was a quarter full and she plunged two hand-towels into it. The water was warm. They could hear people shouting now, but only in intervals between the roar of the fire.

'We must try the lifeline,' he said, tying a hand-towel over his face.

'It's so very short – the line.'

'Well, if I go first, I may be able to break your fall.'

She put her head out of the window but soon withdrew it. The smoke was very much thicker at this side now.

'I don't think I want to go that way,' she said.

He put his arm round her and kissed her on the cheek. 'Courage.'

'Anyway,' she said. 'I'm – sorry you're here but glad you're here.'

'That's a sort of consolation. Even though I was after the first prize.'

The roar of the burning house now dominated everything else. Like feeding Christians to the lions. *This* was what created panic, she thought. You never realize until you experience. She still stood by the window trying to draw at the fresher air.

Then to her ears came a sound she had not heard before. Someone – incredibly at this advanced stage – someone was drawing back the bolts of the staircase door.

She turned, stopped, looked at Christopher, who raised his candle to peer through the smoke. Coughing and breathing through the towels, they rubbed smarting eyes and saw a man's figure come out of the fog. Round the head was a cowl of smouldering towel, which he quickly pulled off.

Simon. Across one cheek ran a series of newly forming blisters. On the same side of his head the thick fair hair had been singed away. He was wearing a long raincoat and one sleeve was alight.

He said: 'I didn't know. I didn't know they'd locked you in. Forgive me. I thought you were safe.'

III

AT FIRST nobody moved. It was as if they were wax figures waiting to melt. The smoke had thickened and then cleared with the opening of the staircase door. Then Christopher broke the spell by stepping past Norah and covering Simon's burning sleeve with the wet towel from his face. The sleeve hissed and went out.

259

Far from appearing to appreciate this, Simon was staring at Christopher with puzzled, tormented eyes. Then he stared back at Norah.

'Oh, my God,' he said. 'So it's all the same again, is it? I thought earlier this week – but after these last two days I never believed . . .'

'Believed? Believed what?' Christopher went past him.

Simon and Norah stared at each other.

Norah said: 'I'm not Marion.'

He shook his head angrily. 'Of *course* not. Of course I know that!'

Christopher was back. 'The landing's a mass of flames! How did you get through?'

'There's another door at the foot of the stairs.'

'Then show us the way . . .'

'It's too late. The floor collapsed as I came through.'

Norah said: 'It isn't what you think, Simon. Christopher came up to see me about tomorrow – that was all. Someone locked him in. He was in the other room until we were wakened by the smoke.'

Simon said: 'This is the end anyway. It's all been wasted. Everything's been wasted. A pity. It might – I believed, I truly believed it could have been a new beginning.'

Christopher grasped his arm. 'Simon! Don't give up. What she said is true . . .'

'I'm afraid that isn't going to matter now . . .'

'You know this house. If we got out on the roof, which way should we go? Is there a way down? And how far has the fire spread? You're the only one who can help us! Surely you haven't come up here just to die?'

Norah thought: to fall twisting through the smoke and darkness. Young and whole – in two minutes broken legs or crushed ribs or death. The impact, what's it like? The snap of bone. But after the first pain . . . Forgot to write that letter. Strange end to a search for independence. Death between two men who love me. A light now on the other side of the lake – some shepherd. Above that, above the mantle of the trees, another star. The moon had set. Like her life.

'Simon,' she said, 'I'm *sorry*. Dear Simon, I wanted to help – to be with you, to care for you. Everything we have said to each other is true, utterly true – remember that. Always believe that.'

He blinked and coughed. 'I don't think it can ever be now. The past won't let it. I've tried. I've tried so hard to rid myself of it. These last two days I'd begun to dare to hope . . .'

He blinked again, almost as if coming out of a trance. 'Sorry. The shock of finding Carew here – and the shock of everything else. Remember me, love. Remember me, Norah. You *nearly* gave me a new life. I came to help, and then the shock of this . . .'

He began to unbutton his tattered coat. They stared at him through the hot, smoky, roaring dark. About his waist was wound a rope.

CHAPTER EIGHTEEN

I

THE TWITTERING of a thrush continued to announce the dawn long after full daylight had come to show up the devastation of the night. A light wind sighed, and away from the pyre of the house it was cold.

The fire was out. A fire engine from Rhayader had been the first to come, followed half an hour later by one from Aberystwyth. They stood now spraying casual jets here and there among the smoking ruins. A couple of local policemen helped.

The main building had largely gone. Most of the outer walls built of solid limestone, had resisted the heat and remained, but many of the minor walls had collapsed, and of course no roof was left. Windows were gaunt and eyeless. A few pieces of furniture which had been dragged out in time dotted the grass, a picture or two, some silver candlesticks, a typewriter and a pile of books. As the ash cooled, firemen were stepping into some of the more accessible front rooms to see if anything more could be salvaged. The only parts to survive intact were the outbuildings, the stables and the garages, and here the fugitives from the house were sheltering. A few sightseers wandered about, farmers and farm hands from the neighbouring vales.

The storm of yesterday had cleared the air, and although there was still cloud it was of a thinner more vaporous character which drifted across a greenish sky and seemed to be waiting only for the coming of the sun to disperse. The ground was still muddy from the rain, and the brook running down to the lake was in spate.

Standing on the edge of the area of blackened ground which had been scorched by the heat, Christopher Carew filled his pipe and lit it. It was the first pipe of the day and the feel of the stem was pleasant between his teeth. He had come out while the maids were preparing some breakfast. Most of the stores had been destroyed but there were eggs and some bread, and fortunately tea, which everyone seemed to have been drinking for the last four hours.

He was about to walk on when someone touched his arm. A fair man in a brown trilby hat and a shabby mackintosh.

'I beg pardon, sir. I wonder if you could give me some more information about this fire. I should be obliged.'

Christopher looked at him. 'Reporter?'

'From Cardiff. I was in Llanidloes covering some sheep dog trials and happened to hear the fire engine when it left. Could you give me details for a paragraph, like?'

Christopher hesitated. 'I don't live here. Staying at a cottage a couple of miles away. What is it you want to know?'

'Thank you. Just the facts, you know.'

'Won't the firemen have told you those?'

'Well, they were not eye-witnesses, sir, if you know what I mean. They tell me the house was called Morb House and the present owner is a Mrs Althea Syme.'

'The present owner is Mr Simon Syme, and Mrs Syme, his aunt, kept house for him.'

'Profession, do you know?'

'His? A painter. And of course a landowner, if you consider that a profession.'

'Well, a *status*, sir. It's a status, isn't it, like? Were they both here last night?'

'Yes.'

'Any idea how the fire started? They were all in bed, I suppose?'

'Yes. It may have been the storm. Or a careless maid. These old houses are like tinder.'

The reporter tutted his agreement. 'At what time were you awakened by the fire, Mr . . .'

'Carew.'

'Mr Carew. Could you see it from where you were staying?'

'About two it must have been. But I was over here last night.' He explained briefly what had brought him here but gave the impression he had never left. Although more than half the refugees from Morb House had witnessed his descent of the perilous twisting rope, helping Norah to go down hand by hand, explanations would be forthcoming only when he deemed them necessary.

'Thanks very much, Mr Carew. I'm obliged. That's

interesting. Do you happen to know who raised the alarm? That's always a point.'

'No, I don't. I was wakened myself by the smoke and the noise of people's voices.'

The reporter glanced down at Christopher's bandaged right hand. 'Was anyone hurt? Serious, you know. Did everyone get clear in time?'

'Gregory Syme, Mrs Syme's son, fell down some steps and is suffering from concussion, and Mr Simon Syme has had to go to hospital to be treated for burns.'

The automatic concern in the reporter's face did not disguise his interest.

'Mrs Syme's son. Indeed . . . How old is he?'

'Fifteen.'

'And it is serious?'

'I think not. He came round an hour ago and is just lying quiet.'

'These – hikers, Mr Carew. Would they be about, do you think, now? A little word with one of them . . . Another angle, you know . . .'

'I think they're all too tired at present,' Christopher said, preparing to move on. 'Why don't you go and telephone your news? You've got a scoop at present. Make use of it before someone else comes.'

'Thanks very much. Thank you . . .'

The brown hat was gradually and reluctantly left behind. When he was alone Christopher stared down the slaty valley at the way it folded into itself and hid the descending road, at the derelict cottages and the decrepit mine buildings. The shale and waste of former diggings surrounded the engine-house like ashes about another and long-dead fire. Once a scene of life and activity, for fifty years there had been nothing here but emptiness and slow decay – except for the house, prosperous, well cared for, a memorial to all that early industry. Now that was gone too, to a desolation even completer than the rest. Would it ever be rebuilt? One could hardly see Simon wishing to do so, whatever Althea Syme might have done in his place.

He looked up at Cader Morb brooding so close over the scene. The cliff face had been blackened by the heat and smoke. Soon that would be washed by the winter rains and the scorched moss and thrift begin to grow again. But the desolation would be complete. The wilderness would have its way.

And as for the people . . .

'I went down to look for something,' Gregory had whispered when he opened his eyes about seven o'clock. 'And – and I lost my glasses and upset the lamp . . .'

A relief of a sort to know there had been no design. Yet, while one obviously believed him, one still wondered how Norah had come to be left up there. Had Althea, confronted with near panic all round her, improved the sudden opportunity by a discreet and malignant silence? After all, however the fire had started, nothing could have suited better than for Norah and Simon to be its victims. Christopher found it increasingly difficult to estimate Althea Syme's calibre. He could well believe her capable of such deliberate non-action; or he could equally believe that the sight of Gregory lying unconscious – perhaps dead – at the foot of the bathroom stairs, would rob her of every thought but the survival of her son.

At the moment she was acting the part of a weak, miserable, ineffectual woman who had been robbed of her house and nearly of her son. All the command, the self-importance, the vigorous authority had apparently gone out of her. Or she had collapsed genuinely into such a state. He could not tell. No one could tell but Althea Syme herself, and perhaps even she did not know. Perhaps the distinction between the two states was not as great as first appeared. Some people genuinely were like that: they had to bully or be bullied; either they impressed by their importance or were impressed by other people's, and each state was part truly felt, part assumed.

Anyway, Gregory would live. He had been sick a couple of times, which the ambulance men had said was a good sign, and he had been put to bed with hot water bottles, and his mother advised that if he could be kept quiet for twenty-four hours where he was the advantages would outweigh a jolting journey to Aberystwyth with hospital care at the end of it. Now Mrs Syme sat beside his bed, the picture of a patient, doting mother.

Simon only had gone in the ambulance. Norah had offered to go with him but smiling sadly he had refused. Of all the people in the house, he was the only one who had suffered serious burns, but they were not dangerous. It was one side of his face, which was likely to heal without leaving a scar, and his arm, which was worse and might need a skin graft.

But while being temporarily attended to he had been much more withdrawn than he had been for some days. He had been smilingly charming to Norah but she had not been able really to get at him. Shutters had come down between them. At first she had thought that his discovery of Christopher in her room was at the bottom of it: he had shown his shock, and all their explanations might not suffice to convince him. Yet she was inclined to think it something more. She realized that, if her association with him came to be what they both hoped, he might still have his moods, his periods of semi-withdrawal. She did not at all mind. She knew that she could help him out of them.

But when they parted he had said: 'Do you ever rail against time? Its inescapable order, its plodding, relentless tread?'

'How do you mean?'

'None of us can ever swim upstream to pre-empt the future nor downstream to alter by a hair what happened yesterday. No wonder men smoked opium or experiment with mescaline. It gives the illusion of freedom. But we are all slaves.'

'Surely the future's yet to be made.'

He kissed her. 'Perhaps the future is already past. Perhaps the cardinal error in this life is to hope.'

Before the ambulance men left Norah had had minor first aid for both hands which had been skinned on the rope and for one knee which had been bruised against the wall of the house. There were a few other casualties. Christopher's right hand was burned across the knuckles, Timson had been hit by some falling debris, Ann

Dawson had somehow contrived to sprain an ankle and Mr Croome-Nichols had been treated for shock. Too late, when everybody had been seen to, the local doctor appeared, looked them over with an absent-minded eye, and went home to breakfast.

So their own breakfast was somehow served in the laundry where a fire had been lit, a table spread, a few chairs assembled. It was an odd meal at which no one seemed to wish to speak an unnecessary sentence. Talk was confined to the basic needs. Mrs Syme was not present, as she was sitting with Gregory. The doctor had had a good look into his eyes and had said he would be all right in a day or two. Tea was served to Althea, but she would not eat.

Norah did not eat either. She was still suffering from the traumas of two days and of the night. Her head felt as if someone had thumped it with a blunt instrument. After yet one more cup of tea she went outside, to stare at the smoking ruin and to shiver in the fitful early sunshine.

A shadow moved behind her.

'You need a coat. Chill on top of shock is not a good idea.'

She said: 'I'm all right, Christopher. It's not really the cold.'

They stood in silence.

He said: 'What are you going to do?'

'I don't quite know . . . Go into Aberystwyth later in the day, get credit at a bank, buy a few necessaries.'

'I've money.'

'Thanks but . . .'

'Can't I even help you that way?'

'Well . . . thank you.'

'I've a duffle coat at my cottage. Might be useful. Shall I fetch it?'

She smiled. 'What are *you* going to do today?'

'What I can to help here. Then have a look at my cottage. Care to come over?'

'When?'

'Now. There's nothing much you can do here, and I imagine your obligations to Mrs Syme ended last night.'

She hesitated. 'Where's your car?'

'Down the slope and round the corner. That's if no one has nicked it.'

'Well, don't you . . . ? I mean, wouldn't you rather just drive off and wash your hands of the whole mess?'

'Not particularly.'

'What about the three hikers?'

'They're all asleep. And I can telephone from my cottage for a car to take them back to Aberystwyth. It's the least one can do for them.'

She hesitated again, studying him. 'All right. Thank you, I'll come.'

He said: 'You stay here. I'll bring the car up.'

'No, I'd rather walk. I think it'll do my knee good to use it a bit.'

As the first clouds moved across the watery sun they began to walk slowly down, she limping but not accepting his help.

He said: 'I can make you some good coffee. That tea was getting monotonous.'

The car was still there. He unlocked it and they drove

off, down the road Norah had come up, innocently, uninvolved, so short a time ago. It seemed to her half a life. At the second gate he turned left and bumped over a field. 'A short cut,' he laconically explained. And presently they rejoined another lane, ran up a valley which left Cader Morb dwarfed by higher bluffs, twisted up a shaly hill with two hairpin bends and ran through a tiny village with a church and a chapel and a pub, a dog scratching in the mud, two cows peering over a wall, some thatched cottages and a few people stirring. 'Llandathery,' he said. It was about a mile beyond that, his cottage, set back from the road and shadowed by some pines.

A typical shepherd's cottage, which Christopher – or someone – had done up. Probably it had been uninhabited, falling down. Neat and clean now though very small, with a fine view over rolling fields to the mountains, which were empurpled with the shadow of gathering clouds.

She said: 'There doesn't seem too much mess. It's really only the kitchen and the corner of the other room.'

'Well, it can stay like that till Mrs Jones sees to it. She's a kind old girl who comes in Tuesday and Friday afternoons.'

Watching him put the kettle on she said: 'Your three hikers can't have thought it worth turning out again on such a wet night.'

'They didn't. They would have been perfectly happy to sleep in my sitting-room dodging the drips. But in the end I got them moving again.'

He telephoned to Aberystwyth on behalf of the hikers. Then they made coffee. Ever since the crisis and the high words of last night their conversation had been restricted to impersonal things, and there was no change now. For his part it was as if he had now accepted her arguments and decisions of last night. However much he might dispute them in his own mind, he would not carry on the dispute with her.

She was grateful for this and accepted his company on that basis, aware of an area of uncertainty within herself which would have resented intrusion. It was not conflict that she suffered but a sense of disassociation from the commitments of the last two days. It might have suited her better to be quite alone, but undemanding companionship had the greater comfort in it. For a while she didn't want to think, she didn't want to feel. The emotion had been squeezed out of her and she had none left.

He knelt by the fire, making it first with sticks and then with good shiny Welsh coal which quickly gave off its heat; and she wandered round the little room looking at the photographs. There was one of a very handsome young woman reclining on an Edwardian couch.

'Yes,' he said, 'that was my second. I'm afraid I'm very susceptible to good looks. But I learned my lesson.'

'Permanently?'

'I hope so. She was – I found her very hard to live with. Not at all because she had a nasty nature but because she had an unresponsive one. Instead of depth of feeling she had – shallows that you couldn't get beyond . . . No doubt it's not quite the thing to criticize one woman to another, but, in spite of your present plans, I think it's right for you to know.'

'And your first wife?'

'She died.'

'Oh, I'm sorry.'

He made a disclaiming gesture.

She said: 'I thought . . .'

'Another divorce? No, no. It all happened in the course of nature – unfortunately.'

'I'm – sorry.'

'Don't be.'

'I mean that I thought the other.'

'It's not important.'

She said no more, dropping the personal chord before it began to sound within her. After a few minutes he pulled the couch nearer the fire and encouraged her to sit on it. She curled up, sleepy in the warmth. The coffee had gone down comfortably but not stimulatingly. Her eyes pricked and she sank into a deep brief slumber in which she was suddenly back in the sitting-room with the rocking-horse, and Marion and Simon in the mirror waiting for her to walk through. She started sharply awake, staring wide-eyed round the unfamiliar room which was now empty.

Christopher came back. 'Sleep if you feel like it. A nap will do you good.'

He pulled up a chair and stretched his feet towards the fire, picked up a magazine and leafed through it, then leaned back and closed his own eyes.

This time she went much more gradually into sleep. It was as if her consciousness was aware of the pitfalls of nightmare and relaxed its grip with caution. Slowly, slowly she was lowered into the dark.

And in the dark was Simon. And he said: 'Take my hands, hold my hands, because you only can help me now. It was to be a voyage of discovery but already we're among the wrecks. If we remember our love and concentrate on that, only on that . . .'

She woke a long time later, not at all stiff in spite of her cramped attitude, and strangely refreshed. It was as if an hour had recouped the loss of the night. She lay there utterly still and felt she had wakened from a nightmare and could welcome gratefully the commonplace of ordinary life. But it was not the nightmare of an hour, it was one that had lasted a week. She was herself again.

In his chair Christopher Carew slept untidily, one arm dangling, hair on forehead, shoe slipped off, breathing like a long-distance runner.

Without moving her head, her eyes roved round the room taking in the photographs, the well-worn furniture, the high mantelshelf with its tobacco jar, its portable radio, the pear-shaped oak clock, the Bristol jar, the candlesticks. Coal in the fire had fallen away but glowed like Aladdin's cave. Take my hands, hold my hands . . . Words from a dream. Had it all been a dream?

The week at Morb House had been a venture in hypnosis, organized by a designing woman but slipping completely out of her control. Somehow the forces within the house had grown too strong for her, for them all. Althea could never have foreseen or wished this end. Who could? Who did?

That moment in the bedroom when they had all seemed trapped, there had seemed to be an inevitability about it; that she should die with Simon did not seem unexpected. Yet now, in the cool light of another day . . .

A piece of coal fell into the hearth with a clatter and Christopher woke.

In a moment he was on his knees, picking up the smoking coal with the tongs, rebuilding the fire. He looked up at her.

'Surprising how heavily one can sleep when one's knuckles are smarting like hell. I feel much better for that. Do you?'

'Yes, a lot. What time is it? Lord, we must have been asleep two hours!' She got up, straightening her skirt, examining without favour her hasty stitches of the night when she had tried to repair damage done during the escape.

'There's plenty of time. Would you like something to eat now?'

'No, thanks. I don't seem to have any appetite at all at present. But don't let me stop you . . .'

He shook his head. 'What would you like to do now? Sleep some more? There's my bed if you want it.'

'No . . . I think we ought to be getting back. Then I need to go into Aberystwyth. As I said, I need clothes and . . .'

'And to see Simon?'

' . . . . Yes.'

He got up. 'I'll take you. There are a lot of things we have to thrash out.'

The early cloud had cleared, and an autumn sun warmed their backs as they walked to the car.

'I'll take you straight to Aberystwyth if you want.'

She hesitated. 'I've been wondering . . . the thought of seeing Althea again isn't very . . . But no, we'd better go back to the house first. I keep thinking – hoping – a few of my things may have survived.'

'I wouldn't expect it.'

They drove off, back the way they had come, through a village scarcely more awake, down the hairpins, along the valley, across the bumpy field. Norah got out to open the gates and presently Cader Morb was in view and the stark cadaver of the house. The blackened chimneys and gaunt walls stood out against the hills like the walls of an old abbey. The dignity of ruins . . .

The firemen were still there, and certainly more things were outside now dotting the grass. A surprising number of chairs, part of a Coalport teaset, a blanket in which were heaped a pile of blackened knives and forks and some relatively undamaged silver teapots; the remnants of the tape recorder, a heap of water-soaked books.

There was also a second police car.

'I'll go in and see how Mr Croome-Nichols is,' Norah said. 'See if I can help in any way. Then we can go.'

She got out and Christopher backed the car to turn round. As they did this a police inspector came out of the ruined door of the house and walked towards them.

'Excuse me, sir, are you connected with this household?'

Christopher explained.

'Oh, well, I wonder if I might have a word with you?' The inspector glanced at Norah apologetically. 'I think possibly alone.'

'Surely.' Christopher got out of the car. He said to Norah: 'Will you go and see how things are in the stables, or d'you prefer . . . ?'

'I'll wait here,' she said, and stared after them as they strolled towards the house. After a few moments she saw Mr Croome-Nichols and another policeman emerge from the stables and walk to join them. The clergyman's silvery white hair lifted like a halo in the light breeze. They all disappeared up the three steps and through the hollow doorway which had once been the front door of the house.

Norah got back into the car, thoughts of arson floating through her head. Then she changed her mind and dismissed the whole thing, left the car again and limped across to the stables.

The car had come and the three hikers had gone; Ted Repple had left a scribbled note of thanks. The servants were dozing, wanting some sort of instructions which Norah did not feel in a position to give. With Simon in Aberystwyth control of the household must still rest in Mrs Syme's hands and Althea was still sitting with Gregory. Doole stared Norah up and down with hostility, as if carrying on the vendetta of last night.

After five minutes, as Christopher did not come she left again, a prey to vague unease, determined to follow

277

them and discover what the mystery was about. But as she walked towards the house they all came out and stood on the steps. Mr Croome-Nichols remained talking to the two policemen, but Christopher, seeing her, came down the steps and approached her.

'What is it?' she asked, seeing his face.

He took her by the arm. 'Let's get in the car. It's – it'll be easier sitting there.'

'What is it?' she asked again.

They reached the car and he opened the door for her. She hesitated on the point of refusal, then sat in and swung her legs; he shut the door.

'It's – bad news,' he said, opening his own door and sliding in. 'Norah – it's bad news. They've found among the ruins two skeletons which seem to have been dead a long time.'

She stared at him, blood draining from her face. 'What d'you mean? Who are they? What is it to do with me?'

'They appear to have been – it looks as if they were buried under the floorboards of the old part of the house – in an upper part. It was not altogether destroyed – a part of the floor remained so that they – did not fall. It appears to have been a man and a woman, and they appear to have been – done to death.'

Her heart was thumping and she felt as if she must suffocate.

He lowered his window. 'Take it easy, my dear. It never occurred to me – but I suppose it was always on the cards.'

'No, Christopher!' she exclaimed. 'No! You're

jumping to conclusions! How can the police know who
– how can *anyone* know? It might – might be anyone –
the house is a hundred and fifty years old – it's not
possible – any sort of explanation! You know there
might be . . .'

He took her hand and held it.

'It's not – that way, I'm afraid. My dear, my dear,
I'm so sorry, but it's not that way. You see . . . both the
bodies were wearing wartime identity discs.'

She stared at him again – at his pale, lean, bony face,
as if there were some falsehood in it that she might
discern. But she only saw truth.

'Oh no, Christopher!' she said, and put her hands to
her face as if to blot out all sight.

He said: 'Quietly, my dear, quietly.'

'Oh, no, Christopher,' she said again, and tears began
to drip through her fingers.

Presently she raised her head and stared across at the
ruins of the house and said: 'So she's won after all.'

Christopher did not need to be told that the 'she'
referred to wasn't Althea Syme. He sat quietly without
speaking for a long time, temporarily content that the
girl beside him was at least alive and safe, and
uncomfortably aware in the presence of her distress, of
the hope growing within him that he too had won.

All Pan Books are available at your local bookshop or newsagent, or can be ordered direct from the publisher. Indicate the number of copies required and fill in the form below.

Send to: Macmillan General Books C.S.
Book Service By Post
PO Box 29, Douglas I-O-M
IM99 1BQ

or phone: 01624 675137, quoting title, author and credit card number.

or fax: 01624 670923, quoting title, author, and credit card number.

or Internet: http://www.bookpost.co.uk

Please enclose a remittance* to the value of the cover price plus 75 pence per book for post and packing. Overseas customers please allow £1.00 per copy for post and packing.

*Payment may be made in sterling by UK personal cheque, Eurocheque, postal order, sterling draft or international money order, made payable to Book Service By Post.

Alternatively by Access/Visa/MasterCard

Card No.

Expiry Date

Signature _____

Applicable only in the UK and BFPO addresses.

While every effort is made to keep prices low, it is sometimes necessary to increase prices at short notice. Pan Books reserve the right to show on covers and charge new retail prices which may differ from those advertised in the text or elsewhere.

NAME AND ADDRESS IN BLOCK CAPITAL LETTERS PLEASE

Name _____

Address _____

_____

_____

_____

8/95

Please allow 28 days for delivery.
Please tick box if you do not wish to receive any additional information. ☐